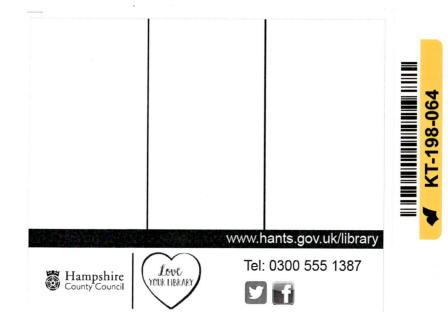

THE ROSE IN WINTER

Recent Titles by Sarah Harrison from Severn House

A DANGEROUS THING
THE DIVIDED HEART
THE NEXT ROOM
THE RED DRESS
ROSE PETAL SOUP
MATTERS ARISING
RETURNING THE FAVOUR
SECRETS OF OUR HEARTS
THE ROSE IN WINTER

THE ROSE IN WINTER

Sarah Harrison

This first world edition published 2017
in Great Britain and the USA by
SEVERN HOUSE PUBLISHERS LTD of
19 Cedar Road, Sutton, Surrey, England, SM2 5DA.
Trade paperback edition first published
in Great Britain and the USA 2018 by
SEVERN HOUSE PUBLISHERS LTD

Copyright © 2017 by Sarah Harrison.

British Library Cataloguing in Publication Data
A CIP catalogue record for this title is available from the British Library.

ISBN-13: 978-0-7278-8748-1 (cased)
ISBN-13: 978-1-84751-858-3 (trade paper)
ISBN-13: 978-1-78010-920-6 (e-book)

All Severn House titles are printed on acid-free paper.

Severn House Publishers support the Forest Stewardship Council™ [FSC™],
the leading international forest certification organisation.
All our titles that are printed on FSC certified paper carry the FSC logo.

MIX
Paper from
responsible sources
FSC   FSC® C013056
www.fsc.org

Typeset by Palimpsest Book Production Ltd.,
Falkirk, Stirlingshire, Scotland.
Printed and bound in Great Britain by
TJ International, Padstow, Cornwall.

One

Barbara flitted across the hall and paused – face to the wall, breath held. Silence lay in the dim rooms all around, rain roared on the windows. She gasped and ran again, pattering along the passage to the kitchen on wings of fear, quick and light as a moth. If she didn't breathe, if her feet scarcely touched the ground, perhaps she would be invisible. Everywhere in the house was unseasonably dark because of the rain, which had been falling all day long and showed no sign of abating. The downpour would obscure the view of anyone looking in, but would it hide them from her, too? How would she know who was out there? And where?

She flew past the pantry and the scullery that looked over the back yard and stopped before entering the kitchen, picturing the space beyond the door. In there, two windows faced one another across the length of the big deal table. Her objective was the larder on the far side. She had to hope that whoever was out there had not yet reached this end of the house. She released her held breath with a sob and sucked in another, before pushing open the door and rushing across the room, looking neither right nor left, closing the larder door swiftly – *softly* – behind her. The click of the latch was like a gunshot. Sweat crept in the roots of her hair.

She had never been shut in here before. Usually she would whisk in and out on a mission – depositing leftovers, taking dripping from a shelf, her mind on her task. Now she stood utterly still, her chest heaving and legs trembling from the effort of silent flight. On this drowned midsummer afternoon, the larder was cold and crepuscular as a tomb. There was a faint smell of overripe food. When she laid her hand on the edge of the marble shelf to steady herself, it struck her dank palm like ice. The small transom window high on the back wall was slightly open, the aperture covered with a fine gauze to keep insects out.

Barbara breathed again, her fists grinding a sob back into her squirming mouth. She should have gone upstairs! No one could have looked in at her there. Instead she had shut herself in this tiny cell, and was trapped! She dared not come out again and if she was found here, there would be no escape.

She realised that she had never, till this moment, been really afraid. She had read of people fearing for their lives, and this – this wild, thundering paralysis – was surely what they meant. The Bad Thing, far more terrifying in her imagination than anything known, was very close and drawing closer, creeping, questing . . . the stuff of childhood nightmares. In her mouth was the taste of blood from her bitten knuckle. Her nose ran and for the first time since early childhood she swiped her cuff over it and gazed at the snail-trail with a sob.

The contents of the larder stood around her like the grave-goods of some ancient burial: Kilner jars full of pickled vegetables – onions, beetroot, cabbage – their contents suspended eerily in the pickling fluid, like body parts in a laboratory; the blackest of dark preserves, bramble and damson; butter, margarine and lard in greaseproof paper; milk in a green pottery jug, the top covered by a beaded net; the remains of the Sunday joint, a leg of lamb (that Maureen had cooked for herself and the Bryants) lay under the meat-safe, shaggy and grey, the exposed bone faintly gleaming; junket seeped water into a pyrex dish; the rhubarb that had accompanied it now like sodden yellow-grey hair; bottles of Camp Coffee, Lea and Perrins and gravy browning had been in here too long – there were ruffs of black sediment around the bottle-tops, and sticky brown rings showing where they had stood before. She must have a word . . .

Barbara!

The rattle of inconsequential thoughts ceased.

Her name, had she heard her name?

The noise of the rain surged, snarling, on a gust of wind. A few drops plopped through the wire netting and spattered on the grey marble. How could she possibly have heard anything? But why would she have imagined it?

She was cold. Her circulation was never good and now her

thin hands looked mauve. At least she still had her coat on. She had only just removed her hat and laid it on the hall table, when she'd heard the footsteps on the gravel, and knew she'd been followed. Her umbrella was standing open in the porch. Did that count as inside? Was it bad luck?

Barbara . . .?

There was no mistaking it this time. Somewhere between the dead silence of the house and the roar of the rain, someone had spoken her name, with the slight interrogative inflection that meant he knew she was here. He had followed her back from the village and tapped once, softly, on the door with his knuckles.

She whimpered. If only Stanley were here – tall and severe and unimaginative, his shoulders pulled back and his brows beetling – to stump outside with his walking stick or a golf club, and then to come back in to tell her she was a goose and it was time to have some tea. In his case, it would have been something a little stronger from the decanter. Stanley, who was incredibly dear to her now and whose very ghost would have been a comfort at this moment.

For minutes, she had moved nothing but her eyes. Now, using the marble slab as a support, she stiffly lowered herself to the ground and sat on the floor, twisting her legs to one side and drawing her coat under her, between her thighs and the frigid stone. She wanted to tuck herself under the shelf, but there was a clank when her foot struck a box of old jars, so she hitched herself backward to huddle against the wall, her face buried in her upturned collar. Ostrich-like, she closed her eyes so as not to be seen.

Time crawled by. The rain eased. She felt even more unprotected, as if her breathing might be heard over its gentle hiss. It was early June and, if the rain stopped altogether, it would be light for hours yet. She thought, *If need be I can stay here till Maureen gets back.* Except that now her right leg, bent under her, was numb and she could feel that she needed to spend a penny, urgently. She had to change position, to ease her leg and take her mind off her bursting bladder.

She braced her arms to take her weight but, as she began to move her legs, she heard a tiny, sharp sound. No more than a scratch, close – so close! – and just above her.

Scarcely tilting her head and not daring to show her face, she looked up.

A hand was spread, spider-like, against the wire mesh of the window.

Two

The Bryants had been most insistent.

'Bar, you simply must come.' Paul placed his knife and fork together with a decisive clink. 'Very good lamb by the way. It's a big occasion, a coronation – the biggest since the war and a happy one too.'

Audrey beamed at her, taking her husband's part.

'Yes, quite right, it's a celebration! That lovely young woman, a new Elizabethan age. Salting will be *en fête*.'

'Then I shan't be missed, shall I?' She realised this sounded sharp, but they were old friends and not easily offended.

'Not true,' said Paul. '*We* shall miss you and Evelyn and Richard. David . . .'

'. . . Lesley, Beatrice, everyone!' added Audrey in case her husband was running out of ideas. 'We're going to watch the ceremony in the parish rooms and be back for a buffet lunch at the Keyes'. Then, if we're all still going strong, we can go down to the Green for tea and watch the Mayor giving out mugs to the schoolchildren to the strains of the town band – how can you resist?'

Barbara smiled. 'I shall be there in spirit. I have my trusty wireless, remember.'

'But if you join us you'll be able to watch it on *television*, Bar, the whole thing, as it happens. Imagine – history in the making!'

She went in the end; of course she did. It had proved imposs-ible to make them understand that she wouldn't be sad, or lonely, or that she didn't mean to be unpatriotic. She'd just prefer to listen to the day's events at home, eating her own sort of lunch at the time she wanted it. The Bryants were dears but she was more different from them than they realised. She had far more in common with Edith Malmay, whom they had failed to mentioned in their litany of friends, and whom she'd actually heard Paul describe once as a 'funny old bat'. Two of those words were true, but the three of them did not begin to sum up Edith.

The rain was coming down steadily, but it was not pig-headedness that prompted her to walk the mile and a half into town. She had only taken her test two years before and was still an unconfident driver; she didn't want the worry of parking or of being asked to run someone else home later. She would leave her beloved, pale green Morris snug in the garage. The walk would do her good and give her a reason to leave promptly.

Getting ready to go out always made her think of Stanley. He was a man of few words and not free with compliments, but she knew that he admired her appearance and she liked to maintain standards in case he was watching. She sat in front of the dressing table in her petticoat and applied a discreet veneer of Cyclax foundation, a dab of powder and the pearl earrings and necklace he had given her on their wedding day. While she improved on nature, her friendly wood pigeons croo-crooed in the trees on the Fort, the little hill in the garden of Hearts Ease.

Before putting on her dress, she brushed her hair. It was the only aspect of her appearance that had changed and which she knew Stanley might not have liked. From childhood onwards, Barbara had had long, silken, mouse-brown hair with the merest ripple of a wave, which she brushed fifty times morning and night. Stanley had liked to watch her and once she'd offered him the brush, but his cheeks had gone pink as he waved it away and she'd never offered again. Three years ago, she'd had her hair cut so that now it framed her face. The girl at Marcelle had complimented her on her decision and on her hair – the slight wave meant that she didn't need a perm or to have it set on rollers – It fell into place just nicely. She herself liked the new style because it was easy and practical, but she could imagine Stanley's reaction, the minute tightening of the mouth that gave him away. He would never have dreamed of criticising her but then he didn't have to, she always knew when he didn't like something.

She put on her navy coat, the matching felt hat with a becoming rolled-back brim and pulled on galoshes over her shoes. She was aware the galoshes were old-fashioned, but she found them useful. Salting being what it was, she was not the only galosh-wearer, though she may have been the youngest. From the stand by the door, she selected Stanley's old golf umbrella and set off.

Her route down to the town was via the old Church Path, which ran over the golf course and between the fields, joining the road just above the nursery garden and the Bay Tree Convalescent Home. There wasn't much cover in the first half mile but, even through the drizzle, she delighted in the view of Salting bay. There were the elegant houses and hotels clustered comfortably along the curve of pale shingle and the buttress of red cliff, with its shawl of trees on the far side of the estuary. There were no golfers out today, so she didn't have to wait to cross the fairway but crossed briskly, sheltered by Stanley's brolly. The fields were fresh and green, the gorse bushes and brambles in flower. Seagulls mewed and wheeled under the weeping, grey clouds. The church path was pitted with rain and puddles were already beginning to collect in the ruts. If this kept up, she would have to take the longer way home, by the road. But she had already decided that she would not accept a lift; politeness would dictate that she invite the person in, when all she'd want by that time was peace and quiet.

Audrey had been right; Salting was *en fête* – or doing its best under the circumstances. Red, white and blue was much in evidence. Union Jacks hung out of upstairs windows, strings of bunting drooped and dripped across the high street and many windows carried a picture of the young Queen. Aside from these shows of patriotism it was quiet, with the shops closed and everyone either indoors or, like Barbara, scurrying through the rain to wherever they were going to follow the proceedings. People with televisions or organisations who had rented them for the day, were few and far between and in great demand.

The Masonic Hall, when she passed it, looked already full, with steamed-up windows and a handful of sodden people still waiting outside to get in. The parish rooms – a smaller and more select venue – were opposite the church, next to the doctor's surgery. Beatrice Talbot had been responsible for hiring the rooms and the television for this private gathering of friends.

She was welcoming arrivals in the lobby.

'Barbara! Good morning – or is it? What a day, at least we'll be in the warm and dry, pity those poor souls in London, such a rotten shame. Don't tell me you walked, you should have asked . . . Brollies in the box in the corner, oh my goodness here's Cecil – Cecil, can you believe it . . .?'

Barbara removed her galoshes, parked the golfing umbrella – like Stanley himself, it dwarfed its companions – hung up her coat and hat on the rack and went through the swing doors. Inside it was pleasantly fuggy, with a strong scent of damp fabric emanating from the thirty or so already there. Two rows of chairs had been placed in a semicircle facing the television, but there was no picture as yet and most people were still milling about inside the door, talking loudly.

Paul arrived at her side at once.

'Well done, Bar, so glad you came in the end. Not much of a day, but are we downhearted? Would you like some coffee?'

The coffee, though instant and not very nice, was hot and she had a little sugar to buck herself up. Everyone was most welcoming and she reproved herself for her earlier grudging thoughts. Of course one should celebrate these things together! As if to confirm this more benign view, she spotted Edith Malmay sitting at the end of the back row of chairs, reading a programme.

'Edith!'

'Hello, my dear. I decided to bag my favoured seat.'

'May I?'

'Please. I'm just running through what we're all going to be looking at.' She glanced at Barbara humorously over her glasses. 'Which is rather a lot.'

'I suppose everyone has to be there.'

'Of course. Everyone who's anyone and some besides, if this is to be believed. Poor girl.'

By this, Barbara knew she meant the Queen. She returned
to the programme and Barbara sat quietly for a moment, contem-
plating the 'poor girl' and the momentousness of it all.

'Right!' carolled Beatrice. 'Take your seats, we're about to
switch on!'

Once Queen Elizabeth II had made her appearance on the
balcony, Beatrice switched off the television, cried 'Long live
the Queen!' and made up-in-the air shooing movements to
indicate they should make a move. There was a general sense
of relief – the picture was very small, the reception poor and
the sound tinny – the whole thing had been something of an
effort. Though 'Vivat Regina!' had been extremely stirring
and the Queen was generally acknowledged to be beautiful and
dignified beyond her years. As they shuffled about picking up
handbags and programmes, Edith leaned towards Barbara.

'I've made my excuses, not going to the luncheon I'm afraid.'

'Oh, I'm sorry to hear that. I was really hoping you'd be
there.'

'How nice of you to say so. I suspect the others can take me
or leave me, though it was kind of the Keyes to ask. What I
need now is peace and quiet and a bowl of soup, not cold
bubbles and chit-chat.'

'I can't say I blame you.' Barbara couldn't hide her envy.

Edith rose, towering over her. 'You're going, I hope.'

'Yes.'

'Quite right. And you will enjoy it.'

'I expect so.' She must have sounded unconvinced.

'Yes, you will.' Edith tapped her arm with the rolled-up
programme. 'That's an order.'

'Right you are!'

'And don't hang about politely for me, for goodness' sake. I
shall take my time and be last out.'

'If you're sure, I can't—'

'Run along.'

At the door, Barbara paused before putting her umbrella up
and glanced back. Edith had changed her shoes for black welling-
tons and put on her long, unfashionable mac, with the hood
that tied under the chin. She cut an odd figure, of no particular

age, time or sex – she might have been an archer from Agincourt, a nun from some obscure order, or a mackerel fisherman straight off the boat.

The Keyes – Evelyn and Richard – lived in Cliff Terrace, only a hundred yards from the parish rooms. In the end, their party was quite enjoyable. In company, Barbara often felt younger than her forty-four years, because of how others treated her. Perhaps they were prompted to by something girlish in her manner, a trait fostered albeit unintentionally by Stanley. She suspected that her widowhood at a relatively early age, combined with her childlessness (something not willed, but not regretted either) conferred a sort of spurious sanctity. Had she been single through choice, let alone a divorcee, the reactions would have been different. As it was, the men were teasing yet chivalrous, the women indulgent. This sense of being petted could be annoying, but today she found it agreeable. Perhaps, in spite of the disparity in age, she reminded people of the new Queen whom she did superficially resemble, with her steady gaze and full, serious mouth.

Then suddenly she was tired and ready to leave. Having decided, she wished to make her goodbyes as swiftly as was consistent with politeness. Evelyn implored her hospitably to stay, but nonetheless fetched her coat from the study. Richard, pleasantly squiffy, was more insistent.

'Now then, Bar, what's all this? Not leaving us, surely?'

'Yes, I'm afraid I must, I'm sorry.'

'Why must you?' he turned to his wife who was holding Barbara's coat. 'Why must she?'

'Pish tush Dickie,' said Evelyn, 'don't bluster.'

They wrangled amiably over her as she put on her hat and galoshes. She was used to this underlying attitude that she never really needed to be at home because, after all, what was waiting for her there? They didn't realise that Heart's Ease was well-named. What they saw as 'that isolated house' that was too big for her up at the top of the hill was, in fact, her sanctuary. The place where she felt safest and most content. Now she longed to be back.

'Thank you so much for a lovely party.'

'Well,' said Evelyn, 'thank you for coming. It's been a memorable day.'

'I had an umbrella . . .'

'Let me guess.' Richard's hand hovered over the sheaf of brollies and selected a coppery silk one with a handle like a twist of barley sugar. 'Yes?'

'Nice, but no.' She smiled and dragged out the mighty golf umbrella.

'Hold your horses — you're not thinking of walking, are you?'

'Definitely, I walked down very happily.'

Evelyn pulled a face. 'Down is the operative word. It'll be a frightful trudge all the way back up and in the rain, Dick will run you home, won't you?'

'Certainly, it would be my absolute pleasure!'

'No thank you. Honestly. It's so kind of you to offer, but I'm completely prepared, and the fresh air's just what I need.'

The Keyes, spurned, exchanged a look of amused helplessness. Richard shrugged. 'If you say so, my dear. Make yourself a hot toddy . . .'

At first, she strode along happily enough, buoyed up by her own resolve and glad to be on her way. Her sturdy galoshes stamped through the puddles, the rain rattled down merrily on her umbrella and the air was cool and damp on her face. There were a few people around, mostly parents with children clutching mugs, returning from the soggy mayoral presentation on the Green. She passed Salting's own simpleton, the affectionately named Hummer from the Denley Estate, singing 'Morning has broken' in the entrance to the ironmonger's. Not for the first time did Barbara think about what a nice voice he had and that, if things had been different, he might have been in a choir, or made a record.

She was smiling as she marched up the high street. But as she left the shops behind and began the long slow ascent from the town, with the comfortable villas looking smug and closed and so little traffic, she became rather dejected. She almost wished an acquaintance, even the garrulous Richard, would draw alongside and suggest she hop in. Her earlier route would be a quagmire by now; she had nearly a mile to go by road, before she could turn off and follow the sheltered path up through the beech wood to the back gate of Heart's Ease.

She plodded on, keeping her eyes on the streaming pavement, until the point where it ran out. For a few hundred yards, it became a track across Little Common, an area of scrub bordered by firs and containing the scout hut. In the lee of the hut, she paused for a moment and looked over her shoulder to remind herself how far she'd come, that she was halfway to the beech wood and so doing pretty well. There was one other person, a man, walking some hundred yards behind her. He wore a hat, but no coat, the collar of his jacket was turned up, a mere token gesture against the downpour. As she looked he stopped and seemed to be consulting his watch, glancing around as if looking out for someone.

Twenty minutes later, she reached the point where she could cross into the beech wood. Though there were no cars coming in either direction, she positively scampered over the road and the moment she'd done so, she closed the umbrella and felt much better. She was almost home and this last part of the walk was familiar as well as sheltered. The trees were old and tall, she could hear the rain on the branches, but down here in the green and sepia twilight, it fell as no more than intermittent drops and splatters. The path was soft beneath her feet. A grey squirrel scuttled about busily in the beech mast.

The path continued through the beech wood for a couple of hundred yards, before emerging to wander up the hill between an apple orchard and a dense, high hedge.

The climb was quite steep and as Barbara emerged from the trees she stopped to catch her breath. She was too warm now and, in spite of the rain, she unbuttoned her coat. She caught a movement behind her in the soft twilight of the wood – the squirrel again?

Quickly, she set off once more, on the last lap, looking forward to the cup of tea she'd make, and how on this dingy evening she'd light the lamps in the drawing room and enjoy the space and ampleness that no one thought she needed.

About twenty yards before the five-bar gate of Heart's Ease, the path levelled out and she glanced back. This time she could clearly see another walker, moving at a good pace, in fact gaining

on her. She realised it was the man she'd seen earlier from Little
Common. A thin man, his suit jacket tightly buttoned, collar
still up, head down, his hands thrust into his pockets. He must
have been soaked, but his step was quick, light and purposeful,
like a fox she sometimes saw trotting over the lawn at dusk.

Barbara's scalp stirred beneath her hat. She pulled her coat
around her and moved as fast as she could without running, she
didn't want him to see her run to the gate. Once she was
through to the other side, she did run, frantically, her feet clumsy
in her galoshes, the half-furled umbrella flapping at her side, her
hat slipping off on to the gravel. As she reached the porch, she
heard the soft metallic scrape of the gate latch and felt the sweat
pop out all over her. She dropped the umbrella, snatched and
scrabbled with slippery fingers for the key in her bag, pushed
it into the lock and burst through into the hall closing the door
behind her.

She thought she heard the stealthy whisper of steps on the
gravel . . . Then nothing but the patter of the rain as she fled.

Three

1929

Barbara's mother, Julia, was looking forward to the season much
more than Barbara herself. She was not a frivolous or socially
ambitious woman, but an intelligent one with rather too much
time on her hands and introducing her only child to society
was a project she could get her administrative teeth into.

She even displayed a sense of humour on the subject.

'Do it for me, darling. I never did it myself and I shall derive
a great deal of simple pleasure from being the mother of this
year's prettiest debutante.'

Barbara, who was not in any case rebellious by nature, could
scarcely refuse. Her father, in shipping and rich as a result,
regarded the whole thing as a necessary evil that would set him
back a few bob, but which might prove an investment in terms

of exposing her to not entirely hopeless husband material. (On encountering some of the young men he wasn't quite so sure, but was by then resigned to his course of action.)

The Delahays' country house was a rambling arts-and-crafts villa in the Surrey Hills. Barbara and her mother lived there most of the time while Sir Conrad was in London at the Regents Park mansion. He came down at weekends to play golf, socialise and renew acquaintance with the locals. When occasion arose, the positions would be reversed and Barbara and Julia would go up to town. Barbara always knew her parents liked London, but she preferred Surrey with its civilised countryside, cosy villages and manicured paddocks, in one of which was Jiggins – her old Dartmoor pony. Throughout a happy and secure childhood, the closest thing she had to siblings were: Jiggins, Myrtle the Labrador, Shamus the border terrier and the cats. When Barbara and her parents attended church at Christmas (the only time they did so) and sang the carol containing the phrase 'all His wondrous childhood' she pictured that childhood as exactly like hers, if a squeak holier.

Nor was she short of friends. As she entered her teens, class-mates from Aggie's – St Agatha's school for girls near Godalming – came to stay, and there were sedate but enjoyable parties, tennis and treasure hunts, not to mention pony club events ranging from adventurous treks to gymkhanas and dances. She knew lots of nice boys, the sons of her parents' social circle, but they were jolly, puppyish friendships rather than anything romantic. Some of the boys might have liked a little more from pretty Barbara Delahay, but she was protected from unwelcome attention by the aura of innocent, carefree confidence of which she was largely unaware.

The season, when it happened, seemed more of a game than anything else. She had left Aggie's at Christmas, just after her seventeenth birthday, to find her mother already planning a cocktail party in London at the end of May and a dance at Ardonleigh a month later. Barbara had no particular ambitions so this seemed as good a way as any to spend the summer, although it was rather overwhelming to have so much attention and money lavished on her. She knew from talking to her friends, Lucia (scion of a noble house in Suffolk) and Rosemary (an admiral's daughter from Weybridge), that her own parties were going to be enviably lavish, which she found rather embarrassing. Also, the guest lists were largely composed of people she didn't know.

'Don't worry darling!' Julia gave an insouciant wave of the hand. 'You'll have met most of them by then.'

'How will I?'

'You'll see them at other people's parties.'

The full implication of this was suddenly borne in on her. There were going to be innumerable parties, a multitude of people, many strangers and countless dresses. Life for the next few months was going to be, as Julia put it, happily, 'one mad whirl'. Barbara was not one of nature's whirlers, but she appreciated her good fortune and was determined to enjoy herself.

The whirl soon became, if not routine, then at least less mad. Several of the girls doing the season were friends and others, if they were not acquaintances already, soon were. The young men were jolly, attentive and some were surprisingly good dancers, with whom she loved taking the floor. She discovered a streak of show-offness which she didn't know she had. Jiggins, gazing glumly over his fence in the Surrey hills, grew rather fat as Barbara became fashionably slim. The current styles suited her, but she wouldn't have her hair cropped; she compromised by wearing it in a neat Grecian coil on the nape of her neck, to which Julia liked to attach a fresh flower – a rose or camellia – preferably in bud, so that it would open over the course of an evening.

One morning in London, the day after a particularly lively dance in the garden of a Chelsea mansion, she emerged from her room to hear a rumble of male voices in the drawing room. It was only just approaching midday and she had on her kimono over her nightdress. The kimono was red and black silk, brought back from Hong Kong by her father, but was definitely not suitable for mixed company at this time of day.

Clarice was hovering helpfully on the landing, passing a duster over picture frames.

'A word to the wise, miss, Sir Conrad's got company.'

'Thanks Clarice, I'll put some clothes on.'

'I would if I were you.'

'Do we know who?'

'Let's see . . .' Clarice pursed her lips, calling the name to mind as she polished the glass on a watercolour landscape. 'Brigadier Govan.'

Barbara ran a swift mental inventory of her father's wartime cronies, but the name didn't ring a bell.

'Is my mother in?'

'I believe not.' Clarice paused in her polishing. 'Would you like some coffee Miss – while you get dressed . . .?'

Back in her room, Barbara was tempted to get back into bed and wait till her father's friend had gone. But the arrival of the hot coffee perked her up. She applied what her childhood nanny would have called 'a lick and a promise' at the basin, put on loose trousers and a shirt, brushed her hair and went downstairs to satisfy her curiosity.

Brigadier Stanley Govan was very, very tall. Sir Conrad was considered an imposing figure, but as both men rose to greet her, Govan towered over him. His big, dry hand enveloped Barbara's with courteous lightness. Far above, his brows drew together above an eagle's beak of nose, his mouth was firm and unsmiling and he had a smoothly-groomed peak of hair. The impression was one of uprightness; he was contained, correct, a little stern, a leader of men. She was quite glad she had put on no make-up, but found herself wishing she had opted for a skirt instead of trousers.

'Sit down, Bar,' said her father easily, 'and tell us about the goings-on last night.'

She gave them a judiciously edited version of the events in Chelsea: the garden, the band, the lights . . . how one girl had lost an earring in the ornamental pond and three boys had jumped in and competed to get it back. Her father nodded benignly and rather enjoyed the idea of his daughter getting up to high jinx. Govan gazed now at his highly-polished shoes, now at her. For a man of his considerable physical presence he seemed ill at ease. He was at least as old as her father.

Barbara thought it quite likely he disapproved of her but, after half an hour, when she excused herself, Govan sprang to

his feet and expressed his pleasure in meeting her warmly and
with apparent sincerity.

It was still a surprise when, a few days later, she returned from
cycling with a friend in the park to find her mother in the
drawing room, phone in hand.

'Bar is that you? Hang on, this may be her . . . Bar, darling?
Telephone for you.'

'Stanley Govan.' Her mother mouthed, in answer to her look.
And then, aloud into the receiver, 'She's coming now.'

Given another minute, Barbara might have made some excuse,
but the receiver was thrust into her hand and her mother was
off, beaming like a cheshire cat, waving one hand in the air and
mouthing, '*Over to you . . .*'

'Hello?'

'Barbara, it's Stanley Govan here. I apologise if you were
hardly through the door. Would you prefer me to call again if
this isn't convenient?'

'No, not at all – it's fine.'

'I have some theatre tickets for the end of next week, Friday
– for what I believe is rather a good new play, "Journey's End",
do you know it?'

'I've heard of it.'

'I wondered, your busy social calendar permitting, if you'd
care to come with me?'

If he had seemed ill at ease before, he didn't now. She was
astonished and taken aback. This friend of her father's and leader
of men? A new play with this old – well quite old – man?

'Thank you, that sounds . . . May I just go and check?'

'Of course.'

Her mother was waiting in the Hall, diary in hand. She leaned
past Barbara and pushed the drawing-room door closed behind
her.

'I think you're free that night.'

'How do you know?'

'Stanley mentioned to your father that he had the tickets.'

'Mummy! You're ganging up on me.'

'You don't have to go. I'm just saying you can, if you want to.'

'He's too old. Why would he want to take me?'

'Not that old.' Julia put down the diary and took her by the shoulders, turning her to face the hall mirror, which was crowned with reclining brazen dryads. 'And that's why.'

Barbara saw a girl with pink cheeks, disarrayed hair and a baffled expression.

'Don't be silly. It's ridiculous.'

'Not at all.' Julia gave the door a push. 'But if you don't want to, simply make your excuses . . .'

A second later she went through and picked up the receiver.

That evening at the theatre was the first of what Barbara would look back on as their courtship. It was a strange choice of opening move, that fierce and uncompromising play that had made her cry; a test of character perhaps.

She soon realised that any perceived lack of confidence in him – from their first meeting – had simply been a military man's thoughtful reconnaissance. Once he had decided to advance his plan, he was determined and single-minded. After her initial uncertainty among the well-heeled theatre buffs, she became gradually aware of the cache of being an interesting couple. Stanley may have been twice her age, but he was a distinguished bachelor, who had had an excellent war (wounded twice and recipient of the DSM and bar) and who was also a man of means. In the dress circle bar beforehand, they were approached by an elegant, older woman who greeted Stanley as a long-lost friend. When introduced, she gazed at Barbara with a sort of charming, kindly curiosity, as if he'd brought a kitten along in his pocket.

'Am I allowed to say I've been admiring you from afar? Who, I asked myself, is that enchanting young thing with the rose in her hair?'

Barbara touched the flower. 'Thank you.'

'How did you two bump into each other?' The woman smiled encouragingly, her large, bright eyes darting back and forth between them with frank speculation.

'At home,' said Barbara.

'Ah, of course.'

'Barbara's father is Sir Conrad Delahay.'

'You don't say?'

The question was rhetorical, but still it was like facing the polite interrogation of her mother's friends. She was glad when the final bell rang and Stanley cupped her elbow gently to lead her back to their seats.

They were both moved by the play and full of admiration for the writing and the performances. It certainly gave them plenty to talk about over supper at the Savoy. She talked at least as much as him, though the production must have raised a host of ghosts and memories for him. He was a quiet, thoughtful listener to her jejune chatter.

As they waited for a cab to arrive, he said, 'When they reopen the theatre here, perhaps I can bring you to see some Gilbert and Sullivan, for a little light relief.'

'That would be fun.'

And so the likelihood of further meetings opened up.

The season continued on its merry way. She felt herself to be quite an old hand now, adept at small talk and a sought-after dance partner, light on her feet and quick to master steps. She had a lot of fun and champagne, and some mildly *risqué* escapades in sports cars, some of them involving kisses, which were exciting only because they were stolen and therefore part of the general larks.

In between all of this, she saw Stanley. He took her to the theatre and to the ballet and dinner at a succession of grand restaurants – the Boulestin and the Savoy, Quaglino's – all of which made a nice change. She began to look forward to these outings which, in contrast to most of her social life, were measured and calm. Stanley was never less than the soul of propriety, but she did not find their time together dull. On the contrary she felt safe and spoiled. The only awkward moments were when Stanley arrived to collect her from the house and fell into conversation with her parents. Then it was impossible to ignore the disparity in their ages and she would feel like a child, waiting in her party dress. But the moment he escorted her out to the waiting car, she relaxed, knowing that for the next few hours she would be the whole focus of his attention and the season seem miles away, a distant hubbub that she was happy to escape for a while.

Her father, a man of the world and a pragmatist, kept his counsel, making no comment except to enquire from time to time how she'd enjoyed her evening. He did however tell her that Stanley was 'an exceptionally fine soldier' and (until now was the implication) 'a rather a solitary chap', so she was given to understand that she had been singled out.

Julia was, by nature, less cautious and more curious and the morning after Barbara's fourth evening out with Stanley, she tapped on the bedroom door.

'May I come in?'

'I'm asleep, Mummy . . .'

'Well you're not now and I've brought you a cup of tea.' Julia put the cup down on her bedside table and sat on the dressing table stool, elegant legs crossed, hands clasped around her knee. 'Did you have a lovely time?'

'Yes thank you.'

'Where did he take you?'

'We went to Madam Butterfly and supper at Rules.'

'Butterfly! Did you cry?'

'Nearly.' Barbara pulled herself up on the pillows and reached for her cup. 'If I'd been with someone else I probably would have done.'

Julia gave a little sigh. 'Your father hates opera, but when it has such lovely tunes and such a gloriously sad story . . .' She cocked her head on one side. 'Did Stanley enjoy it?'

'I hope so. He chose it.'

'But for you, I expect.'

'He did enjoy it, yes. Actually, he did say he hadn't seen it before.'

'There you are then.' Julia watched Barbara sip her tea, with rapt, smiling fascination. 'Do you like him? Do you get on?'

'Of course. I'd find some excuse otherwise.'

'Ah yes, I suppose you would.'

'I do sometimes wonder if he likes me. *Why* he likes me.' Barbara put the cup down. 'And he does seem to.'

'I told you why!'

'That can't possibly be enough. I've met some of his friends – they're elegant, sophisticated, well-read—'

'You had an expensive education yourself.'

Barbara considered St Agatha's. 'Perhaps I mean worldly.'

'Take it from me, worldliness is overrated. Besides, Stanley's no intellectual. He's a soldier.' Julia smoothed the eiderdown with a well-manicured hand. 'And on extended leave, he'll be going back soon.'

'Back where?'

'India. Peshawar.' Julia got up. 'I'm surprised he hasn't told you.'

Barbara was herself surprised. Though on reflection she realised they talked very little about him. He either asked her about herself, or they discussed whatever they had seen, or what was around them. Sometimes they were quiet, but these silences were not awkward. She was far from being completely at home with Stanley, but she felt increasingly out of place with her young friends and their minute-by-minute enthusiasms. She was suspended between two worlds.

After her conversation with her mother, she found herself wondering when Stanley would tell her that he was leaving for the other side of the world. Because he had never so much as mentioned India, she felt shy about asking. The weeks passed and the season, along with summer, was ending.

One stifling day, towards the end of August, he came down to lunch at Ardonleigh. It was his first visit to their country house. She sensed at once that unlike her parents he was naturally at home in the countryside. Instead of a suit, he wore a blazer and flannels and his face had lost a little of its seriousness; both of these made him look younger. Also, there was something in the air, something anticipatory, a consciousness of occasion, like Christmas or her mother's birthday. Everyone seemed light-hearted. They had claret with the beef and sauternes with the apricot mousse. She amused them all with her latest and last batch of stories about the season and there was much laughter. She realised she had never heard Stanley's laugh before, a full-throated bark that creased his face in two.

After lunch, he asked her if she would show him around 'the family acres'.

'Oh do, what a good idea,' Julia said. 'I'll ask for coffee in the orangery in about half an hour, how's that?'

The precise timing of this should have told her something

was afoot, but everything was so agreeably happy and relaxed that she noticed nothing. Myrtle, stricken in years, was too old and fat to accompany them and watched their departure from beneath the chestnut tree, but Shamus trotted briskly beside them as they went across the lawn to the orchard and the paddock.

'You still have your horse?' he asked. 'Shall you be hunting in a few weeks' time?'

She realised he was teasing her, something else that was new. 'He's not a horse he's an old Welsh mountain pony and I've never hunted.'

'I thought you might be a hard woman to hounds.'

'I'm not a hard woman to anything.'

A moment elapsed before she thought she heard him say, 'I know.'

In the orchard, there were a few small early apples, still green. She reached up and pulled one down.

'He can have one or two of these. No more or he'll get a stomach ache.'

He picked another; he hardly had to reach at all. 'We wouldn't want that.'

Jiggins was cropping lazily on the far side of the paddock, but the moment they appeared he looked up and began making his way towards them, head nodding, blowing a soft whuffle of greeting.

'A fine beast,' said Stanley. He offered his apple in a cupped palm. 'A pity you can't meet Beau.'

'You have a horse?'

'I do. In Peshawar.'

This was the first time India had been mentioned. She chose her words carefully.

'When will you see him again?'

'Quite soon as a matter of fact. I go back there in two weeks.'

She was nettled by his and her parents' duplicity. 'I had no idea.'

He turned to look at her. 'I know, and I owe you an apology.'

'How long will you be gone for?'

'Another year, at least.'

'I see.'

'I'm very sorry for not making things clearer.'

Now she felt the burden of his discomfiture, which quite disarmed hers. 'It doesn't matter.'

'I think it does.'

'No, no. Really.'

'I've avoided mentioning my going, because I don't look forward to it.'

'How sad,' she said, meaning not only his departure that but everything – his unwillingness, her confused feelings.

'I don't know.' He pulled on the pony's forelock, pulled and smoothed, pulled and smoothed. 'Maybe I've had enough of soldiering.'

She sensed that this was a heavy, difficult thing for him to say and that there was no reply of hers that would make it any lighter. They were quiet, leaning together on the gate. Then he gave Jiggins' nose a brisk rub and seemed to take a grip, squaring and settling his shoulders and turning his face towards the house.

'This is all quite charming,' he said as they set off. 'This house, the gardens, everything.'

'Thank you, we do love it. I feel like a child though, every time I come back.'

'You had a happy childhood.' It was a statement.

'Yes, very. I've been very lucky all my life.'

'All your life . . .' She felt him glance at her, but there was no smile in his voice, he wasn't teasing her. 'There's a place I'd like to show you before I leave,' he said. 'Would you allow me to do that?'

'Of course,' she said. 'I'd like it.'

A few days later, Stanley drove her down to Devon.

'My house,' he said. 'My father built it. My mother named it Heart's Ease.'

She could tell from the timbre of his voice how important this was to him and how much store would be set on her reaction. The truth was that this place was not as lovely as Ardonleigh, being both older and plainer. But where the garden fell away beyond the terrace and the lawn, was a view of such sparkling beauty that she exclaimed,

'Oh look, how lovely!'

They were on top of a hill, below which a band of trees gave way to chequered fields, some already showing the ochre stripes of early autumn. In the middle distance a broad bay gleamed like a smile, a lazy river estuary joined it on the far, eastern end and was protected by a red bluff fringed with pines. Behind the bay a tumble of roofs and wedding-cake white houses gleamed in the sun. She could hear the mewing of high, distant gulls, and see the white flash of their wings in the clear air.

As she gazed, enchanted, she felt Stanley's hand enclose hers, something that had not happened since they were first introduced.

'I'm so glad,' he said, 'that you like it.'

'Oh, I do! More than I can say.'

'In that case I wonder,' he added, in an uncharacteristically diffident tone, 'whether you might consider sharing it with me?'

Four

Occasionally, over past months, when the extraordinary thought had crossed her mind she had brushed it hastily — perhaps fearfully — aside. Now that it had been put into words she found she was not just taken aback but appalled. Impossible — she could not do it!

He must have read her face, because his voice became urgent, distressed.

'Barbara, my dear — I've been too abrupt. I don't know how to say these things. I've never asked anyone before, never.'

'That's all right, honestly. Stanley, thank you.' She wanted desperately to set him at his ease. What should she say? 'I'm flattered.'

'Flattered.' He understood her all too well, but still she babbled on.

'Yes of course, tremendously. And a little . . .' she sought an appropriate word '. . . over-awed.'

'Please don't be. You mustn't. Let me show you the rest before you make up your mind.' He released her hand, adding gruffly, 'No pony, I'm afraid.'

In spite of the glorious view shining below them, the tour was not a success, and Barbara could not enjoy it. Everything Stanley showed her, his every proud, explanatory remark, had become for her freighted with an expectation she could not fulfil. In the kitchen garden she was introduce to Mr Prayle, one half of the live-in couple who looked after the house.

'When my parents lived here, this was fully cultivated all year round, but for the time being Prayle keeps it ship-shape and with just enough for him and Mrs Prayle.'

'What a lot of work,' she said, 'just to . . .' She realised she had embarked on a remark that might sound rude and finished lamely '. . . keep it ship-shape.'

Prayle was civil and unsmiling. 'Yes miss, but won't take long to get everything planted and ready for when the Brigadier wants to come back.'

Her heart gave a sad, frightened lurch.

'I'm told this is good soil,' said Stanley.

'Proper good soil sir, the best.'

'Is Mrs Prayle in the house?'

'Down the town sir, at the shops.'

'I'm sorry we shall miss her.'

'She'll be sorry too.' Prayle stood patiently, one hand on his hoe.

'We'll let you get on.'

'Thank you, sir – nice to see you. Miss.'

Prayle made an abbreviated gesture towards his cap. As he continued to hoe she saw that he had a bad left leg, the ankle and foot encased in a massive built-up boot. A legacy, she presumed, of the war.

Stanley had seen her look. 'He was with my company at Ypres.'

They went in through the loggia, a tiled veranda containing a scrubbed, wooden table, folded deckchairs and more stuff covered by a faded tarpaulin. The house was cool and twilit, with a scent of polish. Barbara was reminded of a church; a place dedicated to one purpose, unlived-in, but cared for.

A grandfather clock ticked in the hall. In the drawing room, a screen covered in *découpage* stood just inside the door. The sofa and armchairs were well-worn, spotless and invitingly plumped-up, but Stanley did not suggest they sit. A wide mirror, topped with a falcon hung above the fireplace, and the fire-irons below it gleamed. In one corner was a piano, with a closed music book on the stand.

'Do you play?' she asked.

'No. My mother did and could sing quite creditably as well.' He opened the lid and pressed a couple of notes before closing it again. 'I keep it tuned in her honour.'

They didn't go upstairs – 'one bedroom is much like another' – but across the hall into the dining room. Here, there was a long table polished to a high gloss and a massive sideboard carved with frowning angels and the date *1705*, which he told her had been a bedhead bought separately and adapted.

'My father liked interesting old things. My mother was not so enthusiastic.'

'What about you?'

'Provided I'm comfortable, I don't worry about my surroundings. And, after two decades in the army, I'm pretty easy to please on both counts.'

Off the other side of the hall, overlooking the drive, was a mannish study, with framed maps on one wall and a bookcase full of seious-looking volumes on the other. A dark red afghan rug lay on the floor and a globe by the window. The desk with its tooled leather top was neat – like everything here, unused but ready for use. The blotter was snow-white, the brass pen tray polished. There was an inkwell made from a hoof, which she commented on.

'A kudu shot by my father in South Africa. Rather a fine thing in its way, but not to everyone's taste.'

The only other item on the desk was a photograph, a formal study of three people, a couple in their thirties and a child. The man was tall, handsomely whiskered and unsmiling, standing behind his seated wife. She was solemn too, but Barbara suspected that was due to the demands of the photographer. Her face was soft and round, with doe eyes and a full lower lip, a face made for laughter. But it was the third person that made her exclaim.

'Is that you?'

'Yes.'

'How sweet! How old were you?'

'I have no idea. Your guess would be as good, if not better, than mine, what do you think?'

'Two? Perhaps less – look at your curls.'

'Hm.' Stanley ran his hand over his head. 'Will you excuse me a moment? I just want to go down and take a look at the boiler, check everything's in order.'

His footsteps disappeared along the passage that led to the kitchen. Barbara replaced the photograph and went back into the hall. The front door was in a square portico with windows at right angles on either side. One of these afforded a view of the front gate some twenty yards away, a simple white-painted iron, five-bar affair which Stanley had closed carefully once the car was parked in the drive. Beyond it, the narrow lane that led up from the road was bisected by another – scarcely more than a footpath – which led, she'd been told, in one direction to the town and in the other to the Salting Beacon on the cliff. To the left the lane diverged and led to another house a little further down the hill.

As she looked, someone came to the gate. He appeared quite suddenly, his approach hidden by the tall shrubbery, and stood with both hands on the top of the gate, staring in at the car and then – no doubt of it – directly at Barbara. It was a bold stare, as if she, not he, were the outsider. He wore flannels, an open-necked shirt and a dusty black hat which he lifted as he caught her eye. The gesture struck her as mildly impertinent rather than courteous.

Flustered, she opened the door and stepped out.

'Can I help you?'

'Do you know,' he pursed his lips and frowned. 'I have absolutely no idea.' He was well spoken and his voice was light and quick as a boy's.

'Did you want to speak to the Brigadier?' she asked primly. 'He is here today.'

'Is he? Is he really?'

'Yes.'

'And what about you – just enjoying a pleasant run out into the country?'

He was straight-faced but she knew she was being teased. 'May I ask who you are?'

'I'm the Brigadier's neighbour, Jonathan Eldridge – ah, here he is.'

'Eldridge?'

Stanley came out of the front door and strode towards the gate, clipping her shoulder without apology as he passed.

He only barely lowered his voice, but she had the impression she was not intended to hear.

'Eldridge – what do you want?'

'Afternoon, sir. Nothing whatever, I saw the car and was taking a dekko, in case there were intruders, burglars, what have you, just being a good neighbour.'

'Well thank you, but everything's under control. Mr and Mrs Prayle are always here, as you know.'

'Still, you can't be too careful.'

'I'm aware of that.'

There was no doubt in Barbara's mind that Eldridge had been dismissed – almost rudely, in her opinion – but he made no move to go.

'Just down for the day? Beautiful weather for it.' When Stanley didn't reply, Eldridge leaned slightly to the side and directed his next question to her. 'What do you think of it round here? Delightful part of the world isn't it?'

Even shadowed by the hat brim, his eyes were mischievously bright. She realised that she was being invited to collude, in however small a way, with this complete stranger against Stanley.

'I haven't seen much of it.'

Stanley tapped the top of the gate. 'Now if you'll excuse us.'

'But of course.' Eldridge lifted the hat briefly and replaced it rather on the back of his head. His dark hair was lank and untidy, his skin pallid. Apart from the pallor he looked, she thought, like a gypsy. As he moved away, he fished a cigarette packet out of his pocket and raised the hand holding the packet in an airy salute.

'Glad I saw you. If you're down this way again come and knock on my door.'

Stanley watched him go – 'saw him off' was the phrase that

sprung to mind – and returned to her side, breathing noisily like an agitated horse.

'Not for the first time Barbara, I owe you an apology.'

'Why?'

'For seeming rude, to you, and to that fellow.'

'You don't like Mr Eldridge.'

'No, but that's no excuse. I find him aggravating, he has an insinuating manner but he's harmless.'

She considered this and was less sure. Stanley was flustered, not something she'd seen before.

'Why don't we go and sit in the loggia? It's nice and cool there.' She suggested gently.

'I was going to take you to the golf club for lunch.'

'It's not lunchtime yet.' She went ahead of him, out of the garden door and into the loggia. Before he could argue, she had opened one deck chair and he had little option but to open another.

'This is nice, such a pretty garden.' She linked her hands behind her head and they sat in silence for a moment before she asked, 'So where does Mr Eldridge live?'

'Down the lane. He's the tenant at Keeper's Cottage.'

'What about the keeper?'

'These days he has a house on the Barton estate. It's been many years since a keeper lived down there.'

Barbara could sense him settling and regrouping after the annoyance.

'And what does Mr Eldridge do there?'

'Some sort of painter, God knows.' Stanley settled his shoulders. 'I have really no idea and even less interest.'

That had put a stop to her questions, but Stanley had one more. He put it to her on the drive home, following a pleasant lunch in the golf club Guests' Dining Room and a walk up to the Salting Beacon. As they turned inland, away from the shining coast, she said,

'What a lovely day, thank you so much.'

'You thought so? You enjoyed yourself, really?'

'Very much, I can see why your mother gave the house its name.'

He muttered something about that being fanciful and then added gruffly, 'I didn't spoil things for you, I hope?'

'Spoil them, no. How could you?'

'I mean by jumping the gun.'

'No, not at all.' She looked out of the window at the black-berry hedges streaming by, the rounded fields beyond, and thought *Please don't! Please don't say any more about it — please!*

'I want to say just one more thing, if I may.'

'Of course.' Her voice was small.

'As you know, I go back in a couple of weeks and it could be as much as a year before I'm in England again. I would deem it the most enormous favour if you could, perhaps, give some consideration to my proposal before I leave . . .?' She was silent and he glanced at her. 'Would that be out of the question? Barbara?'

Stanley had never been anything but straight with her. She owed him the courtesy of a straight answer.

'I shall. I shall give it very serious consideration and I promise to let you know before then.'

'Thank you.' The happy relief in his voice jolted Barbara's heart. 'And I, in my turn, hereby undertake not to mention the subject again until I hear from you.'

Five

Mutual discretion dictated that no further arrangement was made between her and Stanley until the night before his departure, when they would be having drinks with her parents in London and dinner at the Savoy. The date sat in her diary, a source of quiet but unavoidable dread.

With the Season over, the early autumn days at Ardonleigh trickled gently by, marked by nothing more than walks with the dogs, tennis with friends and the vague idea that she should get some sort of little job now that she was fully 'out' and grown-up. When this idea occurred to her, she always set it aside because of the shadow of the Great Decision.

If she said yes, her job would consist in being Mrs Govan, a role she was even less qualified for than anything else. She had told none of her friends about Stanley in so many words – though their antennae were attuned to such things. Quite a few of them were now engaged and making plans, of the others the well-off were hell-bent on further fun, frolics and foreign travel. The less well-to-do girls headed towards brief courses in *cordon bleu* and Constance Spry in the cheerful expectation that something (or more accurately someone) would come up. Barbara knew that in the eyes of any of these she would be an object of considerable admiration, if not actually envy, but she could not bear to discuss it.

Her father was careful to betray no awareness whatever of the situation, let alone her dilemma. Julia, however, couldn't contain herself and one morning over weekday breakfast *à deux*, she gave into temptation.

'Have you heard from Stanley since your trip to Devon, darling?'

'No Mummy.' Barbara was not taken in by her mother's tone. 'I haven't.'

A moment ticked by, during which Julia poured both of them more coffee. 'He is such a dear.'

Barbara helped herself to milk. The newspaper lay, still folded, at the end of the table; she longed to open and hide behind it, but Julia was launched now.

'He thinks the absolute world of you, you know.'

'I'm not sure about that.'

'Oh *yes*. I'm sorry, but I absolutely have to ask . . .' Here it comes, thought Barbara, lifting her cup like a shield. '. . . how do you feel about him?'

Barbara closed her eyes, sipped and swallowed. 'I like him. We get on.'

Julia gave a little hoot of laughter. 'That's no answer!' She cocked her head. 'I hope . . .?'

'Very well, I give in.' Barbara put her cup down. 'Stanley asked me to marry him.'

Julia's long fingers flew to her cheeks. 'No!' Her mouth described astonishment, but her eyes were lit with delighted satisfaction. 'A proposal! Really and truly?'

'Don't tell me you're surprised.'

'Well, of course—'

'You and Daddy knew he was going to, when he came down before.'

'Before? Oh, then. He had mentioned it to your father; he's an extremely correct man, but as far as we were aware, nothing transpired.'

'It didn't. Not on that day. He asked me when we visited his house.'

'Ah, I *see* . . .'

Julia's face was quite swollen with anticipation; Barbara was suddenly aware of her own power. She was no longer a child, she was the person holding the cards, and the feeling was not invigorating.

'The house is a bit gloomy inside, but the garden's lovely and the position is wonderful. You can look down over the cliffs, and the rooftops and the sea.'

'So, in effect, he was saying "all this can be yours" . . .?'

'He asked me if I'd like to share it with him, yes.'

She paused and let the pause extend until Julia was obliged to end it.

'And would you?'

'I promised to tell him before he left.'

'Poor Stanley . . .!' There was a laugh in Julia's voice. 'Not a situation he's used to!'

'I've no idea.' Barbara realised this was true. 'Do you know—?'

'No, no – goodness no! Your father says he's never lost his heart or his head, at least as far as he's aware.' Julia leaned forward, all womanly sweetness. 'You're the first to have that effect.'

Barbara couldn't help it – she felt a pulse of pride, followed immediately by one of shame. Confusion and anxiety swept over her and her voice when she answered reflected that.

'You're wondering what I'm going to say to him.'

'Of course that's none of my business, darling. But I need hardly say, you could do a great deal worse and many would say not a great deal better!'

A few days later, when Barbara turned down Stanley Govan's proposal of marriage, those words, rather than any feelings of her own, were what influenced her. Her own feelings were unformed and unawakened, she scarcely recognised them. The possibility of doing a great deal worse was uninviting and of not doing much better, uninspiring. If Stanley's previously intact and self-possessed heart was broken, he didn't show it. He expressed the keenest disappointment, but also respect for her decision. His cheeks grew a little pink. They finished their dinner quickly and quietly, and he drove her home in a silence that held no shadow of resentment. She had never so fully appreciated his unwavering concern for her own comfort. He saw her to her door and, as they stood at the top of the steps, she spoke.

'I'm so sorry, Stanley.'

'My dear, there's no need.'

'I hope you understand that . . .' She wasn't entirely sure what it was that she wanted him to understand, or how she would frame it, so it was a relief when he immediately stepped in to the awkward silence.

'I understand everything. These past few weeks have been a source of the most enormous pleasure to me.'

'And to me.'

He took her hand in both of his and, for the first time, kissed her. The kiss was placed on her forehead like a blessing.

'Goodbye Barbara. Please give my regards to your parents, I shan't come in tonight. I look forward to seeing them on my next leave.'

She noticed, with a pang, that she was not included in this hope. Though her goodbye was small and dry as an autumn leaf, her eyes stung. By the time he reached the bottom of the steps, she had gone into the building and closed the door behind her. Both her parents were discreet, barely raising their eyes when she said goodnight. She went straight to bed, where she cried and cried before falling asleep. When she woke in the morning she felt light and fresh, rinsed through by relief.

Rosemary was among those former school friends with whom she had stayed in touch and the only person of her own age in whom she confided. Neither was engaged, nor employed, nor (for the moment anyway) qualified to be so. As others who had done the season moved on, or away, and became at least nominally grown-up, they reverted to a kind of childhood. Rosemary came to stay and the two of them spent days walking the dogs, patrolling Jiggins round the lanes on his lead rope, eating apples in the chilly hayloft and perfecting dance steps to the gramophone. They wore comfortable clothes and shoes and let their hair go its own way. Julia had swallowed her disappointment and wisely said nothing. After Christmas, things would inevitably change.

Barbara's revelation was handsomely rewarded. Ros gaped and then shrieked,

'No! Lawks a mercy!' They were fooling about playing first-to-fifty in the billiard room. 'Were you expecting that?'

'I suspected it might be coming, but sort of hoping it wouldn't.'

'I can jolly well imagine!'

'Please don't tell anyone.'

'Hope to die!'

'No one at all, Ros.' Barbara felt a pang of remorse and what she realised was tenderness for Stanley. 'Please. Promise.'

'I wouldn't dream of it.' Ros replaced her cue in the rack and flopped down in one of the green, leather armchairs, with her legs over the arm. 'But what a dark horse, Bar – you do at least owe me the story.'

'There isn't much of one.'

'Do your very best.'

When she'd heard what there was, Ros said, 'Well, you obviously did the honourable thing. In spite of his brilliant war, his many virtues and his palatial house—'

'It wasn't palatial.'

'All right, his gentleman's residence, what did you say it was called?'

'Heart's Ease. His mother named it.'

'Gosh!' Ros pulled a friendly smirk. 'A romantic streak in the family, then.'

'She certainly had one.'

'In spite of *all that*, you turned him down.'

'I didn't love him. I couldn't . . .' Barbara leaned down, picking at the pile of the Afghan rug by her feet. She added in a practical sort of voice, 'And anyway, I could never have coped.'

'What was that? Coped? Of course you could. If you'd *wanted* to, you'd have coped and Stanley would have helped his pretty, little wife.'

Barbara could hear the tease, which then became a laugh, plucking at the tension of recent days and weeks until she began to laugh too. When Julia opened the door a moment later she found the two of them rocking, shrieking and snorting like a couple of drunks and was far from sure what to make of it.

Gerry Gorringe was a nice, goofily amusing young man, whiling away time in the city, while waiting to inherit rolling acres in Dorset. His invitation to attend a 'house party and treasure hunt' – while his people were in New York – came at just the right moment, when the darkening weeks before Christmas might otherwise have grown tedious. Ros was back at home and suffering from the flu, but Julia positively ushered Barbara out of the house and into the new Sunbeam roadster that was her pride and joy.

'This is exactly the right thing,' she declared, zooming injudiciously round corners en route to the station, she was a dashing driver. 'You need a bit of proper fun after everything.'

Barbara forbore to say that the 'everything' referred to had probably caused her mother more distress than her, but she did point out that she *had* been having fun, with Ros.

'Ros is an absolute dear, but that's hardly the same.'

They both knew that by 'fun' Julia meant mixed company and the opportunities it afforded. But she also meant well and Barbara was looking forward to the weekend. On the telephone the night before her father had enjoined her to 'lark about a bit'. After the school-girlish interlude with Ros, the prospect of jolly, undemanding company and games with others of her own age felt like the natural next stage.

But the next stage of what? She wondered, as she closed the train door and joined her companions – a befurred dowager in a Persian lamb hat and her sweet-faced, paid companion – in the first-class compartment. She and the young woman exchanged a quick, collusive smile. Outside the window, the brown-and-green countryside with pewter-coloured winter woods began to chug past beyond the smoke. Barbara thought, *I am lucky, so lucky not to be at the beck and call of a spoiled old woman . . . lucky to have friends, and invitations . . . lucky to have time . . . Lucky* (she made herself think this) *to have escaped.*

Time, yes. That was why she didn't *feel* as lucky as she should. After this weekend, time spread out as featureless and heavy as the pale sky outside the window. The pleasant sensation of relief could not, by definition, last long. You were embattled, then relieved, then you regrouped and moved forward. But she wasn't doing that, was she? She was replaying the past year like one of those songs you got on the brain, that you couldn't shake off.

The Gorringes' Georgian manor house was freezing. That night after dinner, they danced in the drawing room, to keep warm as much as anything. Fires lit in marble baronial grates looked cheerful, but seemed only to be warming the spinney of chimneys far above. There were twelve of them, including Gerry and his brisk older sister Marjory who, along with Sugden the farm manager, had ferried those arriving by train the three or four miles from the station. About half of them were familiar to Barbara; Gerry was, of course, with his rush of teeth, chortley laugh, gangly legs and paddle-like hands that he employed to such droll effect on the dance floor. There was also the pale, patrician Lucia, who (with Ros) had made up their triumvirate at St Agatha's. Julian and Edgar were two young men from London with enough cash and flash to ensure their attendance at any party. Then there was a fashionable, sarcastic, young woman called Molly (christened Molly the Libertine by Lucia) who was scarecrow-thin in her slippery, stylish clothes, with a cap of raspberry-red hair, slanting, kohl-rimmed eyes and a crackling laugh that could be heard across the room. The rest of the group seemed to be old county friends of the Gorringes, comfortably at ease with their host and his icy house.

Barbara had missed dancing. She took the floor with Gerry, with Ed, with a local fellow named Maurice. She shimmied, she glided, she kicked her legs and whirled her arms. For a while she became the centre of attention and positively revelled in it. After a few records, she took a breather. Molly materialised next to her and offered her a cigarette from a mother-of-pearl case.

'No?' She took one herself and lit it with a tiny, sparkly lighter. 'I thought you might need one after all that.'

'I'll have a drink though . . .'

'Hear that?' Molly tapped the attendant Maurice on the arm. 'Your partner needs a drink.'

'Then she shall have one!'

'And another, if you can manage it.'

'Forthwith!'

'My, oh my.' Molly raised her eyebrows. 'You were a positive whirling dervish.'

'I enjoy dancing and haven't had the chance for ages.'

'Really? That won't do. Whatever have you been up to?'

Barbara suspected that Molly had heard something from someone and was picking up on the scent.

'Nothing much. I've been at home, making plans.'

'Plans, good for you!' The rasping laugh rang out. 'Is it all right to ask what they are?'

'Quite all right, but they're rather fuzzy at the moment.'

'Ah . . . Thanks.' Molly took a drink from the returned Maurice. 'Plans are like that, I find. They hang about in the background, preying on one's mind, demanding attention and generally being a nuisance until one gives them the heave-ho. Aren't I right?'

She addressed this last question to Maurice, who appeared startled to have his opinion sought.

'Very probably – yes, I'd say so.'

'So here's to fuzziness . . .!'

'Do you have any yourself?' Barbara asked.

'Perish the thought. I'm a great believer in Something coming up.'

'Me too!' Maurice put his oar in, nodding fervently. 'Extraordinary how it always does.'

'Quite,' said Molly, her eyes still on Barbara. 'Doesn't it just?'

It was Julian's suggestion that they play Sardines. Mixed reactions only fuelled his enthusiasm.

'This is the perfect house!'

'It's enormous,' said Gerry, 'we'll be sending out search parties.'

'All the better. Bags I hide.'

Molly laughed. 'What happens if *you* get lost?'

'I was a boy scout.'

'Also,' went on Gerry, as if confiding information that might surprise them, 'it's pretty damn chilly away from the main rooms.'

In spite of the laughter, Julian was now into his stride. 'Once we find each other we can huddle together for warmth.'

'And the lighting's not all it might be.'

'Come on Gerry, where's your spirit of adventure?'

'I don't need one,' Gerry pointed out. 'Remember, I live here.'

'Then you hide! You'll know all the best places.'

'If we're going to play, I need to be on patrol with a torch, mopping up the stragglers.'

'No torch!' Molly said, 'that'd be cheating.'

This comment, coming from her, seemed to give the group's imprimatur to the project. Faces turned to look at her expectantly.

'Oh? Shall I? Right you are.' She stubbed out her cigarette and put down her glass. 'I shall hide, but I want a clear ten minutes before you come looking.'

'Righty-ho,' said Gerry. 'Would you like some instructions on where not to go?'

'Of course not. I shan't go outside, far too cold. Nowhere beyond the front door, but anywhere inside is fair game and there's to be no turning lights on.'

'You're a hard woman, Mol.' Gerry consulted his watch. 'Your time starts . . . Now!'

Barbara watched Molly swish from the room. Her stride was long, her feet narrow and pointed in kingfisher-blue shoes. She was like some haughty creature, a giraffe or a unicorn, a law unto herself

Ed hove alongside. 'Want to team up?'

'Good idea,' said Barbara. 'I'd be lost in two seconds.'

'You can get lost in *four* seconds, with me.'

Ten minutes later Gerry flourished his torch.

'Go! Seek! Give a good scream if you fall down any stairs and I'll come and rescue you!'

There was much shrieking and giggling as people rushed off, but Ed held on to Barbara's wrist.

'Hold your horses. I've got a theory.'

Lucia wandered over to the gramophone and began sifting through records.

'Well I'm not going anywhere. I'm going to play sweet music to guide people back to base.'

Gerry stood out in the hall, shamelessly moving the proscribed torch in wide arcs, high and low. The soft beam swept over: stony-eyed portraits; an antelope's head with twisted horns; a couple fleeing hand in hand up the stairs; the balustrade of a high gallery; an open door on the opposite side of the hall and a closed one at the back; a huge mirror that caught the flitting beam like a will o' the wisp. Catching Ed and Barbara's reflection in the lighted drawing room, Gerry swung round.

'Come on you two, what are you hanging about there for?'

'All right, all right!' Ed put his arm round Barbara and raised a defensive hand. 'We're going!'

'But I'm not . . .' cooed Lucia over the strains of 'What'll I do . . .?' '. . . And you can't make me.'

'I wouldn't dream of it.' Gerry passed them in the doorway. 'Go on, what are you waiting for? Care to dance, Lucy . . .?'

He pulled the door to behind him. In the chilly darkness, Barbara tried to remember where the landmarks were: the stairs to their left, with the gallery far above . . . the tall, wide door opposite, like the mouth of a cave . . . beyond the foot of the stairs, at the end of a short corridor, the backstairs door, firmly closed. Was that, perhaps, a forbidden area . . .? The muffled music from the drawing room, the distant whispers, hoots and pattering of the other seekers, emphasised the stillness down here.

'Where shall we go?' she asked.

'Want to hear my theory?'

'Go on.'

'Well, you know Molly, crafty as a sack of weasels. My guess is that she won't have gone far. She could be listening to us right now.' He cocked his head. 'Molly . . .? Mol, are you there . . .?'

The record ended and, for a long moment, there was no sound from elsewhere. A fog of silence enveloped them. Barbara's scalp crawled. For some reason she didn't care for the idea of Molly lurking close by – crouched and contained in her hiding-place – probably smiling to herself.

Ed's fingers folded about her wrist. 'I know how her mind works.'

He began to lead her across the hall in the direction of the servants' door. Behind the sweeping curve of the stairs was a recess, they bumped into velvet curtains which yielded with a soft rattle of rings. Where the curtain brushed Barbara's face it gave off a pungent smell – smoke, old clothing and something fetid and animal. She exclaimed and flapped her hands, beating it off.

'Ssh!'

'Why do we have to be quiet?'

'Because we want to surprise her,' Ed leaned in; she could feel his breath on her ear. 'Because she's too clever by half.'

There was a shriek and giggling from some far-off part of the house, above their heads. Music started up again in the drawing room, '*If you knew Suzie . . .*'

'You have a look in here,' whispered Ed.

'I'd rather not.'

'In that case, I will. Why don't you take a look through the little door, see where it goes.'

'I'm sure that'll be out of bounds.'

'Other door, then, use your initiative, scout around. I'll do the same, back here in a sec. And—' now his face was close enough to see the glimmering holes of his eyes and his fingers were pressed on her mouth '—Sssh.'

Like a pantomime villain, he stepped behind the curtain and disappeared.

I hate this, she thought. *I don't want to be here.* These thoughts surprised her. She entertained a sudden, unbidden mental picture of Stanley and was shocked to find her eyes stinging with childish tears. What was the matter with her? This was only a game, after all, and only a few yards away a narrow ribbon of light showed where Gerry and Lucia were happily dancing to the jaunty music. She could go straight back in there now if she wanted.

But some deeply ingrained notion of correctness – from home, from school, or simply bred in the bone – told her not to be pathetic. She must not wilt, but be a good sport and get on with it. The temperature out here was as Gerry had predicted.

Her feet were frozen, as was every inch of bare skin. Rubbing her arms vigorously she headed for the large open door which led into the library – there had been a fire in the room on their arrival, and a sumptuous tea laid out. Now the fire was no more than a pile of crimson-veined rubble in the grate. The room was huge, far bigger than the drawing room, the tall bookcases marching away on either side, away from the small, dusty light of the embers into blackness. She remembered something her father would say, 'Escape from the light and the dark will be your friend.'

Long windows to her right, at the front of the house, over-looked the broad drive and wooded park. There was a little moonlight and, with her back to the dying fire, she could make out lighter chinks between the curtains. Wind nudged an ill-fitting window. A pattering and hissing, like something being dragged, made her jump and hold her breath, until she realised that it had started to rain.

Drawing the curtains would surely not breach the no lights rule. She went to the window nearest the door and reaching high with both hands, parted the curtains. Torrential rain sizzled down on the gravel and sailed in fluid columns across the park. The branches of the trees churned, but what caught Barbara's eye was a movement to her right. Outside the front door of the house, the Gorringes had adapted their portico into a huge outer porch. The lower half of the porch was stone-work that blended with the frontage of the house and the outer columns. The upper half was glass, divided into long panes which were now, like the rest of the house, dark, and streaming with water. But she could see three pale shapes fanned out against the glass – two high up, another some three feet lower down. She could make no sense of them until one of the higher shapes moved, lifting away from the glass and repositioning itself. At the same time she detected another, more solid black shape, also move and now she realised what she was looking at: hands.

Hands, palms planted against the glass side of the porch, two braced above someone's head, the other, fingers spread down-wards, supporting a second person. And in between, behind the racing raindrops, a creased and flattened pad of material slithering against the smooth surface in a jerky rhythm.

Nowhere beyond the front door.

Shocked, she took a step back, and reached for the curtains. As she did so she glimpsed, between the raised hands, a bone-white disc of face with dark smears of mouth and eyes. Dropping the curtains she stumbled backwards and out of the room, her arms out in front of her like a sleepwalker. When she found the banister she clutched it and lowered herself on to the stairs. Her heart was racing and the blood had drained from her head. She felt faint and a little sick.

'Barbara . . .? Is that you? You here?'

Ed placed a fumbling hand on her shoulder, patting her cheek and hair. 'There you are. Any joy?'

She shook her head. 'No.'

'No one has.' He sidestepped round and sat down next to her. 'They're all still crashing about up there.'

Cold and nauseous she laid her head on her knees and he touched the back of her neck again, this time solicitously.

'You all right Bar?' She shook her head. 'Perhaps you should go somewhere more comfortable.' A couple were coming down the stairs behind them. 'Hang on, don't trip over us, got a casualty here.'

By the time Ed had parked her in an armchair by the drawing-room fire the others – chilled to the bone and, now the excitement had worn off, bored and impatient with the search – were returning in dribs and drabs. Ed found someone more amusing to talk to and Marjory brought her a cup of tea and pulled up a stool next to her.

'Here we are. Strong and sweet – thought it might help.'

'Thank you so much. This isn't like me.'

'Or anyone,' said Marjory in her no-nonsense way. 'No one ever expects to feel faint, but it happens to the best of us.'

In the room behind them, people were chattering over the clink of refreshed glasses, the click and sigh of cigarettes being lit. No music, they were discussing the game and the distinct possibility that Molly had cheated. Gerry came over.

'I'm taking a straw poll,' he said. 'Leave her to stew, wherever she is, or turn on every light in the place and flush her out?'

Barbara closed her eyes. 'I don't mind.'

'Leave her to stew,' said Marjory. 'She's perfectly capable of finding her own way back.'

'What if she's had an accident?'

'She'll yell. She's got a loud enough voice.'

'Let's hope so.'

Five minutes later, the result of the straw poll apparently accorded with Marjory's view, because someone put on 'Someone to watch over me' and Ed and Julian were singing along, doing their double act. Molly's whereabouts were forgotten.

Barbara finished her tea and got up. She no longer felt light-headed, but she wanted more than anything to be on her own, beneath the covers. Marjory stood up too, politely affecting a stifled yawn.

'Up the wooden hill . . .?'

'I think I shall, if it's all the same to you.' She added, 'I want to be on form tomorrow, for the treasure hunt.'

'Fox and hounds, actually, slight change of plan. Still a prize though!'

Lucia met her by the door.

'Are you recovered? Ed said you had a funny turn.'

'I'm fine now, but I'm going to bed.'

'Night-night then.' Lucia proffered a cool, pale cheek. 'Sleep tight.'

'I shall.'

One or two others carolled goodnight and Gerry called, 'Watch out for Molly . . .!'

Barbara closed the door after her. There was now some light in the hall from two standard lamps on either side of the door and from a great spherical brass table lamp by the balustrade on the first floor landing. She was leaden with tiredness. She slipped off her shoes, and pulled the gardenia from her hair as she trudged up the stairs. When she reached the gallery she paused, alerted by a movement down in the hall. The front door opened and through it came a man, who headed swiftly and quietly for the servants' entrance below where Barbara was standing, then Molly. She surveyed herself for a second in the mirror, dabbing at her hair with pointed fingers and smoothing her dress, before heading for the drawing room. A riotous burst of complaint and laughter greeted her entrance but her rasping voice overrode it.

'Now then everyone, don't let's be bad losers . . .!'

The mattress on Barbara's bed had a trough in it and the sheets were cold, but there were down pillows, a comforting pile of blankets and a fat eiderdown. She snuggled down like a dormouse, with one strand of her hair wrapped round her forefinger. What she had seen was nothing to do with her . . . it was none of her business.

But just before falling asleep, a tiny mouse of memory scratched at her consciousness, trying to get in. Something she had missed.

Six

The arrangement for the next day was that breakfast would be between eight and nine, and that, breakfasted or not, they should all meet in the hall, dressed in warm and weather-proof clothes, at nine thirty.

About half the company met over the bacon and eggs and it was pretty clear that Barbara, having 'retired hurt last night' as Gerry put it, was now feeling a good better than the rest. They had stayed up till the small hours and drunk the cabinet dry. Tomato juice, Worcester sauce and a basket of eggs, along with cut-glass tumblers, had been thoughtfully placed at the end of the sideboard by the butler, Streetly. The initial silence was broken only by the clink and swallow of medicinal prairie oysters.

Conversation round the table was desultory. It was warmer, they noted, and it had stopped raining. Just as well, because Marjory poured scorn on their clothing.

'We've got a fiendish fox, he's going to lead you thorough bush, thorough brier!' she announced with steely brightness. 'I suggest you all go and have a rummage in the boot room and under the stairs, there are masses of old coats and whatnot.'

'Dear God,' said Molly, black coffee poised en route to her perfectly painted carmine lips, 'if it's going to be that hearty, I'm giving it a miss.'

'It's meant to be a challenge,' Gerry told her. 'Damn it all, we all came looking for you last night.'

'And failed miserably.'

'We tried our best. Poor Bar had a funny turn in the process.'

'Oh yes.' Molly turned raised eyebrows to Barbara. 'I was sorry to hear about that.'

'I'm fine now thanks.'

'So,' Ed leaned back in his chair, 'are you going to tell us where you were?'

'Certainly not, that's my secret.' *And mine,* thought Barbara. 'And I shall take it to the grave.'

Gerry looked round the assembled pallid faces. 'Time to 'fess up, anyone know where she was?' There were mumbles and shaken heads. 'But we're not all here, anyway – I bet someone does.'

Barbara spread her toast with regular, even strokes.

'Of course,' said Molly. 'But I paid them to keep their mouth shut.'

This got a ripple of laughter.

She's joking, thought Barbara. *She doesn't know I saw and I shall say nothing.*

It was nearer ten when the last stragglers arrived in the hall and Marjory was able to deliver her briefing. Some people – the locals – had thorn-proof tweeds, mackintosh capes and hats of their own. Others had braved the boot room and the collection of old coats under the stairs and appeared looking faintly ridiculous but determined to withstand the jeers. Molly was dressed, quite unapologetically, for a stroll along the *Promenade des Anglais.*

'What? If there's somewhere I can't go, then I shan't.'

'Up to you,' said Marjory. 'Now listen.' She raised her voice commandingly. 'Listen, everyone!' They turned to her like obedient children. All except for Molly, who was sitting on the wooden bench in the porch, one arm resting casually along the back, one neatly-shod foot swinging, as if she were impatient to be off.

'. . . it's a race,' Marjory was saying, 'a contest and, believe it or not, there's a prize. I hope you saw to that Gerry?'

'Yes ma'am!'

'Our fox went off two hours ago, he'll probably have gone to ground by now, but he'd have left a trail. I'm giving you each a piece of paper with the meaning of the signs.' She handed a sheaf of papers to Gerry, who began distributing them. The mood of the meeting was now one of humorous rebellion.

'Hey!' Julian waved his piece of paper. 'Who's a map reader? I want to be with that man. What, no one?'

Marjory pressed on. 'We're going to send you off in your twos and threes at three-minute intervals. There will be false trails from time to time, but if you do get diverted there will eventually be a sign telling you to stop and turn back.'

'*Eventually* . . .*!*' someone moaned. 'How long is all this going to take?'

'Not more than, oh, say three hours?' More good-natured groans. 'I'm taking the car, with hot coffee to a point on the trail – no I'm not saying where. Obviously if you get lost, make your way back to the road and come home.'

'And if we find Mr Fox?' Ed asked.

'He'll give you a token, so we know you're not fibbing, and if you're the fastest you'll get our wonderful prize later on.'

Perhaps put off by what had happened last night, Ed didn't invite Barbara to be his partner this time. Lucia however, sought her out.

'What do you think, shall we? We can make up for brawn with brains.'

'You forgot beauty.' This was Molly, who had returned from the porch and was buttoning the neck of her fur-trimmed, camel coat. 'What do you think; shall we be the Three Graces?'

Barbara found herself tongue-tied but Lucia agreed enthusiastically. 'You won't regret it, I don't like the dark but I'm a country girl at heart – my father was an absolute fiend for long, difficult walks.'

Molly's smile was thin as a blade. 'There'll be none of that with me, darling.' She raised her finger at Marjory, as if catching the eye of a waiter. 'Er – we'll go last, if that's all right!'

'Permission granted.' Marjory glanced askance at her shoes. 'I can't help thinking that would be extremely wise.'

They set off fifteen minutes later, Barbara and Lucia carrying their crib sheets, Molly's left on the hall table. 'How many do we need . . .?'

It was a day of rain-washed sunshine, glinting puddles and soft, heavy clouds. The park gleamed with wetness and the amber leaves appeared lit from inside. High above the trees rooks wheeled and tumbled.

Lucia paused and pointed. 'Did you know that rooks are the only birds known to play?'

'Good gracious,' said Molly without looking up. 'I had no idea.'

Lucia and Barbara watched for a moment. Molly drifted some paces away. She appeared preoccupied. They caught up with her and Barbara tapped her piece of paper.

'We should look out for an arrow.'

'You'd better keep your eyes peeled, then.'

'Here's one!' Barbara found the three twigs at the side of the drive.

'Well naturally,' said Molly, 'we go that way. I can see some people down by the gate.'

There was indeed another group at the end of the drive, first conferring, then moving off. Following Molly, sashaying along in her unsuitable shoes, Barbara and Lucia both felt rather foolish. Molly was humming a tune; there was no doubt she was in a strange mood, but they felt curiously flattered to be chosen.

From the house to the stone gate posts, where they'd seen the others, was further than it appeared because the drive made two long bends between the trees. Before long Lucia was drawing ahead, with Molly dawdling and Barbara (thinking, *this is me all over*) maintaining a pace that kept her equidistant between the two of them.

Lucia looked over her shoulder. 'Found another one!'

'Well done.'

'Why the excitement?' said Molly. 'We know we have to get to the road anyway.'

Lucia wasn't put out. 'It's good practice though, to find the signs.'

'If you say so.'

Lucia reached the gate and started peering around.

'What's she hunting for?' murmured Molly. 'The others went left.'

'They could be wrong,' ventured Barbara.

'No.' Molly stopped. 'No, they're not.' Lucia waved her piece of paper and pointed energetically.

'Come on!'

'Coming!'

'Oh, don't let's,' said Molly.

'What?'

'Why don't we just have a nice stroll and go back?'

Lucia waved again and set off, moving out of sight up the lane.

Barbara looked from one to the other. 'Actually, I think I'll carry on.'

'Up to you.' She let Barbara take a few steps. 'I know exactly where the fox is.'

'Really? How?'

Molly cocked her head on one side like a sleek, sagacious, hard-eyed bird. 'Well, it doesn't take a genius to work out that our Reynard is going to go in some sort of circle.'

'I suppose.' Barbara shot a longing glance at the empty gateway. 'But that's not the point.'

'Not playing the game, what-what?'

'If you put it like that.'

'Remember it *is* only a game. Go on Babs, live dangerously. Take the shortcut with me.'

Barbara was not nor ever had been 'Babs', but she didn't know how to object without appearing pompous.

'All right.'

'Attagirl. Our third – what's her name?'

'Lucia.'

'Lucia, she won't miss us, she'll be hot on the trail by now, overtaking others and goodness knows what. Come.'

Molly linked her arm through Barbara's, tucking her own hand back in her coat pocket as she did so. The gesture was both friendly and domineering. After a few steps, Barbara feigned something in her boot to get free.

'So where do you suggest we go?'

'Let's see . . . Why don't we explore round the other side of the house? Kitchen gardens and stable blocks would normally bore me rigid, but on this occasion something tells me they might reward investigation.'

They retraced their steps, pausing for a moment when the car, with Marjory at the wheel, swept down the drive towards them and paused, window rolled down. Two springer spaniels panted and wagged on the back seat.

'What's this? Dipping out already?'

With dazzling (and Barbara couldn't help feeling practised) presence of mind Molly pointed at her shoes and pulled a face.

'You were right. I'm going back to find something more suitable. Then Barbara and I will run like the wind, won't we?'

Marjory made a noise between a snort and a hoot of derision. As she drove off, dogs barking, Molly drawled, 'Boo sucks to you!'

This made Barbara laugh. She was already an accessory to a lie and probably to further cheating, but what did it really matter? The combination of the fine day, the pleasant surroundings and the sense of being chosen for an adventure, was working on her. She was beginning to enjoy herself.

The house, too, seemed benign, having returned to its workday self after the unsettling goings-on last night. As they crossed the gravel sweep, they could make out the figure of Streetly stalking through the library and a girl in parlourmaid's uniform pushing a carpet sweeper about in the drawing room. One of the upstairs windows was open and a duster appeared and was shaken briskly.

'Isn't this nice?' said Molly, and Barbara found herself agreeing. They fell into step and she realised that if Molly linked arms again, she wouldn't mind.

They rounded the side of the house and passed under the arch that led to the stable yard. Three motors, presumably the property of guests, were neatly parked at the far end. A couple of handsome bay hunters looked over their doors at them and, in one of the stalls, a lad was working on the horse with a straw whisp, whistling between his teeth. Barbara had a slight sense of intrusion, but Molly carolled a merry 'Good morning!'

'Morning miss!'

'We're just exploring!'

'Right-o miss.'

On the opposite side of the yard were the garages, one of them empty, the other containing Gerry's yellow roadster. Facing them, between the parked cars, was a wooden door.

'Ah,' said Molly, 'that way I think.'

They went through and found themselves in a large kitchen garden, perhaps a quarter of an acre, stretching to their left. It was laid out to beds of herbs and vegetables, rows of neatly tended fruit trees and surrounded by grey stone walls covered with elegant fans of espaliered fruits. Immaculate grassy paths threaded the vegetable beds. The wall to their right contained another door, leading to the garden of the house. At the end of the kitchen garden was a long greenhouse reflecting the sunshine, full of what looked like a jungle of vegetation. Molly set off in this direction.

'What on earth,' she murmured rhetorically, 'can one family want with all this stuff?'

'There are estate workers I suppose,' said Barbara, following. 'And perhaps they sell it.'

Molly sighed.

As they drew closer, they could see that the greenhouse contained an enormous vine. Its main trunk was like a twisted anaconda stretching from one end to the other, with a mass of branches reaching out on all sides, curving and straining, pressing tendrils against the glass. Several bunches of small green grapes hung amongst the foliage.

'Look at that, for heaven's sake,' said Molly. 'Do you think they make wine?'

'Chateau Gorringe. We must ask Gerry.'

'Let's go in.'

'Will there be room?'

Molly didn't bother to answer, but led the way to the end of the greenhouse, and opened the door. Inside the humid heat was like dragon's breath.

'Wonderful . . .!' sighed Molly.

The trunk of the vine rose from an Ali Baba-sized terracotta pot to the left of the door and roamed away from them for some fifteen yards, making the end of the greenhouse invisible. The branches reached not only to the side, but overhead, slithering beneath the roof so that they were enclosed in a tunnel of green. There was a sense of powerful, unstoppable growth, as if at any moment one of the sinuous, grey, muscular branches might come curling down and wrap itself round them. Barbara felt compelled to glance over her shoulder to check that the door was still there and visible, that they weren't imprisoned. She noticed a faint, not unpleasant smell that she couldn't identify.

Molly was a little way in front, peering about, head cocked in that birdlike way of hers. Now she stopped.

'Aha, Mr Fox – got you!'

He was perched on a wooden table, near the back wall of the greenhouse. The curtains of vines on either side of him meant that, at first, all they could see were his legs stretched out, crossed at the ankles, a wisp of smoke and one hand, holding a dark cigarette – the smell of which Barbara had noticed.

'Come on out,' said Molly. 'You're well and truly found.'

'I need hardly ask,' said a voice, 'whether you cheated.'

'Of course we did!' Molly turned a gleeful look on Barbara to include her in the victory. 'We have our reputations to think of.'

'We?'

'Come on out of there. Show yourself and see.'

He uncrossed his legs and rose, coming into sight head first. Molly let out a rasping cackle of mirth. On his head was a lopsided circlet of vine and a small cluster of grapes hung over one ear.

'Hello Molly, you old cheat.'

'Am not . . .!' She flapped a hand, incapable with mirth.

He removed the circlet with a formal gesture as if doffing a hat and addressed Barbara.

'I'd say how do you do, but I have the strong impression we've met before.'

'Really?' He was right, she knew he was right, but the thought worried her.

'Yes . . .' He surveyed her through narrowed eyes, tapping a finger against his lips. 'Yes, yes, definitely . . . give me a moment . . .'

Molly, her face still carrying the traces of laughter, looked from one to the other.

'Is anyone going to tell me what on earth you're talking about?'

'Hang on, I'm thinking.'

'I'm afraid I can't help,' said Barbara. She sounded jittery even to herself. 'I honestly have no idea.'

'Well *I* certainly don't.'

'Got it!' He clicked his fingers. 'How is our mutual friend the brigadier?'

'I'm sorry?' Though she knew of course what he meant.

'Brigadier Govan. The man with the empty house. Heart's Ease. You were with him there when I happened to pass by, back in the summer.'

'Oh, then . . .!' The relief threatened to drain coherent thought and she had to get a grip. 'Maybe . . . yes. Yes. Hello.'

'I don't believe we were properly introduced. Jonathan Eldridge.'

'Barbara Delahay.'

He proffered a hand and gave hers a short, light squeeze.

'I have no idea what's going on,' Molly said.

'Our first meeting was rather tense,' he told her. 'For some reason, the brigadier doesn't care for me.'

'I don't blame him.'

'Cruel, cruel.' Eldridge shot Barbara a sideways grin of such brilliance and warm, collusive charm that she found herself smiling back.

'Be that as it may,' Molly went on, 'now I've proved how clever I am and we've tracked you to your lair with no trouble at all, we'd better cut along. Because of course we wouldn't dream of claiming the prize, would we?'

'Whatever is it?' asked Eldridge, as if this were the most fascinating topic imaginable.

'God alone knows – bath salts? A bottle of indifferent sherry?'

'Ah, something to reward effort rather than low cunning.'

'Precisely.'

'Anyway,' said Barbara, 'you're right. The first of the hounds can't be far away and it will be most embarrassing if they find us already here.'

'Yes, go!' said Eldridge. 'Go! I shall settle back and await developments.'

Molly swept out. Eldridge waved a hand at Barbara as he bent to pick up the coronet with the other.

'Hang on. You need a token.'

'Oh, don't worry, we're not in earnest.'

'Never mind. Here.'

He tweaked off the small bunch of grapes and handed it to her.

'I can't believe *you* cheated – you might get the awful sherry.'

She hurried out of the greenhouse, closing the door after her. After the close heat the day no longer felt balmy; the fresh, November air cooled the mist of perspiration on her skin and made her shiver. But the little grapes were warm in her hand and, when she popped one in her mouth, it burst with sweetness on her tongue as she ran to catch up with Molly.

Molly was alight with self-satisfaction. 'Ha! He couldn't fool me.'

'No indeed.'

'How extraordinary that you've met before and with Stanley Govan!' She seemed particularly delighted at this, adding with a chuckle, 'I can just imagine him taking a pretty dim view of Johnny.'

They re-entered the house by the front door, which was unlocked. In the porch, a ceramic nymph clasped an amphora filled with umbrellas, walking- and shooting-sticks and a couple of racquets. The maid had been in here, the floor was swept and mopped and the glass shone; there were no smears or fingermarks. Molly hummed as she unbuttoned her coat and swept through into the hall, the epitome of sangfroid. Streetly appeared.

'Congratulations, miss. You're the first.'

'But of course.'

'The fire's lit in the drawing room. May I bring you some coffee?'

'Please, oh please!'

Streetly took their coats. The drawing room fire blazed merrily, but had not been lit for long so they went to stand near it for warmth.

'So you've only met Johnny once before . . .' Molly cast about for the cigarette box. '. . . thank God, that's better! Was it just on that one occasion?'

'Yes,' said Barbara. 'To be honest I was surprised he remembered. I wouldn't have done.'

'Would you not?'

'It was months ago and only very briefly.'

'Still, I'm surprised.' Molly tapped ash into the fire. 'Most people consider him quite memorable, the rat.'

Barbara agreed with this assessment, though she didn't say so. Eldridge's was a face, and a manner, that stuck in the mind. That was when she realised she had seen him not once, but twice, before and the second time only last night.

Lunch was relaxed yet riotous, the cottage pie washed down with local cider, the rigours of the morning out of the way and departure imminent for most of the guests. One of those staying was Johnny Eldridge. Gerry proposed a toast.

'I think we should drink the health of our gallant fox for providing a great morning's sport! He foreswore the party last night in order to get up early and lay the trail you all had such fun following—' this provoked loud scoffing '—and you must agree he did an absolutely spiffing job, kept you all out of the house and taking healthy exercise—' loud groans '—while displaying all the native craft and cunning of his breed.'

Molly's waspish 'Hear, hear,' was taken up by several others, but Eldridge's expression was one of innocent delight, looking round with his hand spread on his chest as if asking, *Who, me . . .?*

'*So*,' continued Gerry, steady under fire, 'I ask you to raise your glasses and join me in toasting Mr Fox!'

Of course they all joined in with that, except for Molly, who said nothing but tilted her glass very slightly in Eldridge's direction.

The much-decried prize turned out to be not one, but two decent bottles of champagne. It was won jointly by Clive, one of the locals, and Lucia, with chief honours going to Lucia for having overtaken so many others. Each had a vine leaf as proof of completion. Barbara's cluster of grapes lay on her dressing table upstairs.

With cheese and biscuits on the table, there was a certain amount of seat-swapping. Barbara went to sit by Lucia.

'Congratulations. We should have stuck with you.'

'Oh, I'm afraid I'm terribly competitive with that sort of thing,' said Lucia, 'I really am like a hound, I simply take off.'

'Do you know our fox?'

'Not at all. I gather he's staying here while he does a portrait of one of Marjory's horses.'

Barbara recalled Stanley's 'some sort of painter' remark. 'Is he well known? Should I have heard of him?'

'I don't think so. I gather from Gerry they're doing him a bit of a favour. Down on his luck, *noblesse oblige* etcetera.'

'Molly seems to know him.'

'Yes, but Molly knows everyone, whether they like it or not.'

They laughed together at this witty assessment. Barbara glanced at Eldridge. He was leaning forward on the table, his head resting sideways on his hand as he listened attentively to whatever Gerry was saying. His over-long black hair coiled from between his fingers. Neither hair nor fingers looked completely clean but perhaps, she thought, that was painters for you.

Gerry rose and Eldridge sat back abruptly, then looked straight at Barbara. Not for the first time, he seemed to know she'd been watching him. He smiled broadly and, to her consternation, got up and walked round the table to her side.

'Am I interrupting?'

'No, no,' said Lucia, pushing her chair back. 'I'm going up to pack.'

'If you're sure . . .' Eldridge sat down, his eyes on Barbara. 'Are you off this afternoon?'

'Yes. Marjory's taking a few of us to the station at three.'

'What a perfect brick she is.'

This was said straight-faced, but Barbara couldn't be sure he wasn't joking.

'Now tell me,' he said, 'how is the brigadier?'

'Actually I don't know. He rejoined his regiment in India some time ago.'

'No! Has he indeed? Well, well, I thought I hadn't seen him for a while.' He grinned. 'Not since I spotted you in the window that time.'

'We were just taking a day trip.' Why did she feel this need to explain? 'He wanted to show me the house.'

'A pretty decent house, I've always thought. Not that I've ever been inside it. Not beautiful, but ample.' He spread a hand. 'Comfortable.'

'Yes.'

'Pretty views from up there.'

'Yes,' said Barbara, 'there are.' Oh dear, she was not proving scintillating company, but Eldridge continued to gaze smilingly at her, allowing a pause to stretch out, before saying,

'Rather too big, I should say, for one fellow on his own.'

'It's well looked after.'

'Oh, of course, because he's never there. The brigadier.' There was something in the way he said 'brigadier' that made her think he was making fun of Stanley, not just his rank but his person.

'He will be one day,' she said. 'When he comes out of the army.'

'Excellent,' said Eldridge, as if this had taken a load off his mind. 'And what about you, Barbara, have you come far?'

'Only about a couple of hours on the train.' She found she was disinclined to say exactly where from.

'And how do you know all these people?' He glanced around. 'I only ask because, of course, I'm not a guest.' He inclined his head and lowered his voice. 'Trade, don't you know.'

She decided to comment on this rather than answer his question. 'But I understand you're an artist.'

'Really? Who told you that?'

'Lucia, just now. She said you're painting one of Marjory's horses.'

'I am. Pancho. He's a model sitter, no trouble at all. Though, naturally, I'd prefer to be painting Marjory herself. Who knows? Portraitist to the county set would keep me in smokes for a while.'

'When will the painting be finished?'

'It very nearly is. Between us, I'm spinning things out a bit. I'm enjoying myself down here, it's a cushy billet. Trying to make myself useful in other ways, like today. I reckon I was a good fox, don't you? Maybe I could hire out . . . do you think there's a market for that sort of thing?'

Barbara laughed in spite of herself. 'You never know!'

Pleased with this effect, Eldridge laughed too.

'What else do you do?' she asked.

'Anything, I'm not proud. Split logs, clean the car, help in the stable. Do a bit of non-artistic painting around the house . . . You may have noticed the old place could do with it.' He noticed her quick, embarrassed glance. 'Don't worry, nobody's listening.'

'It sounds as if you've made yourself indispensable.'

'I'm good at keeping my head down. Gerry tolerates me – he's the one who asked me after all, so he has to. Marjory's slowly coming round. Below stairs, Streetly and co, regard me as a complete bounder.'

'Why's that?' she asked, though she could imagine why.

'Search me. It's desperately unfair.' He tapped the edge of the table as if he'd come to a decision. 'Would you like to see the painting?'

It would have seemed impolite to refuse. On the way out of the dining room, he said to Marjory, 'I'm taking Barbara to see the picture.'

'Honoured indeed. I'm not allowed to look till it's finished. Be warned – I shall be asking for your very honest opinion.'

This time, he led her through the boot room and out of the back door. They emerged into the stable yard next to the garages and, as before, went through the door into the kitchen garden. Next to the greenhouse with the giant vine was a terraced row of three brick-built outhouses. Eldridge pulled a string with a key attached from the neck of his shirt and unlocked the middle one, which had windows on either side of the door.

'They had to clear this for me, but it makes a perfect studio because . . .' he pointed upwards and she saw that there was a large, flat pane of glass in the roof. '. . . Excellent light as well as privacy. When the old boy was alive he kept this as a sort of

den for his specimens and whatnot, then it was a tool store until
I came along.'

As well as the easel – set at an angle facing away from the
door – there was only a hard chair and two trestle tables set
at right angles to each other. One was covered with a clutter
of oil paints, trays, tins and jars. On the other were scattered
papers with sketches and scribbled notes and what looked
like a wartime primus at the far end. There was also the kit
necessary for making hot drinks: a mug and spoon, a tin
saucepan, sugar and a couple of stained paper packets with
gaping tops.

'Don't worry,' said Eldridge, reading her thoughts as usual, 'I
shan't offer you tea. Come and look at the great work.'

He appeared confident and easy, as he led her round to the
other side of the easel; there was no cloth over it.

'There you are, Pancho.'

'Oh.' Barbara studied the picture with her head on one side.
'That's very . . .' She leaned forward, arms folded. 'Of course I
don't know the subject so it's hard for me to— But that's marvellous. Very striking.'

He stood alongside her, lighting a cigarette. 'Think Marjory
will like it?'

'Yes. Very much!'

'I think so too and, of course, once it's in a nice big, showy
frame . . .'

'Exactly. Like an ancestor.'

'An ancestor – ha!' He stepped forward and flicked a speck
off the corner of the canvas. 'Like an ancestor, but much more
important.'

She laughed and Eldridge joined in, looking at her. 'I'd like
to paint you, Barbara.'

'Me?' She hoped he couldn't see her blush. 'Oh for heaven's
sake.'

'Except,' he quirked an eyebrow, 'I couldn't do you justice
and you couldn't afford me.'

So they were laughing again as they left the shed.

'Shall we go back through the yard? Then you can see Pancho
and judge whether I've caught a likeness.'

Barbara had been a little uncomfortable giving her opinion

on the painting, but animals were more familiar territory. One
of the lads was out hosing down the yard and gave them a nod;
not, she noticed, the cheery greeting she and Molly had received
that morning.

Pancho was sixteen and a half hands of gleaming hunter in
the peak of condition, standing hock-deep in fresh straw, blowing
and stretching his neck as they leaned on the door to admire
him. Barbara stroked the rubbery, velvet-soft patch of nose
between his nostrils.

'Handsome boy . . . You're a beauty, aren't you?'

'That's what I thought. Though, admittedly, I haven't met
many horses.'

'Nor me, or not as big as this. But I rode a lot as a child.'

'And now?'

She shook her head. 'My old pony's retired.'

Eldridge didn't pat the horse. Instead, he turned round and
leaned back on the door, fishing a pack of cigarettes out of his
pocket. He shook one loose and offered it to Barbara.

'You?'

Suddenly she wanted one. 'All right, thanks.'

He lit both their cigarettes with a match from a box.

'So what do you think? Have I captured a likeness?'

'Definitely,' she said. 'You definitely have.'

'What a sweet thing to say, Barbara.' He gazed at her in that
warm, speculative way of his, his jaw resting on his thumb,
smoke wreathing round his head. 'How perfectly sweet.'

It wasn't till she was back in her room that she allowed her
thoughts free rein, as if to do so before would have been to
let them loose all over her face for all to see.

The picture was *awful*: crude, highly coloured, lacking imagination or finesse – what her father would have called 'a daub'.
Not even dashingly modern, just . . . *oh, terrible!* She pressed
her fists to her temples in an agony of embarrassment. She
could not begin to imagine what Marjory would make of it
and as for a big, showy frame – a patch of wall in the boot
room was surely the best that he could hope for. The situation
might almost have been funny, except that (and she could not
begin to analyse or find the origins of this) it inspired in her

a sharp pang of some unexpected emotion: not pity, not scorn, but – yes – tenderness, for the patently unscrupulous, untalented fox, Johnny Eldridge.

Fortunately her reserved window seat on the train was well away from the others. The only other person in the compartment was an old gentleman sleeping soundly, with his chins falling in ripe folds over his collar and his watch chain rising and falling with his whistling snores. She closed the door and put her case on the overhead rack without disturbing him. As the train pulled away she waved to Marjory – poor, unsuspecting Marjory – and leaned her head against the window. The dun-coloured countryside spooled past slowly, then briskly as the train picked up speed.

She had not realised how tired she was. Her body felt heavy, her cheek jolted against the glass. She would soon be as dead to the world as her travelling companion. But as her head swam and her eyelids drooped, she sensed – she knew – that a change had taken place. She was not the same girl who had made the journey down yesterday.

A seed had been sown.

Seven

1953

It must have been another half hour at least before Barbara heard Maureen's key unlock the back door. The sound made her jump and she shrunk even further back, scraping a hole in her stocking on the rough edge of a tile. A click and a thread of light appeared at the bottom of the door. The clunk of keys and her bag on the table, the brisk footsteps across the kitchen and the rattle of water from the scullery tap persuaded Barbara it was safe to come out.

She was so cold and stiff that she had to pull herself up by clutching the edge of the shelf. Upright, her vision darkened for a moment and she leaned on the shelf till it cleared. As she opened the larder door, she came face to face with the startled Maureen.

'Madam!' Maureen took a step back, hand on heart. 'Goodness gracious you gave me the fright of my life!' She put the kettle down with a crash. 'I thought you were in the drawing room!'

'I'm sorry I gave you a shock, Maureen.' Unsteadily, Barbara reached for a chair and sat down at the table.

'Do you feel quite all right? Mrs Govan? Are you ill?'

'No, don't worry. I rather stupidly slipped and fell over.'

'In the larder? What happened? I hope you didn't bang your head.'

'No, nothing like that. Just a fall, but it gave me a shock.'

'Of course it did.' Maureen was all business now. 'I'm going to put this kettle on right away. Is the electric fire on along there? I'll pop and take a look. You need to get warmed up.'

She put the kettle on the aga and bustled off down the corridor. Barbara leaned her head on her hands and was still in this attitude when Maureen came back.

'How are you feeling?'

'Still a bit woozy.'

'Why don't you go and make yourself comfy. I've turned on three bars, I'll bring some tea in a tick.'

'Actually, Maureen, I wonder—'

'What is it Madam?'

'I think I might have something stronger.'

'Oh . . .?' Maureen didn't quite manage to conceal her surprise. 'And why not? It's good for shock and if you can't have a drop of something tonight of all nights,' her face relaxed into a beatific smile. 'Wasn't the ceremony lovely?'

'It was. Most impressive.'

'A pity about the weather, but you can't have everything.'

'No. Maureen, I think there's some sherry on the sideboard in the dining room.'

'Right away. Oops!' the kettle began its thin scream and she moved it off the hot plate. 'Don't get up.'

When she returned, decanter in hand, Barbara said, 'Would you like to join me?'

'Well, thank you Madam, if you're sure?'

'Quite sure. And I'm quite happy to sit here for a moment.'

'Very good. I'll get the glasses.'

Barbara wasn't sure her legs would have carried her as far as the drawing room. Beneath the table, her knees were still trembling and her hands were clammy; she wiped them on her skirt. Maureen came back with the glasses.

'Sit down with me, do.' Barbara's voice sounded flat and peremptory, but now Maureen was satisfied there was no crisis, she was too exhilarated to notice and chatted away for the next several minutes about the events of the day. She and her sister's family had been to the village hall to watch the ceremony, followed by tea, cake, silly games and singing. It had been a wonderful party, with all ages thoroughly enjoying themselves.

Barbara watched Maureen's mouth, as the restorative warmth of the sherry crept through her. The words seemed to be coming from some distance away and the events they described from still further.

'Madam?'

'Yes?'

'I was just asking: how about you? Did you have a nice day?'

'Yes – yes I did thank you. I wonder, Maureen, when you got back just now, did you see anyone outside the house?'

'Outside? You mean in the lane?'

'Either there or even in the garden. Anywhere.'

'No, no one. Not a soul.'

'And you'd have noticed, wouldn't you? If there had been?'

'Of course, I would.' Maureen, now quite pink-cheeked, cocked her head on one side. 'Why do you ask, Madam?'

'It's probably nothing. I just thought I heard someone. You know what it's like when you're alone. Once you have the thought it won't go away.'

Maureen downed the last mouthful of amontillado. 'Well you're not on your own any more. Would you like to go and sit by the fire now?'

It occurred to Barbara that Maureen probably wanted to settle down in here with the kitchen wireless and a further discreet nip from Stanley's decanter.

'Yes, I will.'

'Can I bring you something nice on a tray? Scrambled eggs?'

'No thank you, I'm not hungry. I'll probably go up to bed before long.'

'Good idea, Madam. Tuck yourself up. It's been a long day.' She watched as Barbara rose carefully from the table. 'Want me to come along with you? We don't want you falling over again.'

'I shan't.' Barbara had a sudden unpleasant insight into what it would be like to be old and to have people fussing around her. 'It was an accident, I'm perfectly all right now. And don't feel you have to wait up either, Maureen. I'll switch everything off in the drawing room.'

'Good night then Madam.'

'Good night.'

In the drawing room, the electric fire glowed fiercely red in front of the fire screen with its tapestry peacock. The curtains were not yet drawn. Outside it had finally stopped raining and now, at eight o'clock, it was barely dusk. The garden gleamed with wetness, the rhododendrons sagged. Barbara made herself go to each of the two windows and stand for a moment, looking out, before pulling the curtains. A couple of blackbirds hopped and pecked on the grass.

He could easily still be out there, but all was locked and made safe and Maureen's chirpy no-nonsense presence, even at the other end of the house, was like a talisman warding off bad spirits. Tomorrow the comforting Dexter, Mr Prayle's successor, would be back, taking charge over the garden. She would have people around her.

She was not alone.

In the middle of the night, her eyes snapped open. She lay motionless, with the eiderdown pulled tight around her cheeks, trying to identify the small, careful sound that had woken her.

In a second, she identified it. The metal latch of the gate being raised, then replaced softly – so softly – on its notch. Whoever had been in the garden all this time had, at last, gone.

Eight

1930

The shorthand and typing course took only three months. She was surprised at how quickly she picked things up and how much she enjoyed it – not just the learning but the company of the other girls. They were a thoroughly mixed bag, some of them there for fun or to kill time, others to make a living until they married. They were the dedicated and ambitious ones.

Barbara supposed she belonged to the second group. She wanted to work, because she needed something to do. Marriage certainly didn't feature in her immediate future, but it was out there somewhere, not as Barbara's goal, but it was inevitable. No one else in her cohort had done the season and she kept quiet about that for fear of appearing different.

The secretarial school was in West Hampstead, so while she was studying she lived at the Regents Park house (another cause of secrecy). Ardonleigh, to her great sadness, was to be sold. Conrad and Julia, city people at heart, spent less and less time there and were understandably inclined, now that their daughter had been launched (after a fashion), to spend their time and money on matters other than the upkeep of a large, country establishment. Barbara was forced to recognise that if she wanted independence, she could not have her cake and eat it too. But the imminent loss of her happy, childhood home made her determined to find a place of her own.

She had no idea how to go about finding such a place and didn't want to ask her parents' advice for obvious reasons. Discreet enquiries among her classmates revealed that some were still at home like her (though not, she inferred, in such comfort) and a large group were disseminated among various respectable hostels near the Euston Road. Three shared a flat in West Hampstead and suggested she look for advertisements in local papers and newsagents' windows. Acting on this advice, she used her two free afternoons to look at 'flats' in the area. They turned out to be no more than bedsits, about as bleak and lonely as could be imagined. One in Kensal Rise had a rancid smell, as if something had died in there and the place had been only inadequately cleaned since. The room reeked of the last sad, solitary life that it had contained. She fled.

It was Molly Kidd, the Libertine herself, who came up with a solution. Molly (whose own family and upbringing were a mystery, about which one didn't enquire) was working as a publicist and occasional model for a small but *recherche* fashion house off Berkeley Square. When congratulated on her stylish appearance, her reply was always,

'I'm an advertisement for Maison Luce – do you think I could afford these things myself?'

Barbara bumped into her at a bus stop on Finchley Road. Or, at least, Barbara was at the bus stop when a black cab pulled up alongside and the door was pushed open.

'Can we give you a lift?'

She peered in and saw Molly, elegant in black and white, surrounded by canvas bags.

'Thanks – anywhere near the Park.'

'Jump in.' As the cab pulled away, she said, 'Sorry about all this stuff. I've been showing some of our new designs to a client in Golders Green.'

'And did she like them?'

'She did, poor thing. They'd need to be three sizes bigger, but we can do that.' She rested an arm along the back of the seat to better study Barbara. 'How about you? I haven't seen you since that ghastly weekend at Gerry's. And I must say the last place I expected to find you was at a bus stop on such a filthy afternoon.'

Barbara told her about the course. Molly was a good listener, who gave you her full attention, while giving the strong impression that everything you said was being filed, sorted and cross-referenced, to be processed with advantages on some future occasion.

'So you're going to be a working woman?'

'If I can find the right thing.'

'That's the spirit.' Molly waved a hand. 'Take it from me, you'll be snapped up. And where are you living at the moment?'

'With my parents. Near the park.'

'Very nice!'

'It is,' she agreed, but Molly had noticed her hesitation. 'But lacking privacy, I suppose?'

'Rather. I'm welcome to stay there till – well, for ever – but I've started to look around for somewhere I can rent once I have a job.'

'Seen anything that took your fancy?'

'Frankly, no. They've all been extremely depressing.'

'I bet they have. Believe me, I know. I've lived in some absolute horrors in my time. The reason I worked so hard was to spend as little time as possible in my digs. And no, it's not like that anymore. I have my very own little place in Marylebone, I can't swing even the smallest cat, but it's pretty and comfortable, for me to do just as I like in.'

'It sounds like heaven,' admitted Barbara. 'Look – don't go out of your way, you can drop me off anywhere here.'

Molly leaned forward and slid the shutter back. 'We're enjoying this so much; please can you take us once round the inner circle?'

'Whatever you want, miss.'

She closed the shutter. 'This is so cosy and convenient, why not?'

'I'll pay for the extra.'

'Well naturally . . . Of course you won't! My boss is paying and she can well afford it. Now listen, because I've just had one of my brilliant ideas.'

It turned out that Molly knew of a flat off Edgware Road, bigger than her own, but for two. Both the present occupants were friends of hers and one of the girls was moving out – 'going to stagnate in Tonbridge Wells with her soon-to-be husband' was how Molly put it – so there would be a vacancy and she could guarantee Barbara first refusal.

'Would you like to look? I swear even your parents would approve.'

Four weeks later, Barbara had found employment, and moved out of the Regents Park house into 21b Sussex Court, sharing

with a girl called Cecily, who worked at Liberty's. Her mother
had vetted the premises and her father had paid the required
month's rent in advance. In truth, Julia had been vetting Cecily
too, albeit covertly, but could have found no possible fault.
Cecily was a few years older, sensible to a fault, and wedded to
her work. One never heard her so much as mention marriage
and her ambition was to manage a department in the store.

Molly, of course, had her views about this, 'Thwarted in love.
Either that or she's one of those women who's genuinely not
interested.'

Barbara reserved judgement. She had found a job surprisingly
easily, as an editorial assistant on *The Countrywoman*. The magazine was designed, if not for farmers' wives, at least for provincial
ladies (she had been right in assuming that in this context her
experience of being presented would do no harm). The office
was in Maiden Lane, close to Covent Garden.

There were five other members of staff: Mr Danby the editor;
his secretary Miss Bell; chief 'reporter' Daphne Elliot; advertising
manager Colin Arch; and Terry, the office boy. Mr Danby's
background was in local newspapers, but he affected a patrician
manner and wore a black jacket and pinstriped trousers to the
office, as though editing *The Countrywoman* were an exalted
professional calling. Daphne herself had joined the magazine in
the same lowly capacity as Barbara and moved up the pecking
order. Miss Bell (generally reckoned to be a Mrs, either actual
or widowed) might almost have been *CW*'s ideal reader – neat,
well bred and with unfailingly pleasant manners – except that
she lived in Camden Town. 'Arch' was the oldest member of
staff, former sub-editor on a national paper, some way past his
prime but unable to 'let the typewriter go' as he put it. If even
some of his bibulous anecdotes were to be believed, pulling in
advertisements for weatherproof clothing, gardening equipment
and sciatica remedies for *CW* must have been very small beer
after the heady brew of Fleet Street, but he appeared perfectly
happy with his lot. His chief delight was to tease the others,
especially Mr Danby, by referring to 'scoops', 'straplines', 'door-
stepping' and so on, as if the magazine were an unscrupulous,
popular daily instead of the genteel organ it actually was. Terry
was a sharp-witted lad, smart as paint in his crisp shirtsleeves

and waistcoat, who worked hard and who Arch assured them was destined for greater things. He could whistle any popular tune beautifully; it was like having a resident dance band.

Barbara loved all of it – from her bus ride and walk to work, to the shabby, cosy office, the foibles of her fellow workers and the work itself. No two days were the same. She knew from listening to Arch that this was the softest, smallest journalistic environment imaginable, but to her it was thrillingly new and different. Mindful of her new and lowly status, she was always in a few minutes early and preceded only by Terry with his 'Morning Miss, like a cuppa?'

The Countrywoman was a monthly magazine, so they were not governed by what Arch called 'the tyranny of the deadline'. The content consisted of interviews, accounts of seasonal occasions (such as hunt balls, country fairs, agricultural and flower shows) and 'regulars' (like the letters and etiquette advice, recipes and occasional fashion of a sturdy sort). The advice column, in a question-and-answer format, was sent in by someone known as Lady Fayne (also the magazine's owner), who had never been seen so, for all any of them knew, the writer might not have been female, let alone titled. Recipes were strategically-edited versions of ones appearing elsewhere. These, and the readers' letters, were Barbara's preserve.

She particularly enjoyed sifting through the letters, of which there were over a hundred a week. In fact, for the first few days, she became so absorbed in her task that a backlog built up and Daphne advised her to 'buck up or give up'. Who knew that the wives and mothers of provincial England had so much to say about their homes, their families, their pets, their husbands, in fact the whole weave of their everyday (but not commonplace) lives? You could never guess the subject of a letter from the tone of its opening sentence. Barbara's task was to reduce the monthly intake to a number – ten or twelve – which, after judicious editing, formed a page near the start of the magazine.

Another regular feature was the Editor's Letter penned by Mr Danby in an impeccably ladylike style. For this purpose his byline (and handwritten signature) was 'Anne Montgomery' and a postage-stamp-sized photograph showed his alter ego complete with confiding smile, marcel wave and pearls; even allowing for some photographic enhancement there was no mistaking Miss Bell. When Barbara mentioned the possibility of Mr Danby's being unmasked, the others laughed.

'Our readers, god bless 'em, never come here,' Arch told her. 'We wouldn't let them. They think we're all sitting around in jodhpurs and tea gowns, writing with quills on the finest vellum.'

'Actually,' said Daphne, 'that's not quite true. Remember last year that woman turned up, grousing about the pineapple upside-down cake? She wanted her moment with the editor, so there was nothing for it but for Mr Danby to send Miss Bell into the fray.'

Arch nodded appreciatively. 'She did a terrific job. Breeding will out, you could take her anywhere.'

Barbara was impressed. 'And the reader didn't suspect anything?'

'Of course not, why would she? She met the woman in the photograph, she lodged her complaint, Miss Bell said we'd print a correction and an apology with her name on it, and took her to tea at the Strand Palace.'

There's no doubt about it, thought Barbara, *I'm seeing life.*

Still, by the time she'd been at *The Countrywoman* six weeks, she was getting a little tired of the readers' letters and was monumentally sick of scavenging recipes – particularly because she herself barely cooked and the magazine's readers had experts who could, and would, sniff out errors. She lived in dread of causing another upside-down cake incident and was envious of Daphne, going out and about, meeting people, attending functions and events and writing things up.

It was Terry who encouraged her to spread her wings one morning, when he brought her a cup of tea.

'You should write something Miss,' he told her. 'If it's any good he's not going to turn it down, is he?'

'I've never done anything of this sort. I don't want to tread on anyone's toes.'

'You won't be. You've seen what it's like round here, easy come easy go. You should try, Miss. Go on.'

*   *   *

There was one disobliging thing about her place of work. Now that the nights were drawing in, she didn't care for the entrance to the building. The door, which served two other premises as well, was down a narrow dead-end alley off Maiden Lane. The alley was unlit, so in the evening (and even in the early morning now) you had to dive into the dark, enclosed space, with high, blind walls on either side. It wasn't often that she arrived or left on her own, but there were occasions when this was unavoidable. One night there had been someone there, a bearlike mass emerging from the blackness and weaving unsteadily towards the road. A tramp, the worse for drink and although he was no threat, he had taken her by surprise. She'd nearly bumped into him, feeling the gritty texture of his coat, the greasy tendrils of beard and the stink of his skin and breath. Probably as startled as she was, he had roared something at her in a loud, wild voice and for a second had blocked her path. Her back was against the door and the lighted pavement only just visible beyond his looming bulk.

'Please . . .!' she began, but he was already back in his own world and shuffling, muttering away.

When she mentioned this to Daphne, she was bracingly unsympathetic.

'He's there from time to time, it's a sheltered spot. We've stopped mentioning it to the bobbies, they come and move him on poor chap, but a few days later he's back. Arch gives him a tanner from time to time. Did you see the medals?'

'I didn't see anything.'

'He's got a few. Fancy coming through the whole show and finishing up like that.'

Over those early months of independence, through the first winter of the 1930s, Barbara's life changed out of all recognition. The rhythm and texture of work, the small and diverse group of people with whom she spent most of every day, the different London of which she was now part, all contributed to a feeling of exhilaration. Apart from her colleagues and less frequently her parents, the person she saw most of these days was Molly, who for some reason was taking a lively interest in her. The year of the Season and debutantes, of dances and parties and social 'friends', whom she scarcely knew, was like a bright, impersonal room which she had left behind. She had not seen Ros or Lucia since then, nor any of the young men except for Gerry, whom she had encountered *en passant* one evening in the Strand. They were both rushing, but there was one question she'd felt compelled to ask.

'Did Marjory like her painting?'

Gerry pulled a face. 'You had a sneak preview I believe – what do *you* think?'

'It wasn't much good.'

'That's the understatement of the year. I reckon I could have done better! What a bloody travesty, pardon my french!'

'What did she say?'

'Not much. There wasn't a lot *to* say. Paid for it though – two guineas! The parents know nothing about art and care less, but even they were appalled. Marjory may not look like a soft touch, but when it comes to a lame duck, she's hopeless. She felt sorry for the blighter, just as long as he doesn't expect any references!'

On the bus, Barbara remembered Johnny Eldridge's declared and not wholly unserious ambition to become 'portraitist to the county set'. She experienced a pang of sympathy – for Marjory, and also (she knew it was wrong) for Eldridge himself. But he had his money, so perhaps that was all that mattered. Anyway, she asked herself, why was she troubling her head for a single second about Johnny Eldridge, or his awful picture?

But he was like one of those tunes you got on the brain. Once in there, he was hard to shake.

Nine

After a damp, windy autumn and a rain-soaked Christmas, the new year saw snow and plenty of it. Barbara, used to the opulent warmth of home, discovered that it wasn't only country piles like the Gorringes' which were hard to heat. The Sussex Court flat was freezing and the small, blue flames of the gas fire caused condensation to pour down the ill-fitting windows. It added to the sticky rim of mould already gathered at the bottom of the frames. The office was slightly better on account of a motley array of paraffin burners which took the edge off the cold, but gave off a strong pervasive smell that could make you feel nauseous, if you sat too close to one for too long. At lunchtime, Barbara took to going for a walk to clear her head, returning with her hands and feet hurting from the cold.

It was on one such walk that she saw them. The day was particularly bleak, the pavements cobbled with dirty, hard-packed ice and a gunmetal sky loaded with more unshed snow pressed down on the rooftops. Vehicles had their lights on, even at this time of day, and tyres hissed and threw up spatterings of freezing sludge. Barbara chose a route that took her over the Strand and down to the Embankment, where she could walk along by the river for a few hundred yards and turn back up one of the side roads that came out near Trafalgar Square.

They were standing close together by the embankment wall. She recognised Molly first – tall and strikingly dressed in her persian lamb-trimmed coat and a hat with a brim that swept down on one side. She was talking animatedly, intensely, to her companion, her head tilted slightly as if trying to catch his eye. He was thin and looked downcast, his shoulders hunched and his hands jammed in the pockets of a jacket, with the collar turned up. His clothes looked cheap and inadequate in the bitter cold. As Barbara watched, he drew his right hand from his pocket to take a cigarette from Molly's case, and something about the hand, the glimpse of profile as he leant towards Molly's proffered lighter, sparked a memory.

Johnny Eldridge.

How, and why, do we know when people wish to be unobserved? But we do and instinct told Barbara not to approach. She had an umbrella with her and put it up, pausing a few yards away by the embankment wall, as if watching the river traffic.

Everything about them conveyed intimacy. But not the intimacy of romance or, well, what she had seen that night at the house party. There was nothing romantic in their attitudes. This was something different, deeper somehow, and older. Molly talked on. When she stopped, she continued to stare into Johnny's face and he must have said something, briefly, because she put her gloved hand on his arm and moved it up and down once, fondly, as you might do to encourage a crestfallen child. He threw his cigarette butt down on the pavement and pressed it with the sole of his shoe, both hands now back in his pockets. Molly lifted her chin and clasped the sides of her thick collar together in a gesture Barbara recognised as typical – an armouring of herself. Next to Johnny she appeared taller, vital and brimming with confidence; the contrast between them was shocking.

It seemed the conversation was at an end. Molly turned to go, as she did so, she gave his arm another lighter, quicker touch and then she was setting off smartly towards Westminster Bridge. Johnny turned, head down, he was going to come Barbara's way! Just in time, she angled the umbrella behind her shoulders, a perfect screen. She saw his feet in worn, black shoes come towards her, the soft crunch of his footsteps. When she glanced after him, his head was up once again and his stride had quickened. A fine, sleety snow was starting to fall and his uncovered hair looked wet already.

For a moment she considered calling his name so that he would look round and see her and smile. But the moment passed and he was gone.

Not long after that, Molly suggested they have tea at the Ritz.

'With champagne! My treat – I've had a promotion!'

Sitting in the Palm Court, with the string orchestra playing, the filigree cake stand between them and waiters for whom nothing was too much trouble dancing attendance, Barbara realised that this was in every sense more Molly's treat than hers. Though she would never have dreamed of mentioning it, she had been here before, whereas this was Molly's first time. Her glee was glorious to behold.

'Too marvellous,' she stage-whispered. 'I'm tempted to ask for more cream just for the sake of it.'

'Congratulations!' They raised their glasses and took the first, fizzingly glorious mouthful.

'Now,' said Molly, 'I do hope you don't mind but someone else is quite likely to turn up.'

'It's a celebration, why would I mind?'

'No reason at all! I just thought I'd mention it.'

The little orchestra was playing 'Ain't Misbehavin' when Johnny Eldridge walked in. It was Molly's expression that told Barbara he was arriving and when she glanced over her shoulder she noticed other female heads discreetly doing the same, like sunflowers to the light. With his perfect suit, his shiny shoes and his light, insouciant step, he appeared to move to his very own theme tune.

'Ladies — how rude of me to be late.'

Molly flicked a hand. 'You're always late.'

'Unkind!' He directed a collusive smile at Barbara as the waiter held the back of his chair and fluttered a pristine napkin. 'I hope you ordered for three.'

While another glass was poured and all three clinked together, Barbara marvelled at the difference. The last time she had seen him he had appeared scarcely more than a tramp — dejected, skinny and down-at-heel. The man sitting with them now was as sleek and polished as any West End star, from the top of his groomed head to the toe of his shiny shoes. When he placed his right ankle atop his left knee he exposed a smooth expanse of dark silk sock. His pearl-grey tie was also silk, with the tiniest blue motif. His hands — those thin, expressive hands — were spotless, the nails manicured. Could it possibly be, she asked herself, that the dreadful painting had garnered further commissions? She remembered Gerry's scathing 'no recommendations' and doubted it.

Molly had picked up the conversational baton.

'My stock has risen. They've gone so far as to tell me I'm invaluable. From now on, I shall have a say in the running of the place.'

'My dearest Mol, you *are* invaluable,' said Johnny. 'They've always been lucky to have you and they've finally realised it.'

Barbara agreed. 'I bet the customers—'

'Clients, please!'

'Sorry, clients. I bet they adore you and want to look just like you.' He leaned toward Barbara, so they were surveying Molly with heads together. 'Some of them are famous, you know.'

'Are they? Are they really?'

'No,' said Molly. 'Stop making things up.'

'Make things up? *Me?*'

Molly quirked her mouth sarcastically. 'You. Anyway, I thought I would invite my two favourite people to this little celebration.'

Only later did Barbara wonder exactly when and why she had become one of Molly's 'favourite people'. For now it was sufficient to bask in the moment, the sparkle of the wine and the company, to be included in these teasing exchanges as if she were part of an inner circle.

'Of course,' said Molly, 'now that I'm terribly important and you're Scoop of Maiden Lane I shall be making use of you.'

Barbara nearly choked on her bubbles. 'I'm the most junior member of staff on the least fashionable magazine in London!'

'Ah,' said Molly, 'but we could change all that. Even country-women want nice clothes for . . . whatever it is they do.'

'Walk dogs? Ride horses? Work in the garden?'

Molly waved a hand as if fending off a fly. 'All those ghastly things . . . At any rate, it's a market waiting to be tapped. I've said more than once that we should introduce a small collection of perfectly-cut tweeds, with perhaps a little fur detailing here and there, pretty buttons, clever stitching, that sort of thing.'

'Exactly what Marjory Gorringe would wear,' said Johnny and they all, Barbara included, laughed like drains.

There followed a great deal more laughter, mainly at other people's expense. Encouraged by the scurrilous atmosphere, Barbara treated them to embellished descriptions of the denizens of *The Countrywoman* office. There was something liberating, even exhilarating, in entertaining two people, who were them-selves entertaining and who had no scruples whatever about mocking others.

'Please!' cried Molly, affecting a stitch in her side. 'No more!'

Johnny shook his head. 'Do these poor unsuspecting souls know they've taken a viper to their collective bosom?'

'No, and anyway I'm not,' protested Barbara. 'I like them all, but describing them makes me realise what an ill-assorted bunch we are.'

'Note the "we",' said Johnny. 'Even when shredding her colleagues to pieces, she has to do the decent thing.'

They moved on to the rich dowager, whose lapdogs Johnny was walking daily. He had every inflection and mannerism down pat, to uproarious effect.

Not long after that Molly announced her departure.

'I must dash, there's an equally demanding lady waiting for me in Harley Street, but no need for you two to stop the fun. Stay here and finish the bubbly, it's all taken care of.'

Johnny looked at Barbara. 'I think we should do as we're told, don't you?'

Barbara, slightly squiffy on champagne and hilarity, was in no position to judge whether this was a good idea.

With the founder of the feast gone, the mood changed a little. Johnny sat back, surveying her as if she were the most delightful and intriguing sight in the world.

'How nice this is. Mind if I smoke?'

'Not at all. Thank you, I won't.'

There was no nonsense with matches this time, the waiter was ready with a lighter before the cigarette had reached his lips. He exhaled luxuriously.

'A little high life does a person good, don't you think? From time to time.'

'Yes it does.'

'Although something tells me you're quite used to it.'

'Well . . .' In her present mood she wasn't going to deny it. 'But never tired of it.'

'A good answer.' He widened his eyes. 'Am I allowed to say how elegant you look?'

'Thank you.'

'Not only elegant. Elegant is about clothes and such. Lovely – you look lovely, Barbara.'

'Why thank you.' Buoyant with her new-found confidence, she added, 'You look pretty smart yourself.'

This made him laugh. 'That may not be saying much! Last time you saw me I was living in the Gorringes' attic and spending my days in their garden shed!'

He didn't know, then, that she had seen him since; not long ago and looking far, far worse. The heady shot of relief loosened her tongue still further.

'Did Marjory like her picture?'

'She did. Or she said she did, which I realise may not be the same thing, the upper classes being so polite and all.'

'I'm sure Marjory would speak her mind.'

'That's what I think.' He said this with emphasis, and a slightly furrowed brow, as though she had made a strikingly perceptive observation.

'Have there been any more commissions?'

''Fraid not.' He shook his head, blowing smoke away. 'But no triumph, no tragedy. I'm a jack of all trades, something always comes up.'

'Like the dowager's dogs?'

'Exactly.'

'Maybe she'd like a picture of them.'

'I hope not – they're pugs. It's like walking a brace of hairy frogs!'

They were laughing again. 'I'm sure you could make them look beautiful—'

'Not a chance! Landseer himself couldn't manage it.'

The laughter and light-hearted talk continued as the afternoon grew dark outside, the lights of London came on and the clientele of the Palm Court mutated from the teatime to the cocktail crowd. Molly had provided a second bottle of champagne before leaving and Barbara was surprised to see that they had drunk three quarters of it. She rather dreaded getting to her feet.

Picking up her bag, she said, 'I should be going.'

'Back to that motley crew of yours?'

'No, I asked to leave early today.'

'And they were understanding?'

'I'll tell them I had a meeting with a potentially valuable, new contact. Which is true – Molly and her ideas for county ladies.'

'You see?' He stood as she rose cautiously to her feet. 'These things have a way of happening. Something always comes up.'

Outside, an unexpected wave of *tristesse* washed over her. A taxi was already idling at the kerb. The commissionaire opened the door.

'Madam?'

She turned to Johnny Eldridge. 'Can we share this? I'm going due north.'

'Thanks, but I'll see where the mood takes me.' His expression became serious. 'I do hope to see you again, very soon.'

'I hope so too.'

By the time she'd taken her seat he'd set off in the direction of Hyde Park. Looking out of the rear window his retreating back view, smart suit notwithstanding, reminded her of the last time she saw him – his upturned collar, his hands buried in pockets and his head down. No coat on this bitter city night.

She gave the cabbie her address and leaned back, closing her eyes. She felt a little queasy, not herself. This could have been due to the champagne, but there was something else making her feel light-headed. Johnny Eldridge, who thought she looked lovely. Who wanted to see her again.

Ten

Falling in love, she found, was exactly that – an intoxicating loss of control followed by a sudden, hurtling descent into the unknown.

Not that she had any means of comparison; she had not so much as imagined herself to be in love before. The opportunity for worldly-wise advice from Julia had never arisen (to the latter's mild disappointment it must be said). Until now, Barbara had remained heart-whole and curiously detached from that human experience about which poems, stories, songs, whole operas and plays were written. But from their very strangeness she had intuited something. Perhaps that was why Stanley's proposal had been so easy to decline; she recognised something was lacking, not just in herself, but in him, too. There was no doubting his warm feelings towards her but the calm, considered nature of the request and the stoicism with which he'd received her refusal, spoke volumes.

She had been flattered, but not tempted, and Stanley, well, she did not imagine for a single second that she had sent him back to India heartbroken. The suggestion had been that they form a stable alliance based on mutual affection and respect. Thank

heavens the thought of being mistress of Heart's Ease had so
terrified her. That and some deeply buried unexamined belief
in – well – whatever wonderful, unknown thing was out there.

But this, too, was terrifying. Before, she had known herself just enough to draw back. Now, she scarcely knew herself
at all.

Johnny Eldridge didn't get in touch, but neither did he leave
another meeting to chance. He didn't wait, either. Only two
days later, when she left the office, did he step out of the dark
like a ghost.

'*What*—! Oh, it's you!'

'I'm sorry if I scared you.'

'Don't worry.' She waved a dismissive hand, but she was
trembling. 'Not your fault. There's sometimes a tramp here
and . . . it doesn't matter.'

He stood before her, all benign attention. 'He was here when
I arrived. We were talking.'

'Talking? What about?'

'The way of the world. You know. Interesting fellow, down
on his luck.'

She tried, and failed, to imagine this conversation. 'You could
have come up. You should have rung the bell.'

'I didn't like to disturb and I knew you'd be out before long
anyway.'

The door behind them opened and the editor emerged.

'Barbara . . .' He eyed Johnny. 'Everything all right?'

'Fine thank you, Mr Danby. I just bumped into a friend of
mine.'

Johnny stepped forward. 'Jonathan Eldridge, how do you do?'

'How do you do?' Danby's eyebrows lifted slightly. He
ignored the proffered hand and turned back to Barbara. 'I'll
see you in the morning, then.'

'Yes. Goodnight.'

Johnny was chuckling. 'Thanks to you I knew who that was
the moment he appeared.'

'Really?'

'Scuttling back to his bachelor quarters in – what – Victoria?'

'I don't know where he lives. Or if he's married.'

'Oh, I think not.'

Barbara was suddenly sure he was right, but also sure that there was some other, more disagreeable implication which she failed to grasp.

Johnny went on.

'Is there anywhere round here where I could buy you a drink? I mean, of course, where you would be happy to go?'

The busy cocktail bar of a nearby hotel seemed a good idea, but after the Ritz this place seemed to her too flashy and even a little – there was no other word for it – common. The gilt was too bright, the colours too garish and the waiters brash and hurried. Johnny however appeared at home and amused.

'Looks just the spot for adulterous trysts, doesn't it?'

'I'm afraid it does rather.'

'Wonder what they make of us.'

'You don't imagine—'

'Not being serious. What's yours?'

Cautious after the last time, she asked for a ginger beer and Johnny ordered brandy and soda. When the drinks arrived, he raised his glass.

'To us!'

She clinked. 'Is that what we are? "Us"?'

'Well, we're not, let's see . . .' He glanced around and pointed at a loud, flushed couple at the bar, '. . . them. Thank God.'

'Don't be unkind.'

'Why not? They can't hear.'

'Anyway, that's not what I meant.'

'I know.' He leaned forward, looking down into his glass. 'And I didn't mean to make a joke of your question. Honestly. Quite the opposite.'

The speed with which he moved from heartless humour to childlike penitence took her breath away; she was disarmed and, yes, thrilled.

'It doesn't matter.'

'Oh but it does, we both know it does. Tell me, Barbara,' he glanced up at her from under his brows, remorseful, questioning. 'Have you ever experienced the *coup de foudre*?'

She was going to say no, but something stopped her. 'I don't know.'

'Then take it from me, you haven't.' He set his glass down

on the table, his hands flat on either side. 'I can say that, because you see I have.'

The atmosphere in the bar was febrile, hot and noisy, but she was shivering. His eyes were on her face, tracing a path over her skin, her thoughts.

'Really?'

'A little while ago I was down on my luck. Living from day to day, hand-to-mouth, making a hash of things as I mostly do. No—' Barbara had opened her mouth to protest against him '—not always, but mostly. I couldn't afford the rent on the hovel I was living in and didn't know where it was going to come from. I was pretending to be a rather unsuccessful painter, but I even failed at that.'

'Pretending?' she said, though her eyes slid away. 'Surely, you are a painter?'

He shook his head. 'Listen. After a couple of months, I left the cottage one night and never went back. Never paid the last bit of rent either. Not so good, is it?'

'I suppose not.'

'But here's the thing. Long before that, in the summer, I was at a dance in Chelsea. It was one of those parties full of carefree young people, with nothing to do but enjoy themselves and had the time and money to do it.' He tilted his head. 'You know the sort of thing?'

'I'm afraid I do.'

'Of course you do, because at this dance I saw a girl. She was the loveliest thing I'd ever seen − not the most beautiful, *better* than beautiful − fresh and shiny and sweet as an apple. A girl with a flower in her hair.'

The noise in the bar seemed to recede, to stand at a distance like a hedge of thorns.

'Shall I tell you about her? About how she made me feel?'

Barbara swallowed, 'There's no need.'

'But I'm going to, because I want you to hear it. I wasn't a guest at the party. I was a waiter, so I was invisible. I could gaze at this girl all I liked, because she would never notice. I was standing in the dark, while she danced and played and laughed in the light.'

Barbara remembered the party, the one where the girl's shoe

fell into the fountain. A noisy, hectic party which now she could see through his eyes – eyes which were bright and fierce, never leaving her face.

'I'm going to say something which may sound rude. Everyone else at that party seemed to be silly and spoiled. I despised them, but I was jealous too. Jealous because they could be with this girl, talk to her, dance with her – did I mention she was a wonderful dancer? While I might as well have been on the moon.'

'I'm sorry.' She felt the need to apologise, but she didn't know why. For seeming foolish and carefree and callous when she hadn't even known he was there? Yet his understanding mattered to her, terribly.

'Don't be sorry. To be smitten is a heavenly thing; I was in paradise – isn't that where the sinners hang around waiting to be admitted?'

'So I've heard.'

'I didn't just adore this girl; I wanted to carry her off. I hadn't ever been that young, that fresh and unmarked and full of life. I couldn't take my eyes off her and I can't now.'

'Johnny—'

'Ssh. The strange thing was, that wasn't the end of it. I spent all that night trying to stay where I could see her, but of course it was impossible. I had a job to do and she was surrounded by silly boys, who didn't prize her the way I did.'

'You don't need to tell me any more,' she whispered.

'Oh but I do. A little – there isn't that much. I kept you in my mind for months, taking out the memory and burnishing it like a kid with a shiny brooch, keeping it shiny, treasuring it. And then, towards the end of that summer, when I was in that horrible pokey cottage pretending to paint and doing dirty work for those people with the orchard, I was walking back from the town one day and I noticed the brigadier's car in the drive. It crossed my mind that he might have some work for me, cleaning the car or helping the old boy in the garden. But when I reached the gate, what do you know, there you were again. You were inside the house, looking out. Not bright and blooming and laughing this time, but very solemn and still behind the window.'

She recalled that moment, vividly. The shock of finding she was being watched. She whispered, 'You didn't say.'

'Would you have liked me to?'

'I don't know . . . No.'

'Then what would have been the point?'

'You had the advantage of me.' Why had she used that stiff, old-fashioned phrase?

'But I didn't *take* it, did I?'

'I suppose not.'

'And then,' he went on, raising his hands showman-style, 'lo and behold you appear again, that bloody awful weekend at the Gorringes'. There you were like a good deed in a naughty world, dancing and in demand – what happened to the brigadier, by the way?'

'He rejoined his regiment.'

'Aah . . . Naturally. As befits an officer and a gentleman. Was he hopelessly in love with you?'

'No!' She almost laughed at the idea, but then added, 'not hopelessly, anyway.'

He'd noticed her hesitation. 'You gave him hope?'

'If I did, I didn't mean to.'

'Poor fellow. And now, God help us, there's me.' Johnny sat back, shaking his head at the sadness of it all.

She frowned. 'You talk as if I'm some sort of femme fatale.'

'Surely not.' He looked genuinely puzzled. 'I apologise, I never meant to. You're the opposite of that. You have no idea who you are or what power you have – our recognition of that is, I imagine, the only thing the brigadier and I have in common.'

'In that case, you recognise something I don't.'

'Exactly! Barbara.' Suddenly, he had taken her hand in both of his. In this hot, stuffy place she noticed his calloused hands were cool, almost cold. 'Never change.'

But she was, she thought. She was changing even as she sat there with her captured hand and hammering heart.

'Everyone changes. They can't help it.'

'No.' His voice dropped to an urgent whisper. 'No, they can't.' The waiter hovered and he waved him away. 'Will you do something for me?'

She couldn't so much as bring herself to ask what this favour might be. She was hypnotised. She nodded.

He said, 'I want you to believe in me.'

'I do!'

'No.' He shook his head impatiently. 'You don't, not yet, and I don't blame you. I'm the cove who had the advantage over you, remember, the one who pretended to be an artist, the one the brigadier sent packing. But for you, Barbara, I could be different. If you believed in me.'

It was a simple enough request and yet an enormous one, like being asked to have faith. Could one accede to that to by an act of will? People talked of a 'leap' of faith, when you had to jump off the cliff into the unknown. But if it didn't work, there would be no reward and it would be too late.

'So,' he said, fervently. 'Will you?'

She pushed her anxiety aside. 'Yes.'

Johnny sighed and bowed his head, lifting her hand to his brow as he did so, so that his hair fell on to her wrist. He stayed liked that for a long moment. Then lifted his head again, releasing her hand and his lips brushed the back of it as he did so.

'Thank you . . .'

She wanted to ask 'And what will *you* do?', because surely she'd entered into some kind of contract. The small, dwindling part of her that could still think clearly was telling her she should ask, but the spell was too strong for her. Her hand was like a bird that had crossed oceans, worlds and was now back in its nest.

'You have no idea,' he said, 'what this means to me.'

Shortly after that, they left. On the way out, they passed the pair at the bar. Barbara now saw them differently, as a happy, cheerful married couple enjoying a night out.

In the foyer, a supremely elegant woman sat by herself. She glanced up at them without interest and Barbara saw that the elegance was armour; the woman was not beautiful but hard-faced and dull-eyed.

A bitter wind scurried down the Strand and Johnny hailed a taxi. He put his arm round her as it drew alongside.

'I shall see you again very soon.'

She didn't think to ask why, or where, or how. She had

imagined he would get into the cab with her, but he opened
the door and handed her in.

'Goodnight, my darling Barbara.'

By the time the cabbie had asked her 'Where to, miss?' for
the second time Johnny was already gone.

As they pulled away from the kerb, she leaned back and closed
her eyes. Feelings new, sweet and powerful bloomed inside her,
like flowers in a hothouse.

Eleven

Through the rest of that hard winter, into a fresh, watery
spring and a changeable summer, Barbara had believed. Oh,
how she believed! In Johnny, in love, in herself. In fact, if
belief were all, she would have had nothing whatsoever to
worry about.

Her altered state and awakened heart were obvious. She wore
them on her sleeve, in her smile, her voice and her step. Other
people noticed and were drawn to her. They wanted to bask
in the warmth and light she gave off. But when people asked
and commented on this – her mother, Daphne at the office,
even the unromantic and uncurious Cecily said she was looking
awfully well – Barbara remained silent. Without quite knowing
or examining why, she kept her feelings for Johnny a secret. It
was their secret.

He was secretive about where he lived – Barbara inferred that
it changed, often – and Cecily was rarely out, so they had
nowhere private to retreat to. By tacit mutual consent, they
did nothing that cost money. He rarely had any (the new suit
at the Ritz was a mystery, now losing its shine with everyday
use) and she was sensitive to his feelings. They walked, they
took bus rides, they lingered in museums, galleries, cafés and
even churches; they wanted only to be in each other's company.
She was distracted with love for him. His touch – tender,
exploratory – brought her heart into her throat. He would kiss
her neck, her brow or kiss his fingers to her mouth. Not yet

her lips, though she wanted him to. Feeling so much but knowing so little, she told herself that this was a dance which she had yet to learn. She would abandon herself to it and take his lead. She was now the one in Paradise.

When they talked, it was mainly about her. He was voracious for information about her childhood, her schooling, her friends and family and animals, as if her background − which in his company was a slight embarrassment to her − was an exotic jungle of strange, wild experiences. To her, his fascination was as baffling as it was flattering.

'Until I met you,' she confessed, 'my life was the dullest and most conventional imaginable.'

'Conventional, maybe, but not dull. Never dull. Not to me. Anyway, now look at you.' He did so, making her blush. 'A working woman. Going places.'

Driven in by the cold and finding themselves nearby, they'd taken refuge in her Sussex Court flat. Cecily (who Barbara intuited would not have cared for any liaison, let alone this one) had declared that she was 'just popping out'. Her bright look served notice that she would not be long.

They were sitting in front of the tiny blue and orange honeycomb of the gas fire, Barbara on the sagging chair and Johnny on the rag rug beside her. His arm was draped over her lap, with his fingers stroking her calf. With every stroke she felt softer, more pliant. She laid her hand on his head and he caught it and pushed his face into it; she closed her eyes, the better to feel the heat of his mouth.

'Johnny . . .'

He didn't answer. His tongue was warm and wet in her palm.

'Please . . .'

When she opened her eyes he was looking at her, her own hand covering the lower part of his face like a highwayman's mask so she couldn't read his expression. She slid awkwardly from the lopsided chair, which slid backwards. Now she was off balance, but he caught her and put her arms around his neck. They were kneeling and he put his own arms right around her, so they were pressed together completely, but unsteadily. *We are going to fall,* she thought, *I am going to fall. Oh, let us fall . . .!*

'Hello, you two, ready for some tea?'

Cecily's voice came from the hall (she had that much tact at least). Johnny moved with the speed of a magician, dragging the chair forward and sitting them side by side in front of it. When Cecily came in, she found the two of them blamelessly gazing at the pale fire. Barbara thought she must be able to hear their galloping hearts, to see her chest heaving and the imprint on the air of what had happened – of what, surely, was about to happen.

'Hello there! That needs coins – don't worry, there are some in the jar. I'll get the kettle on, shall I?' Cecily stumped across to the 'kitchenette', which consisted of two gas rings on a rickety cupboard and a tiny sink in the corner.

Once they'd recovered, it might almost have seemed funny, but there was no time for that. Johnny was on his feet at once and by the front door, fists in pockets, forehead against the wall. Barbara gave his arm a gentle tug, but instead of a face creased with suppressed laughter, he turned on her a face white and pinched with fury. She had never seen him angry and the intensity of this rage frightened her. Hastily, she pulled the living-room door shut between them and the brisk rattle of mugs and kettle.

'Oh Johnny, I'm so sorry—' she whispered.

'Bloody, bloody woman!' His whisper was the spitting of a snake. 'Stupid bitch!'

'She doesn't mean anything. It's just how things are.'

He pushed his face into hers, staring but not seeing. All gentleness gone. No comfort.

'I don't like how things are!'

'I don't either, but what can we do?' She was starting to weep, she couldn't bear it.

Cecily's voice called. 'Kettle's boiled, you coming . . .?'

'I'll be there in a tick!' Barbara called back.

'Damn and to hell!' He was fumbling blindly with the door. She released the latch and turned the handle, grabbing his sleeve before he could go.

'Johnny—'

'What? It's hopeless, Barbara!'

Without thinking – unable to think – she put her hands on

either side of his cold, comfortless face, pressed her lips to his and felt, for a split second, his own lips part and a flutter of warm, vital breath pass between them. *The kiss of life,* she thought. The door of the living room opened and he sprang away and was off down the stairs, one hand raised briefly in farewell.

'Has your young man left, then?'

'He had to, yes.'

'Late for something?'

'Yes.'

Gratefully, she drank Cecily's strong sweet tea. The remedy, she remembered, for shock.

She expected things to be strained between them after that, but nothing with Johnny was ever as she expected. For three days she heard nothing from him and the next evening he was waiting for her in Maiden Lane. His hands were behind his back and as she approached he held them out, curled in fists and facing downward, like a child's guessing game.

'Which one?'

She laughed, 'I don't know . . . Left!'

'Right!' He turned his left hand up and opened it. 'A tiny token of remorse.'

'Johnny, there's no—'

'I behaved like a pig. I hope you like it.'

It was a lapel pin, no bigger than her thumbnail and plain grey metal in the shape of a fox's mask with ears pricked and two slanting, holes for eyes.

'It seemed appropriate. Here, let me.' When he'd pinned it on he gave it a little tap and said, 'Now you're wearing my favour.'

That was his first present to her. The second was the kiss that followed, neither of them caring who was there.

She would have gone through fire for him. If a little waiting, for the right time and place, was required, well – that was nothing. At last, thought Barbara, she understood about love, what it was and what it meant: bliss. And she and Johnny were in it, up to their necks. Only when she asked him about his own past did his mouth tighten a little and his eyes slide away.

'You don't want to know.' They were in the carpeted, side chapel of a tiny city church. There was no one else there, but they instinctively kept their voices down.

'But I do!'

'There's nothing to say. I was what your parents would probably call a guttersnipe. My childhood was a grubby business and things haven't been a lot better since.'

He had never enlarged on the 'grubby business', sidestepping her questions or adroitly changing the subject. Now he lay down on the pew, with his head on her lap. She adored him in this puppyish mood. She threaded her fingers in his hair, pushing it back off his forehead so he looked exposed and vulnerable.

'Tell me about the war, then.'

'I was in it for a couple of years. It sort of suited me. War's always been good for misfits. The army can be a good home, even if it's a rough one. And, when it comes to fighting, we don't much care what happens to us and neither does anyone else.'

'Don't say that!'

'Just being truthful.' His voice softened and he reached up to touch her face. 'Sweet girl.'

'I can't imagine you as a soldier.'

'You'd be surprised, I was pretty good. Remember, I'm a past master at pretending to be what I'm not. I can pretty well fool myself and, if you can do that, you can do anything.'

'You must have been awfully young.'

'I'm older than I look.'

'Did you lie about your age?'

'Lots did.'

So he wasn't going to tell her.

'Were you wounded?'

'Let's see . . .' He patted his chest and stomach, as if checking. 'No. My head was rather messed up by it, but whose wasn't? Other than that, not a scratch. I was clever, you see, I ran between the bullets.'

She refused to return his smile. 'You must have lost friends.'

'I don't make many friends. You'll have noticed.'

'What about Molly?'

The instant the words were out of her mouth she regretted them, but if he found them intrusive he didn't show it.

'Ah, that's different.'

He sat up and fished out his cigarettes. Barbara resisted the urge to tell him not to smoke in a church. The snap of the match, the flare of the flame, the breath, the exhalation and the whiff of smoke . . . this was the punctuation of their conversations.

'We're more than friends, Molly and me. We've known each other for as long as either of us can remember.'

'Isn't that the same as friends?'

'Not at all. At least I don't think so. As I understand it you choose friends, you choose each other. I seem always to have known Molly.'

She thought of Ros and Lucia. 'I think that counts as friendship.'

'Maybe.' For a moment he seemed to retreat into his head, considering. 'Perhaps.'

Barbara's mind's eye flew back to the house party – that urgent, covert movement in the darkened porch. Johnny's swiftly striding figure crossing the hall that she spied from the staircase. Had that just been the fruit of an innocent's prurient imagination?

He leaned his elbows on the pew in front, the cigarette between his fingers, his eyes also gazing into the past. Was he looking at the same thing? She wasn't going to ask, not now, not ever.

Molly too had become part of her life these days, though the three of them of them had not met together since the afternoon at the Ritz. Her idea for the line of smart clothing for country ladies had been realised and, as its sponsor on the magazine, Barbara had been commissioned to write a short piece. It would be her first sortie into print. Both clothes and article had been well received. Mr Danby actually suggested she take Molly out to lunch to cement this useful, new contact. It was another first, the use of the company's expense account, though she was put on notice not to push the boat out.

'There's a nice, little French place off Drury Lane that we usually use,' he told her. 'Two ladies can have a very pleasant lunch there, with change from two shillings.'

The little French place was homely rather than chic, with checked tablecloths and thick carafes, but the lunch still felt like an adventure. Molly was greatly amused.

'Who would have thought it a year ago – you and I having a business lunch!'

'More of a thank you, really.'

'But we're women of the world! We know what we're about.'

It was on the tip of Barbara's tongue to ask 'Do we?' Not long ago she would have asked, but now she accepted both the statement and the designation.

'I think we should have a glass of wine,' said Molly, 'to celebrate. Don't worry, we'll order a pichet, that won't break the bank and I shall pitch in.'

They had a jolly time discussing fashion, congratulating themselves and (as usual with Molly) rather wickedly working over their respective colleagues.

Over the crème brûlée, Molly asked, 'How is Johnny? It's an age since I saw him.'

'He's very well,' said Barbara, adding quickly, 'as far as I know.'

To her relief, Molly did not react like someone who had caught her out.

'I'm so glad to hear that. As you may have guessed, I'm awfully fond of him. He's my *special* boy.'

So the secret was out anyway. Barbara knew Molly well enough by now to appreciate that beneath the froth of gossip-mongering lay iron discretion reserved for true friends.

'Molly, I wonder . . . would you tell me about him.'

'But you're seeing him often.' Molly leaned back for coffee to be poured. 'What could I possibly tell you?'

'He doesn't talk about himself.'

'Ha! Does he not?'

'No. He wants to hear about me though, all the time.'

'You don't say? When he's with me we talk exclusively about Johnny.' She helped herself to cream. 'He must be in love with you. It's the only possible explanation.'

'He is.' It was so strange to say it. 'Or at least that's what he says.'

'You don't believe him?'

She hesitated before answering, 'He asked me to believe *in* him. And I do.'

'Believing in and believing are not the same thing.'

'I do both.'

Molly glanced away, as if spotting something in the street. 'Then good. And you love him back?'

Now she could proclaim it, 'Yes.'

'How extraordinary . . .!' Molly sounded both pleased and mystified. 'How wonderful for you both.'

Had she said too much? Her face was fiery. 'Please don't, don't—'

'Never worry. As I said, I hardly see him these days and if I do my lips shall be sealed. You will not be a topic for discussion.'

'Thank you.'

'And to prove it, I shall stop prying and tell you about my ghastly experience with the harridan at Selfridges . . .'

A little later they stood on the pavement.

'Thank you to countrywomen everywhere for my nice lunch.' Molly said. 'Let's see each other again soon.' They touched cheeks and she made to go, then turned back. 'You asked me to tell you about Johnny. I haven't forgotten. One of these days when we have more time I will, I promise. For now, I hope my boy is good to you.'

'He is.'

'And . . .' Molly adjusted Barbara's hat in a way that was almost motherly '. . . you will be good to him too, won't you?'

Walking back to the office, Barbara wondered why there could be the slightest doubt of that; being good to Johnny was her raison d'être.

All of her spare time was spent with him, though they rarely made arrangements. It was always just 'See you tomorrow' and he would turn up: at her door, outside the office, waiting at the bus stop. She still didn't know where – or how – he lived and when she asked he told her he was 'of no fixed abode', which worried her, reminding her as it did of the tramp.

'But, surely, you do have somewhere?'

'Generally speaking, yes. And, if I'm desperate, I can rely on Molly to put me up.'

She wondered how often he was desperate and exactly what it meant. She herself had never been desperate and scarcely had a worry or felt real fear in her whole life.

Johnny didn't like it if Barbara had reason to be away or out of town. Since her minor coup with Molly, she was being given occasional editorial work and it was in the nature of things that this often involved going out of London to interview the county hostess *du jour*, or the president of some particularly successful Women's Institute.

'How long will you be?' he would ask. 'When will you be back?' Or once, quite pitifully, 'Can I come too? I shan't be any trouble.'

She had told him no, he would be bored and she would be self-conscious with an audience. He dismissed the first but accepted the second. 'I'd hate to upset your work.'

She couldn't tell him the real reasons: that he could not afford the fare; that she could not pay for him; that Mr Danby would not approve and that his presence, however peripheral, would complicate matters. When Johnny was with her, he was all she could think of.

'Will you be all right?' he would ask. 'Don't talk to any strange men on the train.'

She was so precious to him and he to her, more than she could say. Though there was little she could do to protect him. When he wasn't with her, it was as though he dematerialised. She lived in a state of longing and heightened tension until he reappeared and then, when she saw him, her heart raced and her limbs grew weak. He could tell – how could he not? He would take her hands in his and bury his face in her palms, as he had done that first time and sometimes she could swear she felt tears. Their kisses were fiercer and more passionate, sometimes she thought she might die of longing; she had lost weight. But if someone had asked how things stood between them, she would have been unable to answer.

And then, one day, as they sat by the Round Pond in Kensington Gardens, Johnny asked, out of the blue, 'Are we near where your parents live?'

'No, our house is by Regents Park.'

'Close to the Zoo.'

'Not far.'

'Can you hear lions roaring in the night?'

'Mummy used to say she had, when I was little, but I think it was just a story.'

They watched a wooden yacht drift past and a small boy trotting between them and the water, keeping pace.

'Could we go and see them?'

'Do let's – I haven't been to the Zoo for years.'

'I mean your parents.'

She was so sure he was joking, that he had really meant the lions and was teasing her that she simply smiled and didn't answer.

'Barbara?' He gave her arm a gentle shake. 'Honestly, I'd like to.'

She looked at him and saw that he was in deadly earnest. Why? This was their secret, surely. She had not so much as mentioned him to her father and mother, even when Julia had asked about 'having fun'. And besides, if she were to introduce him, what might they assume? And would they approve? She examined her feelings. She wasn't ashamed of Johnny – no, surely not – but she did feel protective of him. She did not wish other people, especially people she loved, to mistrust or disapprove of him, to try and discourage her from seeing him.

'Barbara.' He took her hand in his thin, cool one. 'I won't let you down, I promise.'

She almost flinched at how close he had come to the truth. 'Of course you won't! I wasn't thinking that.'

'But the idea worries you.'

She hesitated. 'A little.'

'Why?'

It was important, she knew, to be both truthful and careful. 'Because I want them so much to like you.'

'And you think they might not.' This wasn't a question. He was looking down at their joined hands, stroking hers with his thumb.

'They're like me. They're conventional.'

'And they're like me, too.' He let the unspoken question hang for a second between them. 'They love you.'

Her heart compressed, expanded. Since meeting Johnny she had become conscious of the heart as an organ, not simply an idea – a muscle that could ache, pound, plummet and skip a beat . . . Perhaps, yes, break.

'Not in the same way, I know that,' he went on, 'but they want you to be happy, don't they?'

'More than anything.'

'So Barbara . . .' his smile was like a sunrise, he raised his arms '. . . what's the problem?'

Twelve

There was no problem, well, not one that she could adequately express.

Two weeks later, they were walking along the road by the park, beneath a shared umbrella. Barbara was abuzz with nerves, but Johnny was cheerful and enthusiastic. The visit had been his idea and he appeared simply to have decided that all would be well. And more – that he would take responsibility for its success. He wore the newly-cleaned suit, with a fresh shirt and polished shoes. There was a shaving nick on his right cheek; he had even, she noticed, had a haircut. Still, it was odd to reflect that the last – the only – previous suitor her parents had ever met had been Stanley, a distinguished middle-aged man whom they already knew. Their reaction to that liaison (especially in Julia's case) while it may have been one of slight surprise, was generally favourable. Vitally, it had been of no importance to Barbara herself. Whereas this – this was a leap into the unknown.

Johnny paused, holding her arm. 'Hang on.'

She stopped. Were they about to call it off?

'Listen.'

'What?'

'Can you hear them?' He put his face close to hers, his eyes were brilliant. 'The lions!'

She shook her head. 'No.'

He laughed, he sounded elated. 'Me neither.'

★   ★   ★

Over the next three hours, Barbara had almost to pinch herself several times. The dinner was a success beyond her wildest dreams. Johnny charmed both her parents, though she could hardly have said how. His manner on first arriving was uncharacteristically diffident, he gazed about him with frank admiration and asked Barbara – quietly, but clearly enough to be heard – who was the Edwardian beauty in the portrait over the mantlepiece.

'That's Mummy.'

'What a perfectly lovely picture.'

'Many years ago,' said Julia, clearly gratified. 'Very different times.'

'It's glorious.'

Barbara was glad he hadn't offered a direct compliment on her mother's appearance, which her father would have found suspect. Also, that did not mention his own unsuccessful stab at painting, though she feared the topic was bound to come up. Before dinner, there was general and light talk over sherry (Johnny barely touched his). They spoke of the wet spring, the proximity of the zoo (yes, Barbara really had heard the lions all those years ago), the merits of town versus country and the sad but ultimately satisfactory disposal of Ardonleigh. Johnny sat on the edge of his chair as if poised for flight, paying close attention to every word, brow slightly furrowed, speaking when spoken to. On the subject of country life he was gently self-deprecating.

'I'm out of my depth – pretty hopeless I'm afraid'. He confessed himself dazzled by the 'quite wonderful' house. Conrad was affable – also mostly listening – but, in her father's case, Barbara caught the unmistakable whiff of powder being kept dry. However polite and personable Johnny appeared to be, the moment would come when her father would want to know a little more. This small anxiety, combined with her elation at how well things had gone thus far, resulted in her having small appetite for dinner.

Johnny however ate hungrily: celery soup, wiener schnitzel (a particular favourite of Conrad's), queen of puddings (Julia's contribution, it was her speciality) all went down with expressions of warm appreciation. This was unsurprising, Barbara knew he didn't eat well or even that often, he was always strapped for cash and careless of his own well-being, but she could tell her parents were impressed.

'You're a good trencherman,' observed Julia smilingly.

'Everything is so delicious. Especially this,' he indicated the pudding with his spoon, 'the best I've had.'

Conrad was waiting for the cheese. 'You know the way to my wife's heart. I'm no pudding man.' He paused. Barbara sensed the inevitable enquiry coming down the line. 'Tell me Eldridge, what do you when you're not eating us out of house and home?'

Barbara's stomach churned, but Johnny replied quickly and easily.

'I'm a jack of all trades, I'm afraid, sir. But my excuse is that, by not having any special talent or much formal education, I have to make a living by trying things out.'

Conrad nodded.

'That sounds exciting,' said Julia for whom, it was becoming clear, Johnny could do no wrong. 'What sort of things?'

Barbara's hands clenched tight on her napkin.

'Well, I do odd jobs. I'm pretty handy about the house. For instance, I could build you a shed if you wanted one. Or paint your window frames. Sort out your garden, though actually . . .' he smiled quickly and apologetically '. . . I imagine your garden wouldn't need sorting out. And I'm good with dogs,' he added, as if this was an important point he had omitted to mention. 'They like me and I like them, we get along famously.'

Throughout this description Conrad listened and watched with an expression of polite neutrality. As it ended, the cheese arrived and he cut and speared a slab of cheddar.

'We used to have dogs, in the country.'

'I'd like one now,' said Julia, 'but since we spend all our time in London . . . I miss them rather.' She sighed, turning to Barbara. 'You remember, don't you?'

'I loved them dearly.'

And to Johnny, Julia mentioned, 'they were Barbara's playmates, inseparable.'

'I can imagine.'

'Have you ever owned one?'

Johnny shook his head. 'No, never. Not the right circumstances. I have to content myself with befriending other people's.'

'It sounds as if you make yourself indispensable,' said Julia. No one but Conrad was having cheese, but he was taking his time, cutting and munching appreciatively, perhaps making the most of a reason not to offer an opinion.

'You have some wonderful pictures, Mrs Delahay.' Johnny pointed to one over the sideboard. 'That beach scene is enchanting.'

Enchanting. Barbara's face was hot, but her mother was duly enchanted.

'It is pretty, isn't it? It's by Piers Tredegar, do you know him?'

'I've not come across him before.'

Conrad dabbed his mouth with his napkin. 'He was very popular in our parents' time. That one belonged to my wife's mother.'

'He gave it to her,' said Julia. This was a familiar family story. 'The beach is Holkham, in Norfolk, and she used to say that the group of children included her and her brother – you remember Uncle Geo, Bar?'

'Who could forget?' Great Uncle Geo had been a colourful figure of her youth, given to waistcoats and song, both of them loud. Although much younger than her grandmother, he had predeceased her. He was the first person Barbara knew who had been taken in the midst of life.

Johnny pushed his chair back. 'Would you mind if I took a closer look?'

'Of course. Please do. In fact, I shall do the same. It's so nice to have someone who's genuinely interested in these things.'

The two of them went to the sideboard and studied the picture, Julia pointing out the child believed to be her mother, the boy who might be Geo, the fisherman sewing nets whom she remembered as a rather frightening, whiskery, old man.

'That beach was wonderful, a huge playground, we ran wild as hawks. My parents were not typical Victorians.'

'It sounds an idyllic childhood.'

'I suppose it was . . .' Julia sighed happily as she returned to her place. 'One takes one's childhood for granted, rather. It's only later you realise that it was in any way different from other people's.'

'That's true.' Johnny sat down and glanced at Barbara, for almost the first time. 'Very true.'

'You seem to have an eye for paintings,' Conrad said. 'Did you ever do any yourself?'

'I've played at it, that's all.' He pulled a smiling grimace. 'As Barbara knows. One or two people have been kind enough to encourage me, but I'm realistic enough to see it was just that – kindness.'

'Realism can be a spur to success, unlike false modesty.'

'Believe me, sir, no modesty required!'

Her father chuckled. Yet again a potentially uncomfortable moment had come and gone and the awkwardness had been averted, Barbara wasn't sure how. No lies had been told – on the contrary, Johnny had been truthful, and somehow made a virtue of the truthfulness. She felt proud, touched and bursting with love as she sat there next to him. His skin was so thin and so white she could make out the blue veins on his temple and see them pulse. His hands rested on his knees, the long fingers stretched forward like antennae; she longed to touch them.

'Now, then,' Julia clapped her hands and clasped them beneath her chin. 'I am wondering whether you would like to see some more pictures. Just a few, the better ones, we do have quite a collection.'

'May I? There's nothing I'd like more. Would that be all right with you, sir?'

'Carry on.' Conrad gestured. 'I'm no expert but I'm told there's some quite good stuff, either that or various elderly relatives and gallery owners lied through their teeth. Bar, shall we leave them to it and go and await coffee . . .?'

Julia bore Johnny away and Barbara followed her father back into the drawing room. He pressed the button by the fireplace that would, in turn, shake the left-hand bell in the box in the kitchen (she'd loved watching this as a child) and let Clarice know they were ready. In other houses, ones bigger, grander and colder than this, she thought, Johnny would have seen such a bell ring often, he would have occupied a strange middle realm between up and down, master and servant. Even at the Gorringes he had been on the edge – the fox, the nimble prey, the man in the outhouse. And yet here he was amid the marble and turkish carpet and cherrywood and crystal of her parents' house, taking a tour of paintings with her mother. She was light-headed with relief and something else – a sort of happy confusion.

Conrad offered the silver cigarette box. Barbara hesitated, then took one. He held the silver-gilt lighter to her cigarette, then his. Clarice tapped.

'Come.'

She pushed open the door and carried the tray from the table outside to the one near the bookcase.

'Thank you.'

'Shall I pour, sir?'

'No thank you, Clarice, the others won't be long.'

She arranged a thick, linen napkin around the outside of the jug and withdrew, pulling the door to behind her. Everything was soft, quiet and warm. Everything, as Johnny had observed, was quite wonderful.

Conrad drew on his cigarette. 'Your Mr Eldridge seems a nice fellow.'

'He is.'

'He knew how to charm your mother. First dinner, now paintings.'

Barbara smiled, but the word 'charm' had alerted her to possible reservations. Charm was crafty. Charm was suspect. Charm would require a counter-balance.

'Did he have a war?' Conrad flicked ash. 'It's not something one likes to ask in company.'

'He did. He doesn't talk about it much, but he told me that, in an odd way, he liked being in the army. Not the war itself, but the military, the organisation.'

Her father nodded. 'Stability, of a sort, at a price. A regiment has often filled the space where a family might have been.' He let a pause open, stretch and close. 'You know much about his background?'

'Almost nothing.' She tried not to sound flustered. 'That probably sounds awfully odd. He doesn't seem to want to talk about it and I don't like to press him.'

'Quite right. Everyone's entitled to their – let's say – their privacy. Not so sure about secrets, though.' He tilted his face, scrutinising hers. 'Would you agree?'

'Of course.' She'd told one lie and now added another, 'I don't believe he has any.'

'Though of course by definition, if he had, you wouldn't know. Are you sweet on him?'

Her father had never asked such a thing before. Had never, for instance, asked her this in relation to Stanley. Now, because she intuited that he already knew the answer, there was no point in a third lie.

'I am, a little.'

'There's no such thing as a little.'

The door opened and Johnny and Julia came in, Julia talking animatedly over her shoulder. Fleetingly, powerfully, her mother reminded Barbara of someone, but she could not think who.

'Coffee!' cried Julia gaily. 'But you shouldn't have waited!'

'Don't worry, Clarice swaddled it against delay.'

'I shall pour. You must come and help yourselves to cream and sugar.'

'Let me pass it round,' said Johnny, accompanying her and standing in attendance.

'So what do you think of the Delahay collection?' Barbara asked.

'I adored it,' said Johnny, coming over with the tray. 'There's one of your grandmother that might be a Sargent. Beautiful.'

'Now,' said Conrad, 'I'm going to be brutally honest—'

'Please Con don't!' protested Julia, cheerfully enough.

He raised his hand. 'I want to put forward a topic for debate.'

'Oh dear, if you must.'

'Here goes. "This house moves that truthfulness in a portrait is more important than beauty."'

'If the subject is beautiful, then there's no debate,' Barbara said. 'Indeed.'

Julia arched her eyebrows towards Johnny. 'I'm afraid he's being rude about Mamma.'

It was now Johnny's turn to speak and they all knew it. Barbara's warm feelings towards her father curdled somewhat. How could he be so mischievous as to put a guest, and an unfamiliar one at that, on the spot? But Johnny, with a thoughtful expression, finished stirring sugar into his coffee before replying.

'No, it's a fair point . . . I suppose it depends on whether you consider the artist's genius to be of itself beautiful.'

'Very few artists are geniuses, surely.'

'Perhaps they have talent, then, or are gifted.'

'Can't say I agree,' said Conrad. 'I want him to present me with something that's easy on the eye: a woman, child, landscape, horse, bunch of flowers (if I must). I want something that I don't mind sharing my house with.'

Johnny seemed to be considering this, as he lifted his cup to his lips.

Barbara interjected, 'Isn't that like saying art is just interior decoration?'

'Absolutely!'

She recognised her father was not being completely serious. His mood was genial, but meddlesome. Having watched Johnny for the first part of the evening; Conrad was now of a mind to provoke and see what happened. Julia had seen all this before and was having no truck with it.

'Don't be pig-headed, Con, you don't really think that.'

'I most certainly do. That's why I'm happy to concede that Percy Snell did an excellent job on your mother.'

Julia laughed, tried to catch Johnny's eye, but he declined to smile.

'I can tell you don't agree,' said Conrad.

'I think you're teasing, sir.'

'Teasing?' Conrad tipped his head back. 'That shows how little you know me.'

'Well, of course, I don't know you at all,' said Johnny earnestly. 'It's a guess.'

'Well said!' said Julia. 'Con, stop it.'

'I will, I will, not another word from me. But we must continue the discussion another time, eh Eldridge?'

'I should enjoy that.'

Half an hour later, they left. Johnny's thankyous sounded sincere and were warmly received, with benevolent smiles all round. Unusually, her father placed a kiss on her cheek, taking the opportunity to say quietly, for her ears only,

'My girl. Nice to see you looking happy, take care of yourself,' and added something that sounded like, 'might be a case of Eldritch by name, eldritch by nature.'

On the whole, it had gone better than Barbara had dared to hope, though she would have liked to be a fly on the wall of her parents' room when the post-mortem was taking place. Conrad had offered to call a taxi, but they had elected to walk a little way. Outside, the air was full of the fresh, poignant, green smell of the park. The odd car purred past. A policeman wished them goodnight.

They went some way in silence, side by side, not touching, a little self-conscious after the events of the evening. After a couple of hundred yards Johnny reached for her hand and they stopped, facing one another, in the soft darkness between two street lamps.

'That was a wonderful evening. I do so love your parents.'

'And they liked you, my mother especially.'

'Did I do all right?'

She put her hands on his shoulders. 'Johnny, it wasn't a test!' But he wouldn't buy that any more than she did herself.

'It was, of course, it was. I put myself up for it. Did I pass?'

'With flying colours.'

'Because, you know, it means a great deal to me. You mean a great deal to me. And they, well, I never had anyone like them. Their good opinion matters to me.'

'I suppose I take them for granted.'

'Of course. That's natural.' They began to walk on. 'You don't think I offended your father?'

'Not in the least.' Of this much, at least, she was confident. 'He was goading, a bit. You'd have been entitled to take offence yourself.'

He laughed and she could hear in his laugh that he was relaxing, buoyant with success. 'I'm un-offendable.'

They reached the Euston Road and he put his arms round her, hugging her so tight she could scarcely breathe.

'My Barbara.'

'Will you come back with me?' She whispered and felt him shake his head.

'That woman will be there and I want to do everything properly.'

She wanted to say *but we don't have to be proper all the time, not when no one's looking.*

'What do you mean by "everything"?'

'Us.' He leaned back and smoothed her hair with his hands. 'Everything to do with us.'

It began to rain again, softly. Pools of lamplight became freckled with raindrops. He put up the umbrella and placed it in her hand. They stood for a moment, he with one arm round her shoulders, until a cab came by and he hailed it.

'Will you be all right?' she asked. 'Where do you have to go?'

'Not far.' He waited while she settled the umbrella. 'And anyway, I have wings on my heels.'

This scene was becoming familiar to her, where Johnny sent her on her way and went on his own.

He was walking in the same direction and as the cab passed he gave a little Chaplinesque jump, tapping his heels together at the side. The cabbie quested for her eye in the mirror.

'That's a very chipper young gent you've got there, miss.'

She kept her face averted as if she hadn't heard. She didn't care if he thought her prissy. What did he know?

She was about to put her key in the lock when it came to her, who her mother had reminded her of as she came beaming, glowing into the drawing room, ahead of Johnny.

It was me.

Julia had reminded her of herself.

Thirteen

1907

'What's that?'

'Don't you mean who? Who's that?'

Molly didn't answer. She was busy directing a silent, black bullet of hatred at the intruder.

'Listen young lady.' Molly's mother shot out her free arm and grabbed Molly's shoulder with a hard, pinching hand. 'You'll be civil if you don't mind and—' a tighter pinch, this time with a shake, nails digging in '—even if you do, all right?'

'Who is he?'

'This is your new brother.'

'What? He never is! I never seen him before!'

'*I've. I have* never seen him before. Well that's a nice surprise then, isn't it?'

'No!'

'You want to know something, madam?' Her mother gave her a shake that jolted her head and made her bite the edge of her tongue. 'It doesn't matter what you think or what you want. He's coming to live here, do you understand?'

Molly could taste blood in her mouth, but swallowed it. She shrugged.

Nothing infuriated her mother more than a show of indifference. She gave Molly a sharp push followed by a poorly-aimed smack that glanced off the side of her head, ruffling her hair, which Molly hated more than the blow itself.

'Steady on Netta,' said the man. He'd been standing with his son in front of him, his huge hands on either side of the boy's neck, but now he moved him aside and came to lean over Molly. A constellation of rusty-brown stains spattered his shirt, just below the collar. She could see the black dots in his skin where the bristles grew, the crimson veins on the inside of his nostrils and hairs curling in the greasy whorls of his big ears. He'd made his eyes wide, round and staring. His breath smelt of spit, old food and tobacco.

'It'll all be hunky-dory, won't it?' He tweaked her cheek. His fingers had the texture of stale bread. The gesture was meant to seem affectionate, but she wasn't fooled; he was pinching, just like her mother, holding her face still so she had to pay attention. She shut her eyes.

'Don't be like that, now.'

'What's she doing?'

'Nothing. Are you?' He let go Molly's cheek but she could still smell him there and hear the small creaks and hisses of his great, gross body. 'We'll be right as rain, won't we, Molly? Eh, Molly Malone – won't we?'

He cuffed her hair, in the same place. Her eyes flew open.

'That's not my name.'

'It's a joke. Can't you take a joke?'

'She gets a lot of that Malone business,' said her mother. 'So maybe not.'

Molly liked her mother for saying that. It wasn't much, but she was used to making the most of crumbs.

The man – his name was Percy Eldridge but she would never, ever, call him by it, or by anything if she could help it – stood up, enormous in the little kitchen. He turned to the boy, who had been completely silent through all of this, watching through the hank of black hair that hung over his eyes.

'You going to say hello, son?'

'Hello,' said the boy, docilely. He had a soft voice, a little deeper than she'd expected, maybe it had already broken, though he was a squeak shorter than her. Anyway, she wasn't interested.

'How about "Hello Molly"?'

'Hello Molly,' he copied parrot-fashion. His eyes were bright and dark, sizing her up.

The scorn and loathing she felt at that moment filled Molly's mouth with bile. She turned and ran up the stairs, with her feet hammering on the steps, grasping the banister hand over hand, propelling herself forward.

'I'm sorry, I'm not having that!' her mother hissed.

'All right, Netta, it's all right,' the man said in his heavy, pretend-soppy voice 'nothing to worry about, don't go after her, she'll come round . . .'

Molly closed the door of her room quietly and propped the back of the hard chair under the handle. She would never come round. Never.

After a long time and a lot more hissed conversation, Annette came up the stairs and rattled the door handle ferociously.

'Open this door.'

'Go away!'

'I will not. Move that chair, young lady, or I'll have the door broken down. You know I will.'

Before this might have been an empty threat, but thinking of Percy Eldridge (who was presumably still lurking about somewhere) Molly realised it could be carried out. Better to admit her mother on her own terms than give him the satisfaction. She removed the chair and stood back from the door.

'Thank you and about time.' Her mother closed the door behind her and kept her voice low, but venomous. 'What was that all about? I didn't know where to put myself.'

Molly's lip curled. This, of course, is what it was all about: her mother's embarrassment. Annette was a woman whose nature had been irrevocably warped by a sense of injustice. She had been born to better things and life had cheated her. Her father had been manager of Bournes, the gentlemen's outfitters. He was a leading light on the town council, a director of the football club and a pillar of the community, with soft hands and a spotless white collar. Her mother ran a lovely home and was always beautifully turned out. The fact that Annette herself worked – as a seamstress in a tailor's in New Cross – was a source of both pride and shame. She was proud of her ability to earn her own living (her stitching was immaculate, the tiniest in the shop), but mortified that it was necessary. She did not feel herself to be independent, so much as making the best of a bad job. She was a woman for whom the phrase 'keeping up appearances' might have been invented. She drove herself to exhausting lengths to look smart, to keep the rented terrace house in Savernake Road spotless and 'nice', and to inculcate good behaviour into her wayward daughter – the legacy of her first husband, Barry Flynne, from Cork. Barry had swept Annette off her feet, into bed and up the aisle in that order, a sequence of events predicted by her parents, as they never failed to remind her. When, also predictably, he took off after only a year of marriage, there was a distinct cooling in the family. She wouldn't ask for money and, when her father suffered a fatal stroke in the council chamber, that became academic. Her mother declined in a genteel way and, within a year of his death, she had gone too. Rather shockingly, there was no money to come Annette's way – they had been living beyond their means. To her credit, she put her shoulder to the wheel, but the disappointment of reduced circumstances was bitter indeed. Her neat good looks became pinched, her trim figure shrivelled to thinness and her nature turned sour. She had married the widower Percy Eldridge without her daughter's knowledge because, she reasoned, he was a good hardworking man who was going to look after them. She hadn't mentioned the boy, whom Percy had characterised as 'no trouble at all'.

Molly and her mother were fond of one another, but each was the cross that the other had to bear. Now they faced one another across five feet of threadbare rug and a chasm of mutual suspicion.

Molly said, 'You never told me there was a kid coming.'

'He's older than you and he's going to be making himself useful.'

'That skinny oik?' 'Oik' was a word of her mother's, which Molly was using against her.

'Yes. Some of the time. His father's going to be taking him to the factory on a Saturday.'

'What about school? Doesn't he have to go?'

'I dare say.'

Molly didn't know which would be worse, the boy going to West Street Junior with her, or being out of her hair but pulling rank as an earner. She was dizzy with rage and resentment.

'I don't want him here and he's not my brother.'

'Call him whatever you like. His name's John and he's staying.'

'I shan't call him anything!'

And she didn't. Or not for some time. The boy moved about on the edges of her life like a corporeal ghost. She could always feel when he was near. He did something to the air in a room, like the game they played at school, a group of them staring at someone until the person felt it and began looking around. Not that she ever actually caught him staring, she didn't need to. She knew when he was there.

Her decision to ignore him was less satisfying than she'd hoped. After that first unpromising introduction, he never showed the least inclination to speak to her or even to acknowledge her presence. In fact, he rarely spoke at all. It was impossible to overlook the uncomfortable disparity in their statuses. John Eldridge slept in the tiny room, no more than a cupboard, between the kitchen and the privy at the back. Skinny but surprisingly strong, he lugged in the coal, hauled the mangle, swept the yard, emptied the slops, went out for tobacco and sometimes beer for his father. He kept himself to himself. During these menial, messy activities he was always expressionless, inward-looking and unreadable. When blacking the grate, he crouched over the task, his head bent almost between his knees, rubbing the metal rhythmically, his hair over his eyes, his breathing just audible. He concentrated and displayed no resentment.

Except then there was school. Molly groused about school, but she didn't mind it. She was clever enough not to be designated a swot (and was even prepared to do other people's homework for them, for a small consideration) and sufficiently sharp-tongued to annoy the teachers, a sure route to playground popularity. She didn't court or inspire affection, but she did enjoy respect. The last, the *very last* thing she wanted was some hard-to-explain, guttersnipe oik cramping her style. The Eldridges had taken up residence in the short Easter holiday and she dreaded the start of term. The week preceding it had been bad enough because, in spite of being now 'looked after' by Eldridge, Annette continued to go out to Premier Tailors. Eldridge himself, of course, was at the fancy goods factory supervising the production of china cats, cabbage-shaped cruets and cheap apostle spoons (he had brought home a set). Molly and John Eldridge were left to their own devices. Molly had acolytes up the road, so on the first of these mornings she took herself off to visit them as soon as she could and had a good moan. When she got back, the boy wasn't there. He came back into the house not long before her mother and then Eldridge.

'So what have you two been getting up to today?' Her mother asked, over the watery hotpot.

Molly could tell from the grim brightness of her tone that this was less of a question, more of a prompt or even a threat. Anything short of the right answer would not be countenanced, but who knew what that was?

'I went to see Flo,' said Molly. 'We played jacks.'

She looked at the boy. His turn.

'And you, son?' asked Eldridge, wiping his moustache. 'Been getting to know the place? Playing with your – with Molly here?'

'No,' said the boy in that voice she heard so seldom it surprised her, as if a cat had suddenly spoken. 'I don't want to do that.'

The oik – *the pig* – had hijacked her superiority, made out that the decision was his. She felt robbed, mortified!

An aghast expression bloomed like a thundercloud on Annette's face, but Eldridge cut in jovially.

'Just so long as you rub along eh? No nonsense, no squabbling. Happy house, eh? That right, Molly Malone?'

Molly closed her eyes, but not before she'd seen a swift flash of something in the boy's face. A hot, bright glint intended, she was sure, for her: a glimpse of something like understanding. Perhaps (she was scarcely ready to admit it even to herself) she had an ally.

But the remaining days of the holiday continued without communication between them and when school began they left the house separately, Molly first, accompanied by her friends Edna and Flo from down the road. Her scathing complaints meant they knew about him and halfway there Edna gave her a nudge.

'Is that him?'

He was perhaps fifty yards behind them, hands in pockets and head down, dawdling past Meekins the tobacconist so as not to catch up.

'Yes.'

'Will he be in our class?'

'Don't know. Don't care.'

She did care though and hoped he wouldn't be. She couldn't imagine how it would feel to have this skinny interloper hanging off the edge of her life at school, as well as at home. Or worse she *could* imagine it – the embarrassing, annoying, shaming situation to be explained to a far-from sympathetic audience, who would enjoy bringing Molly Flynne down a peg or two. The mere fact of her mother's remarriage would attract some mean teasing and chi-iking, she had done it to others herself. Even Edna could turn Judas. Molly could hear it in her voice and see it in her gloating smile, the glance that flicked between her and Judy (a sneak would always stick to whoever was riding high).

There were three classes at the school and John Eldridge, being a year older, was put in the one above, with Mr Brayne, the headmaster and butt of many jokes. Mr Brayne was known to be fair and therefore soft, everyone took advantage of him. The teacher of Class Two was Miss Calloway, a tiny, sharp-eyed weasel of a woman whose relations with her pupils were on a permanent war footing. The strap with its grooved end that hung from the side of her desk was not for show. Her lightning-swift, whippy action was greatly feared, even by the boys – and it was boys she mostly picked on.

But the oik was in Sir's class, so it was out of sight out of mind for most of the school day. In the playground, Molly did not concern herself with him. She got on with organising jelly-on-a-plate and Nebuchadnezzar-the-king-of-the-Jews and pretended he wasn't there. It was like in the house – from time to time she would be suddenly aware of him without exactly seeing him. She told herself she wasn't interested, which was more than could be said for Eldridge *père*.

'How are you getting on at school, son? Paying attention, minding your ps and qs?' Mr Eldridge asked. Annette's eyes swung that way, but Molly didn't look up.

'It's all right.' John replied.

'Learning something I hope?'

'Yes.'

'That's the ticket.'

'Learning that I don't like it.'

This was so coolly candid, that it caught even Molly's attention. She looked up to find the boy was staring at his father steadily. Meaning it. Not cowed.

Eldridge chortled. 'What boy likes school? I ask you!' He looked around. 'I didn't. Doesn't mean I don't know the value of education.'

John continued to gaze for a moment and then returned to his plate, scraping gravy and potato on to his fork slowly, with that familiar air of concentration.

'Just keep your head down,' said Eldridge over-emphatically, 'and pay attention, and do as you're told. Can't go wrong.'

Which showed what he knew.

A couple of days later the cry went up in the playground, 'Fight! Fight!' and when Molly and the others rushed with everyone else to see, there was Johnny, bashing seven bells out of Colin Dunkley. To be fair, it looked like Johnny had already had about six bells bashed out of *him*, he was bloodied all around his mouth and nose, the blood viscous with snot and he was staggering like a drunk on his long skinny legs. With his arms flailing and hair flapping across his face, he was howling like a banshee, making harsh, high-pitched war cries, which were dotted with the sort of swear words no one was supposed to know (though they all did, of course). Everyone stood there gaping, aghast at the thrill of it all. The best that could be said of Colin Dunkley was that he was still standing, just – but only because a couple of his cronies were catching him when he tottered and shoving him back into the fray for more punishment. One eye was no more than a puffy, purple egg that was oozing red and the other rolled about like a gobstopper beneath a monstrously split eyebrow. His mouth was a wet crimson and black hole, with at least one tooth sticking out at a jaunty angle. His hands, protruding from the stained cuffs of his jumper, flapped about uselessly like slabs of meat.

Molly saw Mr Brayne advancing from the building at as near a run as dignity would allow, with Miss Calloway in attendance, because of the disparity in their heights Miss Calloway *was* actually running with a silly tittuping action. Miss Leigh, the young Class One teacher, peeped palely from her classroom window, transfixed by the to-do, but mercifully not obliged to be part of it.

'Johnny!' screamed Molly – she'd never called him that, or anything, before, and didn't quite know why she did so now – '*Johnny! Stop!*'

He didn't, but her scream caused everyone else to turn away from the entertainment for a moment. The full-blooded shouting of encouragement was one thing – it was expected, you had to do it – but yelling at someone to stop was being a spoilsport. Molly felt Flo, Edna and Judy move the tiniest bit away from her, distancing themselves, joining the herd.

But because Johnny was still swinging away, yelping and grunting, she screamed again into the lull, recklessly, 'Stop it. Stop it. *Stop it! You stupid bugger!*'

The lull became a goggle-eyed silence through which Mr Brayne wove his way with an automatic, 'Excuse me please . . .

excuse me . . .' and grabbed the collar of Dunkley who was subsiding yet again.

'Dear me, this boy is in a parlous . . . Dunkley? For heaven's sake. Miss Calloway, would you . . .? Thank you. That will do. That will do! Eldridge!'

Miss Calloway had relieved her superior by simply taking Dunkley's collar in her hand and then releasing it so that he went down like a bag of coal. Brayne glanced down and flapped a distracted hand.

'We shall have to do something. Will someone please fetch Miss Leigh and ask her to find the first-aid box from the shelf in my office? Thank you, Agnes. Now.' He huffed a sigh and glanced round, his soft gaze pausing on Molly, moving on to Johnny, then returning to her with a small frown.

'Molly Flynne, I'm shocked. I will not have that language from any child at this school and I am horrified to hear it from you. Please wait for me outside my office.'

'Yes, sir.'

She took a couple of steps backward, just enough for the rest of Crewe Street Juniors to close in front of her and then remained where she was, knowing she could still make it to Brayne's Office before him. Peering between the others she could see that Miss Calloway, the cow, was quite pink-cheeked with excitement. No doubt she was imagining when she might be Head and dishing out the punishment to the likes of these two .

'Eldridge, would you like to tell me what all this was about?'

Fifty-odd pairs of eyes flicked to the scraggy, bloodstained scarecrow in the centre of the circle.

'No.'

There was an audible intake of breath – thrilled and incredulous. Mr Brayne cocked his head, eyebrows drawn together in a wriggly line, genuinely baffled.

'I beg your pardon?'

'No, *sir.*'

Brayne folded his arms, prompting more.

'I wouldn't like to tell you sir.'

Even to the pupils this comment seemed to miss the point. Calloway looked in astonishment from one to the other, Molly fancied she could almost see her bony little hand clenching around an imagined strap.

Mr Brayne frowned. 'It's a figure of speech, Eldridge. Do you know what that is?'

'No. No, sir.'

Brayne sighed heavily. 'Very well. Please tell me what this fight was about? Oh – here comes the first aid box – Dunkley, get up please and go with Miss Leigh, come on lad, on your feet!' between them he and Calloway hauled Colin upright. 'I shall hear your side of the story when you're cleaned up. Eldridge, what do you have to say?'

'We had a row.'

'Well we can see that!' barked Calloway, unable to contain herself. Brayne pinched the top of his nose, Molly felt almost sorry for him.

'Come with me Eldridge. Miss Calloway, perhaps you'd be kind enough to see these children back to their classrooms and give them some work to do.'

Calloway would have made a good sheepdog, nippy, hard-eyed and ruthless, Her excited flock were soon chivvied back into the building. Molly pushed her way through the rest, flew along the corridor and plumped down on the bench outside the head's office just in time. On the way, she caught a glimpse of Miss Leigh in the green-tiled washroom gently dabbing disinfectant and applying lint to Colin Dunkley's wounds. When Brayne arrived, with Johnny in tow, he looked surprised as she sprang to her feet before recollecting why she was there.

'Molly, I don't ever want to hear that language again from you. Your mother would be shocked and ashamed. I shall forebear to tell her this time, but this time *only*. Run along.'

As she bobbed and made to go, she caught Johnny's eye and there it was again – the sharp, brilliant look that told her they were on the same side.

'I think that's when I knew.' Molly stretched out her arms before her and spread her thin, elegant hands, like fans. Her eyes were soft when she looked at Barbara. 'Under the skin, you see, we were two of a kind. He seemed always to know it, but it took me a bit longer.'

They were sitting on their coats – the weather was just warm enough to take them off – and leaning against a tree near the bandstand in Hyde Park. The tune from beyond the ranks of deckchairs was 'What'll I Do?' Directly in front of them sat a fat woman, overflowing her chair, holding the leads of two tiny, bat-eared dogs with curly tails and bulbous eyes. The woman was enjoying the music, her head resting back, hat tilted, her foot bumping in time on the grass, but the dogs sat facing backwards, staring at Molly and Barbara, trembling in expect-ation of some nameless possible excitement. Barbara wondered if they were the dogs that Johnny walked and, if so, whether they knew they were talking about him?

'What was it about?' she asked. 'The fight?'

'Oh . . . about me. Or anyway about Ma.'

'What about her?'

'Thought she was too good for everyone, apparently, and that I thought I was, too. There was something in that, but then, of course, Ma had moved Eldridge in to help with the rent. So according to those little ruffians, she was no better than a pros-titute. Nothing kids like better than someone getting their comeuppance. We were always saying that sort of thing, without knowing exactly what we meant. We just liked being part of the crowd that was saying it. So I've no reason to feel superior.' She looked at Barbara. 'I don't suppose people said that kind of thing at your school. No reason to. Anyway, Johnny decided to stick up for us. He didn't have to and he was probably spoiling for a fight anyway, looking for a way out, which he got.'

At school, things went from bad to worse very quickly. Fighting and backchat apart, Johnny was sullenly idle in lessons and suffered the ignominy of being moved down a class, where Miss Calloway lay in wait with her strap at the ready. After two weeks of poker-faced insolence and beatings born with magnificent disdain he was sent home with a letter from Mr Brayne, which everyone knew meant only one thing; he had achieved his goal. But Molly was left with the aftermath, tarnished by association. The sly, verbal bullying of the girls and the more overt name-calling of the boys reached new levels. Even though Molly was tough she was used to being a leader and was now being brought down.

Annette was appalled, but Eldridge accepted the situation with equanimity. The day it happened Johnny hadn't gone straight home, he turned up after tea, digging Brayne's sadly creased letter out of his pocket and handing it over.

'Here you are. Now can I go to work?' He said in his laconic, grown-up way.

Eldridge went through the letter and the motions – disappointment, the benefits of education, going to have a word, and so forth – but Molly could tell he didn't really care, he wanted the boy out from under and some sort of menial job would do just as well.

Not long after that, she and Johnny had a conversation – their first.

The days were getting longer and she was out in the street, sitting on the front step. Annette hated her doing this, but was prepared to turn the occasional blind eye; it wasn't a big house and in rooms, as in life, Eldridge took up a lot of space.

Molly wasn't used to feeling left out and unhappy. In fact, even now, she couldn't quite recognise these feelings in herself. She was, though, indisputably alone and with no one to call on. The acolytes had withdrawn their support and if they retained any admiration it was now covert. In the house, her mother was preoccupied with her new life, which Molly intuited was not all plain sailing and she knew better than to rock the boat. So she sat there, with her knees bent up and her skirt wrapped round her legs in a condition of animal withdrawal. The woman opposite was also out in the road, toddler by the hand, new baby on her shoulder, jigging and humming. Every so often a snatch of 'Lily of Laguna', slightly off key, would drift across to Molly.

His boots appeared in front of her before she heard his voice.

'Hello.'

'Oh . . .' She screened her eyes briefly with her hand. 'Hello.'

There was room on the step, but after a moment he sat down cross-legged on the pavement next to her.

'You all right?'

'Why shouldn't I be?'

'Those kids at school. That was my fault, they didn't like me no more than I liked them and, after I beat that big idiot, you got roped in.'

She shrugged. 'I don't care.'

'Don't suppose you do, but I'm sorry anyway.'

There followed an awkward silence – awkward not through animosity, but through a sense of change. Molly picked at the buckle on her shoe.

'So what have you been doing?' she asked a trifle grudgingly.

'Errand boy, down at the Castle.'

The Castle was the pub on the corner. Molly was impressed, in spite of herself. She glanced at his sharp profile with its surprisingly thick lashes.

'What do you do?'

'Wash glasses, sweep the bar, fetch and carry. Go in the evening some days.'

'Have you got money then?'

'Might have. A little.' There was no mistaking the gleam of pride.

'Lucky you.'

'Not lucky, I have to work hard for it.' Suddenly he turned to look at her and she felt the impact of his attention, like a beam of light. 'You want some?'

She fired up with embarrassment. 'No thanks.'

'Want anything?'

'Don't be silly.'

'I mean it. We're pals, aren't we? Pals help each other.'

This was such a leap it took her breath away. What had he been thinking all this time? What had he been feeling? Something had been going on and she had had no idea. No one had ever spoken to her of friendship in such a direct way before. Indeed, no one had ever spoken of it at all. She had been handed something, some sort of present, and scarcely knew what to do with it or how to react.

'I suppose.'

He was still looking at her intently. 'I won't let anything happen to you, Molly Flynne.'

'Thanks,' she muttered. He got up and went into the house. She heard her mother's voice talking sharply about time, boots, tea . . . Eldridge's more ingratiating growl . . . Lad . . . day . . . Molly Malone . . .

What was it she wondered, puzzled, as she waited for her mother to call her in, that Johnny would not allow to happen?

There was a rustle of applause and some appreciative murmurs as the band finished their number. It only emphasised the silence between Barbara and Molly.

'Did he keep his promise?' Barbara asked. 'Or maybe, if he did, you'll never know.'

'Oh, he kept it,' said Molly. 'And I knew all right.'

The first time was so quick, that it was over and she was alone again before she'd had time to think. She'd been asleep and didn't hear the door open. She felt the heavy weight of someone sitting on the edge of her narrow bed. There was a looming extra-darkness over her, the smell of breath and the rummaging of a long arm and a heavy hand with prying fingers. A juicy, wheedling whisper in her face.

'Came to say goodnight to you, Molly Malone. Let me have a sweetie, yes, let me have a sweetie, yes, there's a good girl . . . Little Molly Malone . . . Ooh what a lovely sweetie!'

There was a grunting sound, a shifting of the weight and then the door opening and closing, with only the tiniest most careful 'click'. She lay paralysed with horror and shame, unsure of what exactly had happened and what it meant, except that her most private place, her peeing place, felt scoured and no longer private, and there was something sticky on the sheet.

She didn't cry, but she didn't sleep either and the next day she couldn't eat her breakfast. Neither Eldridge nor Johnny was there, but when her mother questioned her lack of appetite and put a hand on her forehead to see if she was ill, she knew she couldn't tell her anything. She didn't know how. What would she say?

That afternoon when she got back from her long, lonely day at school she still had no appetite and felt strangely cold and weak. She went up to her room and put the hard chair under her door handle again. When she heard her mother come back she removed the chair quietly – explaining its presence would have been too complicated.

'You're not right are you?' said Annette, that firm, judgmental hand on her forehead again. Molly could tell she was genuinely worried. 'I must say you look very cheap. You get into bed and I'll bring you up some beef tea.'

She didn't argue, though she knew she wouldn't be able to drink the horrible stuff. Eldridge came in and her mother said something about her.

'Sorry to hear that, I am indeed. Poor lass . . .' he replied. The sound of his soupy, guttural voice made her sweat, she thought she might faint. The moment her mother had left the hot drink she put the chair under the handle again. Next to come back was Johnny, there was another short conversation, this time in the kitchen and then the light tick-tock of his steps coming up the stairs, softly, two at a time.

He tapped on the door. She moved the chair carefully and opened the door a couple of inches. His face was right there, up against hers, his black eyes like mirrors.

'He been up to his tricks?'

Molly couldn't answer. Her face and neck ached and swelled with what she couldn't say. She let out a sound she didn't recognise as tears ran down her face, her mouth stretched and dribbled in helpless, nameless misery.

'Johnny!' Eldridge's voice from downstairs.

'Don't cry.' He wiped her tears with his fingers, with quick, jerky movements. 'I'll stop him, don't you worry. Promise.'

She closed the door, replaced the chair and lay down tense and shivering on the bed. She heard the sounds of tea, the voices – what were they talking about? Her? What would Eldridge say? The trembling was so great that her jaw ached and then her head. She had not been ill, but was becoming so.

It was springtime, therefore still light in the early evening. She heard the clatter of the dishes being cleared and washed by her mother and Johnny. Eldridge's steps in the hall, at the foot of the stairs, pausing – she whimpered. But no, he went into the parlour for his evening pipe. In the street were other voices, boys playing football, over-the-road's toddler bawling, the clatter and clop of a horse and cart, the clang and swoosh of slop buckets. All that everyday life was going on so close, so unknowing, while she lay up here with the secret inside her like a disgusting growth.

A little while later, she heard Johnny go out and Eldridge's usual admonishment to 'Be good and do as you're told!' So he had deserted her anyway, he didn't understand. She cried frantically, silently, pushing a handful of sheet into her mouth.

The evening began to darken and the children went in. She heard her mother climb the stairs and got out to move the chair.

'You didn't drink much.'

'I tried, I couldn't.'

'Have you been crying?' She scrubbed at her swollen face, she couldn't deny it.

'There's nothing to cry about. We'll raise you Molly, but you should eat something or you won't get better.'

She wanted to say that nothing she ate or drank could help – only protection could do that. Safety. But to ask for those things, she'd have had to say so much more and that was beyond her.

'I'll leave it here. Is there anything else you'd like? There's a bit of seed cake in the tin.'

Molly nodded, just to have her mother go away and come back. When she did, she put the cake on the little wicker table by her bed and touched her head gently, stroking her hair. She wanted to grab her mother's hand and hold on to it, to keep her there in this sympathetic and affectionate mood.

'You take those clothes off and put them on the chair,' said Annette, absent-mindedly moving the chair back to its usual place, 'and get under the covers properly. I'll come in again before we go to bed.'

She said 'Yes,' but she didn't remove her clothes. She had a deadline now, a moment after which she would not be safe. After the next time her mother came, she would be truly alone in the dark.

Johnny hadn't meant a word of it. He lied to her and what could he have done anyway?

An hour went by like an eternity. The tap on the door was so soft that she wasn't sure if there was anyone really there. She'd heard no footsteps, so she lay still as death. Then came her name, whispered,

'Molly . . .'

She held her breath.

'Oy, Molly!'

The second she opened the door he was in and had closed it behind him.

'Quiet. Get into bed.'

'I thought you—'

'Ssh. I said quiet.'

He pushed her back on to the mattress, yanking up the thin eiderdown as he did so. Urgency made him rough and for such a skinny kid he was strong.

'You don't know I'm here.'

He ducked down and she felt him slither under the bedstead. He wriggled around under there, making the thin metal frame rattle and bump. She was glad there was nothing in the chamber pot.

An hour later her mother came to say goodnight.

'How are you feeling? Bit better?'

She nodded. 'A bit.'

'That's the way.' Her mother plonked a brisk kiss on her forehead. 'Sleep tight, you'll be all right in the morning.'

'Night, Ma.'

Not long after that, she heard Eldridge call up the stairs.

'Nice evening, just going out for a pipe . . .!'

Now the deadline was past. She trailed her hand over the side of the bed.

'Johnny . . .?'

No reply. What if he'd fallen asleep under there?

'Johnny, are you awake? Mum's gone to bed.'

Still no reply, but this time his cool, dry hand closed around her fingers and gave them a squeeze, releasing them with a little push, telling her to lie doggo.

Another half an hour – she heard the kitchen clock give its single 'ting' – and the front door closed. A pause, while Eldridge took his boots off, and then the soft heavy creak of his feet on the stairs.

The door opened and shut and he was in, so quick and quiet for a big man.

'How you doing Molly Malone . . .?' The edge of the bed sank down as he lowered himself on to it. 'Been poorly, eh? Got a sweetie for me, have you?'

She thought of Johnny under there, crushed. They were both going to be crushed. Eldridge's arm was under the covers, his fat, dry fingers were rummaging, his breath was coming quicker, she clamped her legs together, but his scrabbling hand pushed its way between them. She thought that, this time, she might die because he was going to break her apart.

She couldn't stop him and neither could Johnny. At least, like last time, it was quick. Less than a minute and his breathing jolted and calmed and he tucked the covers back under her chin.

'Sleep tight Molly Malone. See you in the morning.'

'I've seen you. I can see you now.'

It was Johnny's voice, not raised but not whispering either. Eldridge stood up. Molly could make out his big head swinging from side to side.

'What the bleeding—?'

'I been watching you.' Johnny emerged from beneath the bed on the far side. His arms were held slightly away from his body, his eyes were gleaming. 'I know what you do. You can't do that. I'll tell.'

'You didn't see anything. Get out of here.'

'Won't.'

'I'll make you.'

'Go on then. I'll tell. Not just Mrs, I'll tell everyone. You're disgusting.'

Molly lay between them. She'd feared she might die and now she wanted to. She would die of fear. Eldridge's breathing was ramping up again.

'You get over here you rotten, filthy, little toad . . .!' Molly whimpered. 'And you shut your mouth! Hear me?' He spoke in a snarled whisper and she felt his spit on her cheek.

'Percy . . .?'

It was her mother's voice. She could hear that their bedroom door had been opened. The three of them were still as statues.

'Percy?' She was out on the landing now. 'Is everything all right?'

'All well Netta.' He was out there in a split second, his voice cheerful and matter of fact. The door shut behind him. 'Just went in to say goodnight to the invalid, but she's out like a light, must be better.'

'I thought I heard voices.' Her mother had turned, or been turned, away.

'Told those lads in the road to keep their language down.'

'Quite right, I bet you got some back . . .'

The bedroom door closed. Johnny came round the bed and replaced the chair under the door handle. He sat down on the key-pattern rug by the bed, with his back to her, his arms around his knees. He sat very still but Molly could hear his quick breathing, his bony shoulders moving in time.

Minutes went by before she spoke.

'What's going to happen? What will he do?'

'He won't do that again.'

'But if it's his word against yours, then . . .'

'And yours.' He glanced over his shoulder. 'Your Ma will believe you.'

Molly knew this to be true. Whatever Annette's shortcomings she loved her daughter and had brought her up right, she wouldn't for an instant think she was lying.

'He'll go. He'll be off tomorrow.'

'Poor mother,' she began silently to cry again.

'Good riddance for both of you.'

'What about you?'

He shrugged. 'I can look after myself.'

The band were packing up, people were moving. Barbara and Molly carried on sitting beneath the lengthening shadow of the tree. Molly's voice had a rough, uncertain edge, but she was dry-eyed.

'The thing was he couldn't. Not really. He looked after me, but not himself.'

The little dogs trotted past, towed in the considerable shadow of their mistress. A discarded, open newspaper fluttered and fanned between the deck chairs. Barbara found she had to clear her throat.

'What happened?'

'They went, both of them, not right away. Johnny got a terrible beating, his father didn't say why but we knew. He couldn't do his odd jobs, he hung around the house and I saw him in the street now and again. I stayed out of school a couple of times to keep him company. He was light-fingered, but he never took anything from us.'

'When did Eldridge go? Did he – did you –?'

Molly shook her head. 'He didn't come to my room again. A couple of weeks later, I got home from school and my mother was crying, and they'd gone, both of them. But for a long time, I went on seeing Johnny.'

'You stayed friends ever since?'

Molly moved her legs to the side and leaned her shoulder against the tree, looking directly at Barbara for the first time.

'There is one thing I haven't told you.'

That same night, Johnny curled up to sleep on the rug, like a dog. A long while passed and Molly knew that neither of them were asleep. When she could actually hear Eldridge's snores from next door she hung an arm out and tapped Johnny on the leg. He jerked up as though she'd fired a shot.

'What?'

She shunted back and lifted the bedclothes on his side. 'Want to get in?'

He hesitated for only a second.

'All right.'

They tried putting the pillow between them but that didn't work, the bed was too narrow, so they put it back beneath their heads.

'Do you mind?' he asked.

'No.'

In the end, they put their arms around each other so neither of them could fall.

'So that,' said Molly, 'is how it is between Johnny and me.' She narrowed her eyes. 'And now he's in love with you.'

'I sometimes think he doesn't know me.'

'Any more than you know him, though perhaps you understand a little more now. Remember I asked you to be careful?'

Barbara nodded.

'Please do. And *take care* as well. You can hurt Johnny, terribly,
and he can hurt you without meaning to.'

'If he doesn't mean to, then it doesn't matter.'

'Perhaps,' said Molly. She moved to rise, stiffly. 'But God help
you if he does.'

Fourteen

1931

With Molly's revelations in the park that day, Barbara felt she
had been given a gift, but one that had been handed over in
trust. There followed a summer that brought change on its warm
and languorous breath. It would test that trust to the full.

She was delighted that her parents had taken to Johnny.
Her fears in that direction had proved not just unfounded,
but were banished. Her mother frankly doted on him and,
for this reason, alone her father – whatever his misgivings –
reserved judgement.

She had never expected this, nor that Johnny would be
equally taken with them. All through May they visited them at
the weekends and it wasn't long before Julia had asked Johnny
to make some changes in the garden. She wanted to create a
rus in urbe, a city sanctuary that mirrored the artful ease of
Ardonleigh, and Johnny was full of ideas for honeysuckle and
old-fashioned, rambling roses, an arbor, a cloud of tall delphin-
iums in blue, purple, pink . . .

Soon, while Barbara was busy with her job at *The Countrywoman*,
he was at her parents' house, discussing plans and working in the
garden. The evenings were growing longer and he began to
suggest she meet him there. She would find him outside with
one or both of them, expanding on his ideas, a glass in one hand,
rubbing his brow with the kerchief that had been round his neck.

All this was pleasantly unexpected, but increasingly Barbara was unhappy. Their secret had been shanghaied, was no longer a secret, nor even theirs. She had feared disapproval but this enveloping net of not just approbation, but delight, was too much. There had been a reversal of roles and she had become the outsider.

As well as that, she couldn't forget Molly's story and was sickened to realise that she was jealous. She and Johnny had never done it – never lain together! *It's they who have a secret,* she thought. Whatever she did with Johnny, it would in some sense be with Molly's permission.

Molly had sworn her to secrecy about the events she'd described.

'If you say anything, to him or to anyone, I'll lose him,' she told her. 'And, what's more, so will you.'

Still, her foolhardy heart blundered on. There was foreshadowing, but at the time she was aware only of a coolness, as small clouds passed between her and the sun.

The first of these concerned Hannaford. George Hannaford was the gardener in Regent Terrace, a man who stood in a particular and special relationship to his employers, especially Julia. She gave instructions, or at least expressed her wishes, and he listened patiently and responded with advice. The garden was his domain. Any mention of that earlier garden, in the country, let alone the rude mechanicals in whom Julia had put her trust down there, was met with the shortest possible shrift. The appearance of Johnny on the scene, full of ideas and basking in Mrs Delahay's affection, was calculated to get his goat.

One late afternoon, Barbara had arrived after work. She was hot and bothered after a long and strenuously diplomatic interview with one Lady Seaborne (a Lady solely through her businessman husband's elevation) and searched for the others. She found her parents were out, but from the drawing-room window she could see both Hannaford and Johnny down in the garden. This was unusual in itself because Hannaford, having arrived at eight o'clock would normally have gone home at four. He was standing near the end of the garden, feet apart, facing the house, holding a rake as if it were a pike. From his stance alone, she could easily infer his dissatisfaction. Johnny was nearer the house, with his back to it. He had been pushing a wheelbarrow containing plants but, just now, the legs of the barrow were on the ground and he was standing between the shafts. It was perfectly clear that he was speaking and Hannaford listening, the one enthusiastically, the other with extremely poor grace.

Just below the window was a terrace with chairs and a table set out with a jug and glasses, the jug covered with a plate. Lemonade . . . she could almost taste it. This was presumably left out for Johnny and any visitors, Hannaford would apply to the kitchen for a glass of water or a cup of tea.

She went out into the hall and along to the back of the house where a glass-panelled door opened on to the short flight of stone steps leading to the terrace – a flight which, like a stream passing through a pond, continued on the far side and down to the lawn.

Taking the plate from the top of the jug, she caught the sharp fragrance of lemons and sugar. After the first deliciously refreshing gulps, she carried her glass to the edge of the terrace. They hadn't seen her. From here she could no longer see Johnny, but she could hear his voice.

'. . . if we can do away with some of these hard edges, create more of a wave . . . a swirl . . . I think it will be tremendous. And with the statue placed, what do you think, about here . . .? Like a Beardsley print . . .'

Johnny was treading the lip of a volcano and, she was sure, knew he was doing so. *What* had he just said? *A wave . . . a swirl . . . a Beardsley print . . .?* Hannaford's face would have been comical if it hadn't been for his expression of thunderous insult.

'Couldn't say I'm sure.' The words darted jerkily through almost-closed lips like tickets from a bus-conductor's machine.

'I just have this feeling . . . You know, George? You're a man with a feeling for growing things, all your years of experience . . . And you know Mrs Delahay, too, and her tastes, far better than me. I'm a Johnny-come-lately after all!'

Barbara could bear it no longer. She put her glass down on the wall and went down the steps.

'Hello.'

'Evening Miss.'

Johnny turned round. He hadn't known she was there, didn't quite have time to hide the split-second's uncertainty as if she'd caught him off guard.

'Barbara!'

'Am I interrupting?'

'Not in the least, I was just explaining some of my ideas to George here.'

'And what do you make of them?'

She didn't really need to ask, but whatever else he was George wasn't a fool. His expression of sullen disgruntlement had been replaced by stony-faced neutrality the moment she appeared.

'Could work miss. Won't say otherwise.'

She raised her glass. 'Can I get you a cold drink?'

'No thank you Miss, I'll be off shortly.'

'I will though.' Johnny left the wheelbarrow and bounded up the steps, catching her hand as he passed. Her last glimpse of Hannaford, over her shoulder, was of him turning away in disgust, with a look on his face of pure, sulphurous loathing.

The other occasion could not have been more different, nor more unsettling; yet another example of her new position as outsider in her family home. By the middle of August, some of the proposed changes in the garden had been made. They were by no means as radical as Johnny had implied, but there were certainly curves and new, extravagant plants set to romp over walls by the following summer. There were also a couple of romantic, quasi-classical statues that hovered on the borders of good taste, yet Julia expressed herself thrilled with the statues. Barbara was glad she had not been there to observe her father's first reaction to them. By the time she next saw him – and them all together – he was claiming, straight-faced, to find them 'rather fine'.

Over the past weeks, the excitement had gone out of her work. The challenge and independence, which had been such a pleasure to her last autumn, had palled. She chafed against being behind her desk, but felt curiously agitated when required to go out of town, as if she were in some way deserting her

post. She couldn't work out why this should be until one afternoon, when she was visiting a dog-breeder in Sussex. Barbara
was standing, in the sensible shoes she had bought for such
occasions, gazing at a litter of black and yellow Labradors. She
was listening to but not hearing her subject's dissertation on
the honing of pedigree, because her mind had flown back
to the Regent's Park garden and to Johnny. He was not
working, but playing and doing as he wanted in pleasant
surroundings. He was basking in the sunshine and her mother's
approval, being completely at home in her home.

'. . . not being too technical?'

The dog-breeder was regarding her with an expression of
quizzical apology; she must have been looking quite blank.
Politely, Barbara explained that she probably had enough for
The Countrywoman's little piece and the photographer had some
delightful pictures, which the readers would love.

On the train back to London, she sat in her corner seat, her
face turned resolutely away from her fellow-travellers. She and
Johnny had made no arrangement for that evening. There were
rarely any arrangements these days, she realised. She knew
where he was likely to be. From the station she went straight
to the house, Clarice was in the hall.

'Only Sir Conrad, miss,' she said, answering Barbara's question.
'He's in the drawing room.'

Barbara glanced at her watch. Six fifteen was early for her
father to be back and on his own.

'Thank you, Clarice, I'll see myself up.'

He was sitting in the green brocade carriage chair by the
window. This was unusual in itself, because she thought of this
as her mother's chair. Julia liked to sit there and watch the world
go by: the changing colours of the trees in the park, the lamps
being lit on winter afternoons and the sun go down in summer.
Next to him, on the windowsill, stood his glass of whisky and
next to that a copy of the Times, still folded. He was sitting
still, his hands resting on his knees. For that second, she saw
her father as an old man.

'Daddy?'

'Bar!' The moment passed. 'My dear girl. You know your
young man isn't here.'

This wasn't quite a question. Her father was being tactful, not wishing to imply that she'd been left in the dark, although of course she had been.

'I do, Clarice told me.'

'He and your mother have gone to purchase some frippery or other for the garden.' It was the first time she'd heard him disparage Johnny's work, however glancingly. 'They should be back soon, I have no idea what's keeping them. Would you care for a glass of sherry?'

She accepted and, once he'd handed her the glass, he didn't return to the carriage chair, but indicated they should sit in their habitual places away from the window. He asked her, with more than usual interest, about her work and what she had been doing. Then listened to her answers with close attention and smiling briefly when she said something amusing.

Barbara thought, *he needs diversion, and I am it.*

Some fifteen minutes, later Clarice knocked to say Conrad had a telephone caller and on being told the name, he apologised and went to take it in his study. Barbara returned to the window and perched on the sill.

The cab must have only just pulled up, because Johnny was still holding the door, a large bag in his other hand, and her mother emerged like a butterfly from a chrysalis, carrying flowers, holding her pert little hat and laughing. As far as Barbara could see, Johnny was in his gardening clothes: black trousers, worse-for-wear tweed jacket and collarless shirt, with a blue handkerchief knotted round his neck. A woman walking past glanced at them with that sparkle of envy one reserves for beguiling couples.

Barbara watched her mother take money from her bag and give it to Johnny to pay the driver . . . Watched her dip her face sweetly into the soft, pink and blue flowers as the cab pulled away . . . Saw her make some smiling remark to Johnny and rest her hand for a second on his shoulder. Saw Johnny . . . what? What did she see exactly? He had his back to the house but she could tell from the angle of his head, the set of his shoulders, the very displacement of air around him, what the expression was on his face; how he was looking at Julia. She

knew because, in the past, he had looked so often at her in
that way.

*Oh Johnny . . . My handsome, winsome Johnny . . . You're
just a tawdry, street Arab making fools of us all . . .*

'Aha,' said her father, putting his head round the door.
'The great gardeners are back.'

That was nowhere near the end. The summer was too lovely
to spoil and Johnny was so happy. If Barbara's work had lost
its lustre the same could not be said of his. Julia invited a
stream of friends round to admire his handiwork. She made
him a present of a little, eighteenth-century patch-box, with
a red and gold enamelled lid, which he'd admired on his first
visit to the house.

She thought she would never understand him. He was mercur-
ial, protean: a creature that appeared entirely different, depending
on where one was standing. These days she saw less of the
wounded, wary Johnny who had so captivated her and even less
of the sly charmer she had first met. He was caught up in
something else, a mission of his own, and she was only a part
of it. Her heart felt as though it were being crushed, pushed
down in her chest until it ached and yet she lacked the will
to go. She feared that she might lose not just Johnny, but all of
them and everything she had.

In the end, the decision was made for her.

The first theft was a small amount of cash from Julia's handbag.
Julia told the story as one against herself, she 'could never do
arithmetic' and Conrad was *always* telling her she was 'a soft
touch' with the fiddle-player on the corner of Primrose Hill.
Then there was the silver jam spoon that Clarice couldn't find
and the little, mother-of-pearl key, usage and provenance
unknown, that hung on a hook behind the door in the dining
room. Johnny searched, sympathised and speculated, but Barbara
was certain he'd taken them and the thought made her feel sick
and cold. Molly's words in the park came back to Barbara.

'*He was light-fingered, but he never took anything from us . . .*'

Her family was different. She could scarcely ask him, because
she had no proof and she couldn't even look for the things in
his room since she didn't know where that was. Her father was

pensive and poker-faced. In her mother's eyes, Johnny could do no wrong.

His mistake was in stealing from Clarice. Just like the Gorringes' house staff, she and Hannaford had no time for him. Barbara suspected that Clarice might even have set a trap by leaving her purse unattended on the kitchen table. He had taken half a cake from the tin and six shillings from her purse. The cake didn't matter, he 'helped himself all the time' according to Clarice, but he had been the only person there for the quarter of an hour during which the cash had disappeared.

Clarice's righteous wrath and her boldness in confronting her employers was something to behold. She pointed the finger with complete certainty and with that pointing finger she demoted Johnny from Barbara's young man, her mistress's favourite, to just another employee and a light-fingered one at that. Johnny smiled in astonishment. Clarice was thanked and told she could go. The drawing room was a little hell of shame and embarrassment, and despair.

Julia wept. Barbara's father was white with a cold fury. Johnny, feigning furious offence, left the house, banging the front door in Barbara's face. She ran after him and caught his sleeve. He stopped, not looking at her. There was spittle at the corner of his mouth.

'Don't tell me you believe her, that stupid bitch!'

She had scarcely any breath left. 'I don't know what to believe, or who!'

'*Me!*' he snarled. 'You might try believing *me*, instead of the maid!'

'I'm sorry, I'm so sorry . . .' Why was she apologising? 'Clarice has been with us such a long time. She's like one of the family—'

'Something I could never be.' He picked her hand off his arm as if it were a burr, an insect. 'Could I?'

He walked away from her, fast. For years, decades, that remained her most enduring image of Johnny – disappearing, shoulders tight, hands in pockets, coiled against the world.

At one a.m. that night, he beat on the front door of Sussex Court so loudly that Mr Jeffries – from the ground-floor flat and donned in his dressing gown – was already in the hall as she ran down the stairs.

'What's all this about? Do you know anything about this?'

'I may do, I do apologise.'

'Stand back then while I see who it is.'

Mr Jeffries opened the door a few inches.

'Who are you? What in God's name is all the noise about? Do you know what time—?'

'I know, I'm sorry,' Johnny shouted over the man's shoulder, 'Barbara!'

She had known it would be him and now she could see his white, frantic face through the partially opened door.

'It's all right, Mr Jeffries. He's a friend of mine.'

'You need to take more care who you make friends with!'

'Let me in! Please Barbara!'

'Are you quite sure?'

'I am Mr Jeffries, there's nothing to worry about.'

'If you say so.'

Jeffries, with an air of morose impatience, left the door open and stumped back to his flat, closing his own door with a final threatening glare. Outside it was raining and Johnny was soaked, but the moment he was in her arms Barbara could tell he was weeping. His frailty as always squeezed her heart. But when he spoke his voice was fierce and harsh.

'Don't leave me!'

Only twenty-four hours earlier, she could have given him that promise. Now she could only say, 'Come upstairs. You need to get dry.'

She never asked him about the stealing. She couldn't bear to give him yet another opportunity to lie to her. When he left that night, she knew that she would never see him again. She thought she might die of the pain.

With Johnny gone, Julia's humiliation was terrible to see. She could only lick her wounds. It was her father who talked straight to Barbara.

'The man's a cheat, Bar. A cheap, common fraud. We've all been taken in by an expert. There's no shame in that, but there would be in letting it happen again. This is where it has to end. You do understand that.'

It was not a rebuke, but an order. She nodded.

'I thought I was making a joke about his name . . . You know what it means, Eldridge?'

'No.'

'Strange, sinister, not of this world. A bad lot. Look it up, you'll see I'm right.'

He could see he'd gone too far, as the tears ran down her face. He held her close and kissed her forehead – blessing and absolving her, his child.

Child!

She understood the meaning of a heart 'turned to stone'. Hers had cracked but not broken. It became a petrified, useless, senseless lump of matter that sat heavy within her. At all sorts of unexpected moments, she could feel Johnny beneath her hand: the texture of the soft hair that curled on his collar; the skin of his cheek; his threadbare work jacket; his cool, calloused hand, with its long fingers.

The stolen things were returned, left one night in a chocolate box on the table on the terrace: the silver spoon, the key, a sad, little handful of mixed change . . . even the patch box, Julia's gift.

'Now we know,' said Conrad, 'if we didn't before.'

Julia couldn't look at them and her voice was bitter. 'I'm only surprised he hadn't sold them.'

Barbara wasn't surprised. The things in themselves (except for Clarice's money) were pathetic – hostages not only to fortune but to a dream.

Molly, whom she hadn't seen in months, met her in a Lyons Corner House and listened expressionless, to the story, smoking cigarette after cigarette.

'Have you seen him?' Barbara asked. 'Have you heard from him at all?'

'No.' Molly shook her head. 'But then I often don't. He comes and goes. I must say that as time went by I suspected all might not be well.'

'You warned me.'

'I did, but I didn't seriously expect you to heed the warnings. Who would, with Johnny? I didn't, but then I have my reasons to be eternally grateful to him, as I told you.'

'If you're in touch, Molly, will you tell him—?'

'No.' Molly raised a hand. 'I'm not going to be your messenger.'
Her tone was matter-of-fact, rather than sharp. Barbara had
been cut adrift.

Fifteen

1949

Johnny's arms were submerged to the elbow in greasy, opaque
water, on the surface of which scraps of food floated, some of
which had certainly been in people's mouths. Saliva, he tried
not to think about that. The worn soles of his shoes were planted
in a slick of the aforementioned grease, plus gravy, custard, slimy
strands of fish skin, fat and vegetable matter, and whatever else
had slithered from the piles of plates, before they were plunged
into the filthy water. His feet were already dank where the
moisture had seeped through, though not as bad as they would
have been on a Saturday night. Codger, whose thankless and
Sisyphean task it was to clean the kitchen during working hours,
was mopping over the other side near the chefs. There he could
make the most difference and be seen to be doing so. Any
attempt to shift the culinary slurry by the sinks was generally
accorded a waste of time until service was over.

The water in the sink needed changing, but Johnny was
putting it off. If there was one thing worse than the disgusting
soup he was delving around in, it was clawing out the slimy
debris from the drain hole and transferring it to the nearly-full,
galvanised tin bucket on the floor. And then the tap ran so
slowly that further towers of plates would build up on the side
while you waited. To his left was the rinsing sink, which also
needed changing, and beyond that Aldo was on cutlery. Another
thing you didn't want to dwell on was what survived between
the tines of forks and on plates that arrived at the tables, with
food already covering dried-on scabs of what had been there
before. Glasses, the state of which was easily apparent to
customers, were washed in a separate corner by Micky and

Moira, who wore clean white overalls and wielded special cloths.

It was eleven p.m., another couple of hours before they finally saw off the after-theatre crowd. But on a Tuesday, the load at this hour was beginning to lighten at least. The day, even in early July, the height of summer, had long gone. Up there, way overhead and beyond the pavement grille was the jumbled clatter of pedestrians. The heave of traffic was as great as ever, but the light was the patchy, sulphurous yellow of the street lamps. Hubert Gregg's lyrics came back to him as he washed up.

'*I'm gonna get lit up when the lights go on in London . . .!*'

Johnny'd been lit up all right, drunk as a lord up there in the West End, spinning and weaving and kissing and dancing, a succession of girls (and a few men) in his arms, with no cares. The bad times over and the world free again, it was a kaleidoscope of swirling demob-delirious humanity with everything to live for. Looking back, those crowds were more like the food-scrapings swirling towards the sink's blocked plughole. Human detritus. The golden future turned out to be not up, but down. Down and dark.

And here he was, four years later, back in another warzone. It was like France, the show before last, because this was what life there had been like: filthy, nauseating, soul-destroying, repetitive, much of it boring. The kitchen of the Bay Tree just off the Bayswater Road had everything in common with war, except violent death, and even that was probably only a matter of time, given the nature of the people working here and the range of weaponry at their disposal. Blood was regularly shed in the chefs' zone and burns and scalding were commonplace.

The Bay Tree was a popular spot with the arty crowd. Every night was a battle against time, against conditions, against the chefs and the waiters, against (if they weren't careful) the customers. The basement kitchen was very like the trenches but, at least when he was there when he looked up he could see the sky, the occasional bird, a tough, flowering weed, a cloud or two. Here, the pavement grille let through nothing but the thinnest stripes of light and the odd cigarette end.

⋆   ⋆   ⋆

He'd been only in his teens and looked younger, since he was small for his age. He never thought about death, perhaps that was why the bullets and the shrapnel swerved round him – because he didn't care, so what was the point? The other blokes liked him and one or two of them liked him quite a bit, because they thought he was girly. That was fine, he took their cigarettes and the presents they made him out of their parcels from home, wrapped up by their mothers and sweethearts, the women they forgot about when they were rutting their socks off.

Clenching his jaw against the gag-reflex, he clawed the muck out of the sink and began running the tap again, shaking in the powder that made his hands raw and his nails crack.

They'd treated him like a mascot, but there was one chap who became a friend; the only person in his life he could properly call that, apart from Molly and she was a special case. Reg Nicholls was a big, raw-boned, lanky cockney, a bloke so straight he seemed almost innocent. He was not a fool, but decent through and through. The sort of bloke who never said a bad word about anyone and you just knew that was because he didn't think ill of anyone in the first place. It wasn't in his nature. To begin with, when Reg was kind and friendly towards him, Johnny had him marked down as another pansy. Yet as the weeks went by, in rest camp, marching, hanging about in reserve, even in the front line, he came to realise that here was someone who had no ulterior motive, who didn't see him as a lucky charm or a quick poke. Reg liked him. He laughed at his jokes, listened to his stories and looked out for him. Reg was a gent, just about the only man in the squad who never lost his manners. Other blokes respected him for it and even modified their language a bit when he was around, though he didn't mind what they said. Johnny once heard one of the officers say in a baffled drawl that 'Nicholls has the milk of human kindness running through his veins,' which seemed about right. But even allowing for that, Johnny knew he and Reg had a real friendship.

Reg had been in France since almost the start, January 1915, and been back with a Blighty one twice and still come back. You might almost have thought he liked it, or at the very least found something in the blackness that he hadn't found elsewhere.

Perhaps, thought Johnny, that was the source of their instinctive comradeship – there was nothing here they missed and you were so close to the edge nothing mattered. It turned out he was only partly right. Reg was a Barnardo's boy, said he had no complaints about that – the teachers, the chaplain, they'd been good people who'd taught him and cared for him – so being in the army was kind of home from home. The war suited Johnny because, forget the enemy, it was every man for himself and he was already beyond corruption. Reg saw it differently, he was institutionalised, a team player.

Johnny reckoned he could deal with pain, if it happened, and he wasn't scared of death; there was nothing he planned to do with his life, no future he had in mind. But when Reg began to lose his nerve, well, that scared him. It was like seeing a tree you thought would always be there start to die, struck down by nasty unseen blight for which there was no cure. First of all, he became withdrawn. In rest camp – a huddle of derelict farm buildings on the edge of a village – he no longer wanted to play soccer (Johnny didn't blame him for that) or British Bulldog. And you no longer heard him singing any of those bloody hymns he knew by heart, either with or without the alternative words. He just sat and smoked, his hand trembling slightly. He held the shaking right hand propped on the other one. His long forearms were like a couple of thin, knotty sticks that had nothing to do with him, that he was just using for the purpose of holding the fag. His homely, lantern-jawed face was dishwater-grey and empty. When Johnny went to sit by him he would give him a quick, distracted look, acknowledging him almost fearfully, as if anything or anyone coming too close was a threat.

'How you doing, Reg?'

'Not too bad. Not too bad.'

'Get you a cuppa?'

'No thanks, son.'

'Got a fag?'

Reg rummaged in his shirt pocket and brought out a wizened pack containing only two cigarettes. Johnny's hand hovered.

'You sure? Don't want to leave you short.'

The pack was shaken slightly, Johnny took one.

'Coming into town tonight? Drink at the Carrifer?' The *Carrefour* was the most-frequented bar on the crossroads at the far end of the village, the one with the prettiest, friendliest girls and the least disgusting *vin ordinaire* and sausages. Reg's role was usually that of benign non-participant, he didn't drink much and kept a smile on his face and his hands to himself. One thing he would do was sing in his yodelling tenor – one of those sturdy hymns which always got him a roar of affectionately teasing applause. Now he shook his head.

'Don't reckon so.'

'Might do you good,' said Johnny. 'Back up, the day after tomorrow.'

He should never have said that. The hand tremor turned into an uncontrollable shudder and Reg lurched to his feet, tottering for a moment so that Johnny jumped up, thinking he might be crushed along with the half-finished cigarette.

'I'm not going!'

This couldn't have been plainer as regards the bar, but a couple of days later it was as clear as daylight to Johnny that there had been more than one meaning. He stuck like glue to Reg on the march up, chattering like a monkey, looking up into his face for signs and portents, grabbing his sleeve now and again when he seemed to be flagging. The chaps began singing 'When this bloody war is over', that usually got Reg joining in with the proper churchy words, but not this time. He was a walking corpse.

They had a twenty-four-hour behind the lines and then it was on and into the trenches, passing the other lot on the way down, filtering into the bays and alleys, trying not to look at what was under your feet and stuck into the walls and the parapet. For now, they were reasonably clean and well fed, but that wasn't going to last. The weather was hot and after the clean air of rest camp the stink was enough to make you gag, but after a few hours they wouldn't notice that.

They were in the Wipers area, part of a little sub-salient that stuck out like a thumb – a sore thumb ho-ho – towards the German line. There weren't many trees left in their world, but at this particular point there was a thin spinney, a fringe of elders running along the top of the thumb. God knows how they'd survived. Johnny thought they were just plain lucky, like him.

They were all on edge, all jumpy, but Reg was in a proper mess. His spoon clattered on his mess tin, his breathing was sticky and shallow like a man with a fever. He spoke when he was spoken to and was never less than civil, but you could just tell his heart wasn't in it, there was nothing behind the words. Johnny feared for him, dreaded the moment they had to make an advance. The moment when the terror was going to finally burst out of his friend like a dose of the shits, shaming him in a way he didn't deserve after all those years of putting his life on the line for King and fucking Country.

They had a long wait, dug into the filth with beautiful, high summer weather hovering over them: a sky of opalescent blue, feathery clouds, a few brave, scrawny meadow flowers sticking their heads over the lip of the parapet, little bobbing faces looking down on them. Three days went by with barely a squeak from the other side. Johnny looked after Reg: kept an eye on him; made sure he ate; pushed him about at stand-to and inspection; patched up his feet which were in a terrible state; scrounged some socks from someone else; talked and talked and tried to keep him from sinking altogether. No one liked the look of Reg, they all reckoned they knew how it was going to end, but there it was. If Eldridge wanted to play nursemaid that was his look-out.

On the fourth day, a recce party went out and came back quite excited with the news that Gerry had extended their trench by a couple of hundred yards, so the end of it was now just below the fringe of trees, itself about a quarter of a mile away. It didn't take a genius to see that whoever could get up among the trees had won themselves a nice little vantage point, from which to take pot shots or even launch a full-blown attack. The officer in charge, not many years older than Johnny, fresh-faced and a bit startled-looking to find the silver spoon wrenched untimely from his mouth, decreed that, well chaps, they'd better get up there first and make the most of the element of surprise.

The days were long, not fully dark until after ten o'clock, and there was usually a desultory exchange of fire around eight, just to show no one was sleeping on the job. That was about the time when, back at the farm, the bats came out. Tiny pipistrelles flitting and swooping almost faster than the eye could follow in the dusk. The order came along from Captain Dench that they'd be going over, quietly mind, immediately after the half-hearted evening barrage. That the enemy might have exactly the same idea seemed not to have occurred to him, or to anyone. To be honest it was good to be doing something, taking some action, not just being a sitting duck in a hole in the ground.

Waiting to go over, Johnny's main preoccupation was how to get Reg to move. A complete funk wouldn't do him any favours. This wasn't a charge. There'd be no whistle and no rallying cry. Dench would get out there first, poor sod, with his little tin hat and revolver, at least as terrified as the rest of them and rather less prepared. Then they'd follow, keeping low and weaving from side to side, because if Gerry had got there first you wanted to present a moving target. If he had. They hoped not.

Johnny could hear Reg just behind him on the steps. Each breath carried a squeaky moan, like a child with a bellyache. He was shot to buggery. Everyone was pretending not to hear, wishing he'd fucking put a sock in it, he was making them nervous.

Everything happened quickly. Dench went over, hoisting his arm in a beckoning motion. Over they went, Reg stumbling and now almost sobbing. Johnny fell back a few paces, prodding him along, saying daft things like 'get a move on' and 'nearly there' and 'watch yourself', meaningless empty phrases, pretending it wasn't dangerous.

They'd gone about a hundred yards, when there was a volley of shots from the trees. Johnny saw Dench fall over at the same time as he saw Reg spin round and start to run back the way they'd come. Only he could run quicker. He sprinted, caught Reg, pulled him round. He was gibbering, no other word for it. When Johnny shot him, from the front, he was aiming for his shoulder, a nice, Blighty one from the enemy to send him home for good. Reg's look of twisted, frantic panic turned in an instant to one of surprise, as he first reeled, then fell down. Safe as houses.

Johnny, stumbling on between the ribbons of smoke, didn't know that. He'd done his bit for Reg now he had to look out for himself. They'd passed Dench, gobbing up blood, and were returning the business-like fusillade with scattered fire of their own. Corporal Hayley was about ten yards to his left, ducking and weaving like a punch-drunk boxer, but with Dench gone there would be no more heroics.

'Halt! Give over! We're wasting our time lads! Dig in for as long as you need to and get back when you can – got that?'

Johnny threw himself down and brought his Enfield to his cheek. He felt almost snug, with the dark falling and old Reg taken care of back there. He heard the stretcher bearers jogging out to pick up Dench, who was making a horrible racket like a half-blocked drain. He hoped they'd got Reg already and the two of them would soon be on their way to the clearing station.

An hour later, they began to make their way back, creeping and stooping towards their trench, under cover of the stealing dark. Johnny nearly trod on someone, it happened all the time, except now – in the summer weather – the bodies stayed on the surface for longer. On this occasion, something made him glance down, to find Reg's calm, glassy-eyed face looking back at him, his tin hat tilted back like an open lid, his mouth slack. In fact, for a non-drinking man, he looked amazingly like a drunk. In the half-light, the whole front of his tunic was black with blood.

Safe all right, but going nowhere.

Johnny began slotting the steaming, dripping plates into the wooden rack over his head. After the eighth plate, he left his hand up there for a moment, leaning on it, eyes closed. He'd accounted for his share of the enemy, but that one unintended death still had the power to make him feel sick. What the devil had gone through Reg's head in the split second before he went down? Did a man taking a bullet to the heart have time to ask what the fuck was going on? Had his last thought been that Johnny was a traitor? Or did he know him well enough to realise that couldn't be the case – that this was an act of kindness and Johnny was doing him a favour?

'Get out of it Johnny-boy, move yerself!'

Codger shunted his mophead into the side of Johnny's left
shoe. He stepped to one side without looking, let the sodden
grey ropes swirl through the muck, submerge in the bucket,
drain, swirl again. Codger breathed through his mouth, a loud,
adenoidal crackle.

Which reminded Johnny, Dench had died too.

An hour later, around one thirty a.m., he was sitting in his usual
place in the corner of the Pink Parakeet. He couldn't really
afford private drinking club prices, but the hotel kitchen did at
least provide a plate of fried leftovers, a kind of sinister hetero-
geneous bubble-and-squeak, which if you were wise you wolfed
down without thinking. One plate a day was all he needed and
his present room was not much more than a cupboard in Camden
Town, so he reasoned he was entitled to a couple of drinks after
work, when most places were closed.

The Parakeet was conveniently situated on his route home
and he'd come to rely on his small hours gin-and-french.
The place was at its busiest between one and four, there could
be as many as sixty packed into a bar not much bigger than the
Gents' at the Bay Tree. In amongst the misfits and no-hopers
and lushes and ageing good-time girls there were always a few
bona fide artistic types – actors and painters – that you might
recognise. The management, Lewis Calhoun – a Welshman who
often said he'd opened the club to satisfy his own prodigious
thirst – liked them and encouraged them with preferential prices.
To begin with, because of Johnny's appearance and well-spoken
manner, he'd encouraged him too. But now that Lewis knew
he was just another boozer and an out-at-trouser one at that,
he'd been relegated. He didn't even drink that much, so he
made himself popular by mixing in, flirting with the old turkeys
and making the actors laugh, telling tall stories. As in France,
he'd become a sort of mascot. He'd never been good at anything
else, but he was good at that. He didn't tell them he was a
dishwasher by night and a thief by day.

Tonight, this stretch of seedy, sociable small hours' time was no
different. The club was hot and crowded, the air smoggy, the
faces febrile and the noise, appropriately, like a parrot house. A

black chap in a pork pie hat was playing the saxophone in a far corner God alone knew who was listening.

Johnny was too tired. He couldn't be bothered to be amusing so he affected an aesthetic gloom. That got him a couple of drinks, one from an old queer who was always sniffing around, the other from an actress. She was not half bad for her age, with a lovely voice and smile. He wouldn't have said no, but she had the breeding not to offer.

He wasn't really a thief, not a pro. He was an opportunist who took whatever was easy. The things that people were too lazy or stupid or preoccupied to keep an eye on and which he sold on as quickly as possible. The war years, the second show, had been good to him like that. His chest had kept him out of the army, though he wouldn't much have minded, and the black market was there to be played. Nylons, chocolate, fags, he could get hold of them and flog them easily. It helped that he wasn't like the other spivs. He wore a plain black coat and a red scarf, he was well spoken. It was easy to give the impression he had just happened to come by these things and was happy to let them go for a tiny profit to an attractive woman, who deserved a bit of luxury in her life.

Molly, as always, had bailed him out from time to time. She worried about his health, gave him money to buy better food, keep warm and bent his ear about going to see a doctor. He truthfully didn't give a flying fuck about health and usually squandered the money, though he knew Molly was the only other true friend – besides poor old Reg – that he'd ever had. He was letting her down, but then they both recognised she was forever in his debt. He reminded himself of that when he was pinching some old boy's silver cigarette case.

But Molly was on his side of the fence. Molly had made a success of herself, but she'd still come from roughly the same place, the place in life where nothing was safe and anything could happen.

The trouble was that he'd had a glimpse of something else – a different place to be, a different life. That something was Barbara, sweet, rosy, shiny-as-an-apple Barbara.

In the fifteen years since their parting, the memory of which still had the power to flood his mouth with bile, he'd kept tabs on her. Not that she'd ever known. He'd often watched her come and go from the magazine office over the year she'd continued to work there. It was sad, in a way, that she'd abandoned that job, when she'd struck out on her own to become independent, but then she was never like Molly. There was nothing driving her and a big part of him was glad she'd gone back to being the glowing girl he wanted her to be.

The wedding – that was harder to take. She'd married an old man! That crusty old brigadier, probably not as old as he looked, but still. How could she bear it? What did she think she would get from it? But then he always reminded himself – what did she ever think she would have got from *him*? And what could he have given her? He had adored and coveted her. He wanted to cling to her like a barnacle to the hull of a beautiful, fleet yacht, to be carried wherever she went. He made a small, rough sound, dropped his head in his hands and dragged them harshly over his face.

When he removed them the actress was on her way back – perhaps this was the night, then. She reminded him of someone he couldn't at that moment recall.

'Johnny, I hate to see you so sad. Will you come and join us?'

The actress looked over her shoulder, indicating the group she had arrived with, all of them bursting with the wit, laughter and confidence of talent.

'Please.' She pressed her palms together. 'Do.'

He followed with a show of reluctance. She seemed a nice woman. She wasn't to know she had just joined a big club. He remembered now who it was that she reminded him of: Barbara's mother. Jennifer . . . Juliet? Julia.

He often asked himself why he'd done that and concluded it was simply because he could. He'd been *that* close to what he wanted and still he couldn't stop himself.

Oh Barbara. My beautiful girl.

'Now,' said the actress, placing her hand lightly on his shoulder as she addressed her friends. 'This is Johnny, and you're all to be very nice to him!'

Sixteen

1953

On Wednesday, the day after the Coronation, the weather improved. People said, 'Typical, isn't it always the way?' and added ruefully 'Well, it could hardly have got worse.'

Maureen was busy around the place, throwing open windows and shifting furniture to the loud drone of the hoover. When that went off, the strains of *Housewives Choice* on the light programme took over: Anne Shelton, Burl Ives, the Vienna Boys' Choir . . . Barbara might not have turned it on herself, but the cheerful popular tunes were a comfort, as was the sight of Ron Dexter's thermos perched on the wall in the backyard, a sure sign that normal service had been resumed.

Knowing Prayle's agreeable successor was there emboldened her to go out into the garden. Would there be signs? Traces? A message of some sort that only she would understand? She walked round the house in the morning sunshine expecting at every stage to come across some evidence of last night's intruder.

Of – *oh God, oh God!* – Johnny.

She found only one thing and she came upon it at the same moment that she encountered Ron, who was cleaning his tools. He was a man in his late fifties who'd worked a chauffeur since coming out of the RAF but who, happily for Barbara, had decided to swap his smart uniform for dungarees. He'd also retained the impeccable good form and politeness of his previous occupations. He was sitting on an upturned bucket when she appeared, but stood at once, and touched his right hand to his forehead.

'Morning madam.'

'Good morning, Ron.'

'Just getting a bit of housework done.' He indicated the tools. 'Before I get started.'

'What a lovely day,' she said, 'after that terrible rain.'

'Went well for her though, didn't it?'

'It did. I thought it was splendid and so moving.'

There was a short pause.

'Anything special today, madam?' he asked. 'Or shall I just get on with it.'

'Oh, just get on please Ron. You know what needs doing much better than me.'

This was a formality. There never was 'anything special'. The garden was far too big really and it continued exactly as it had been when Stanley was alive, with masses of fruit and vegetables – most of which she gave to the hospital, the convalescent and nursing homes and various deserving acquaintances.

Mr Dexter nodded at the bucket.

'This was here, so thought I might as well perch while I did my polishing.' He was a man who hated to be thought in the least soft.

'Good idea.'

Barbara surveyed the convenient bucket and then looked up to about six feet above, where the narrow transom window of the larder broke the high, blank wall like a squinting eye. There were no finger marks on the glass that she could see, but then the torrential rain would have washed them away.

She telephoned Edith to invite her up to Heart's Ease that afternoon, but she sounded uncharacteristically weary.

'To be perfectly honest, my dear, I'm not at my best.'

'I'm sorry to hear that.'

'Only blooming anno domini. Why don't you pop down and see me here?'

'Thank you, well, why don't I?' The prospect of getting out, a spin down to Salting in the sunshine was pleasant. 'If you're sure?'

'Sure as eggs. I could do with brightening up.'

Edith herself was usually the brightener. Today, she did indeed look a little tired, though she answered the door, after a long interval, with her usual panache.

'Ah *there* you are!' She cried, as though Barbara was the one person she'd been looking for.

The small house in Coastguard Road, overlooking the estuary, contrived to be both eccentrically cluttered and peaceful. Barbara, used to more space than she needed or could use, liked the snug embrace of the small sitting room. Its shelves were full of ornaments and mementoes (Edith's self-proclaimed 'awful old junk'), piles of books and magazines. The walls were covered in wonky pictures, many of them with picture postcards tucked into their frames. The back window afforded a view of the broad, shining sweep of the estuary and the slick bronze mud flats dotted with flashing birds.

'The kettle is on, the cups are there and there's some ginger cake under the cover.'

'Let me.'

'I was hoping you'd say that. A poor show inviting a friend round and obliging her to make her own tea.'

Barbara took the tray through and put it on top of the pile of magazines – *Illustrated London News*, *Punch* and *The Lady* – on the low table by the window. Edith remembered *The Countrywoman* and was tickled by Barbara's brief foray into journalism. She sat in her usual faded red armchair and Barbara pulled up the lloyd loom with its frayed seat.

'Shall you be all right on that my dear?' asked Edith, as she always did, and, as always, Barbara answered that she would and promised to be careful.

Tea was poured and cake passed. They spoke of the previous day. Their conversations always started small before unwinding in all kinds of unforeseen directions.

'Nice party at the Keyes? I take it you got home all right in the deluge?'

'I did, though I rather wished I'd accepted a lift.'

'Lord, you must have been drowned.'

'I was. My own silly fault for being stubborn.'

'Oh, don't say that.' Edith downed the last of her tea. 'I'm a great believer in pig-headedness and it's not done me any harm.'

Barbara went to fetch the kettle and topped up the pot. Afterwards, as she placed the kettle in the hearth, her eye was caught by the framed photograph of Edith's husband. It was a studio portrait in full dress uniform, taken on his first, unscathed, leave when they had both believed in a shared future. He was about the same age as Stanley would have been at the time, but even in a formal pose he conveyed the genial openness of a warm-blooded, young man.

'Such a charmer, my Kit.'

'I can tell.'

'Can you . . .?' Edith leaned forward, pushing herself upright on the arms of her chair. Once standing, she straightened up and took two steps to retrieve the photo from the mantlepiece. Before sitting down, she passed her hand over the glass a couple of times, both cleaning and caressing it, then placed it on the side table next to her cup.

'Your Stanley was a fine figure of a man. So tall and imposing,' she said.

'Yes. Yes, he was.'

After a little pause, she continued, 'Mind you, we all have our one that got away, don't we.'

It was less a question than an observation and Barbara let it hang there.

'In my case that one was Kit.' Edith went on, 'He got away good and proper before there were any disappointments, or squabbles, or compromises. So there he sits, lucky chap, beautiful and new, and beyond reproach.'

There was a question that had to be asked and Edith was a person with whom one never needed to be shy.

'It's been such a long time. Have you never wanted to get married again?'

'No "again" about it. We were never married.'

This information was delivered plainly and simply, not as a bombshell, but she must have noticed Barbara's tremor of surprise.

'Not even engaged. That's not to say we wouldn't have been, if things had turned out differently. I call myself Mrs, but people know jolly well I make it up.'

Barbara could still blush. 'I've known you for a long time and I had no idea.'

'Why would you, my dear? I don't bruit it about. Kit and I were each other's. It doesn't much matter how, not to me anyway. What about you?'

'What about me?'

'Dear Stanley was devoted to you and I'm sure he was the man for you, but I wager if you think about it there's been someone else, some time. "The man at the crossroads" is what I call him.'

Edith's voice was matter-of-fact and she didn't look at Barbara, but was absorbed in pinching up crumbs of ginger cake between her fingers and thumb.

What is she saying? thought Barbara. *What does she know about me that I scarcely know myself? And how does she know that this is why I wanted to see her, why I'm here?*

'There is, actually.'

'Of course.' Edith met Barbara's eyes directly. The slight downward droop of the outer corner of her eyelids gave her face an inscrutable, sagacious air. You always knew, when Edith was looking at you, that you had been seen. Barbara felt she should add something, but Edith put up a hand.

'But don't tell me anything,' she said. 'Why don't you let me tell you something instead?'

'Please. Do.'

'A simple thing based on my own experience and it's this. When you have a hard choice, choose for the future and what might be to come, not on account of the past and what has already happened. The first is freedom and the second is pretty much enslavement.' She leaned forward slightly, peering out of the window as if looking for something. 'Hark at me, I'm being sententious. It's the prerogative of the elderly. You don't have to agree.'

'I do,' said Barbara. 'Or anyway, I understand.'

'Good! And as I said, you don't have to tell me anything, anything at all. Not now, not ever if you don't want to. I only want to hear what you wish to tell me.'

'In that case . . .' Barbara took a deep breath. 'There is one thing.'

'Fire away.'

'I think,' Barbara chose her words carefully, 'that I can see the man at the crossroads again.'

'How extraordinary.' Edith wasn't fooled. 'When we'd just been talking about it.'

'But he's not waiting, he's coming towards me.'

'Really? Putting you on the spot.'

'Yes.'

'Oh Barbara, my dear . . .!' Edith laid her head back and gazed beatifically upward. 'How I envy you.'

Edith had both correctly intuited her feelings and placed any decision firmly in Barbara's own hands. Barbara knew her friend well enough to realise there would be no more forthcoming in the way of advice. Not long afterwards, she took the tea things to the kitchen and washed them up. As she put on her jacket in the narrow hall, Edith said 'Remember I don't ask you to report back.' She clenched her fist. 'But I shall be *thinking* of you.'

On the drive home and more than a little shaken, she tried to think of Stanley as if at this late stage, she needed to, before it was too late. What had Edith said? *A fine figure of a man, tall and imposing . . . devoted to you . . . the man for you. . . .*

All true, after a fashion. They were each what the other had and it was not in their natures to question how things had fallen out, or why. All those years of companionship and domestic peace. The war had not disturbed them much. Stanley was out of the army and Salting had attracted no unwelcome attention from the Luftwaffe, though they had seen the planes go over in forty-four. Like most people in the town, they had involved themselves in the war effort. Barbara had knitted, baked, made up parcels and participated in little musical shows to raise funds. Stanley had helped set up fortifications on the promenade (you never knew) and, with Prayle, laid down even more of the garden to vegetables. They had taken an evacuee, but that had not been a success. The boy, poor lad, had been rude, difficult and when he 'borrowed' a bicycle that put the tin hat on it as far as Stanley was concerned. Barbara would have been more forgiving, but the whole episode had made her glad that they had never had children of their own.

In the spring of forty-six, Stanley had become ill and suffered the most terrible pain that even he was no longer able to conceal. He point-blank refused to go into the hospital. At the end of June that year, he died quietly in his own bed, in the early morning, with a summer haze over the bay and the pigeons calling softly from the Fort.

Barbara had cried, mourned and recovered. Everyone was very, very kind.

But that was a long time ago she reflected as she turned into the lane by Keeper's Cottage. *And this is now. And Johnny is at the crossroads.*

When she got home there was a note from Maureen on the hall table.

'Dear Mrs Delahay,
   Mr Dexter wants me to tell you that someone came round to offer some pruning and other things, he knows about trees. Mr Dexter thinks he might be useful and asked him to come back tomorrow when you are here, his name is I think Mr Ellridge.'

She lowered the note and saw her own face, white as milk, in the hall mirror. It was as if Johnny had put his finger in her mouth.

Seventeen

She broached the subject with Dexter the moment he arrived next day.

'I don't understand. It's so peculiar. Did this man simply appear? He just showed up and offered his services?'

'In a way he did madam. He came to the front door, as a matter of fact, and then Maureen brought him round. He said he knew this house and the Brigadier, when the Brigadier lived here. Used to be down at Keeper's Cottage for a while, apparently. He seemed a pleasant sort of chap, madam, and he did point out that some of the trees on the Fort could do with tidying up before the autumn, I've been thinking the same thing myself.'

'Still, it was rather impertinent of him.' She regretted her choice of words and added, 'Don't you think?'

'I don't want to give the wrong impression, madam. He was very polite, not pushing himself forward. We were chatting.'

She could almost hear the conversation; Ron Dexter would

have been putty in Johnny's hands and, of course, Johnny had uttered nothing but the truth. Plausible, charming, self-deprecating, slightly down-at-heel but a gentleman for all that . . . Her skin prickled.

'So is he coming back?'

'Sometime today, that was how we left it.'

'All right, but please tell him we don't need his help. If you don't mind, Ron.'

'Very well madam, I will.'

She could tell that he wasn't comfortable with having to give the brush-off to a former acquaintance of the Brigadier's. Perhaps she hadn't been forceful enough. Wherever he was, Johnny was pulling the strings.

She couldn't settle to anything: the bills that needed paying; the calls to be made; the letters to be written; the silver to be polished; house flowers to be changed; spare bedroom curtains that needed turning . . . In fact, the thought of all these activities filled her with wild, resentful boredom. That they constituted a large part of her life made her want to weep. She was, however, on the church flower rota this month. Although she would not normally have done hers until Friday, she used this as an excuse to get on her bike and pedal down the lane to St Catherine's, in whose tiny rural parish Heart's Ease stood. She told herself could see what was worth saving from last time, at least, and what she would need to bring fresh.

The church was empty and she was glad of it. She sat down in a pew for a while, steadying her breathing in the peace and quiet, and gazing at the east window over the altar. The window depicted a winsome, doe-eyed Jesus, with a sheaf of lilies cradled like an infant in his left arm. There had not been much church-going in Barbara's upbringing – except at school where it was obligatory – but Stanley was a regular attender ('church parade') and they had walked down the lane most Sundays to matins or evensong. A simple, brass plaque commemorated Brigadier Stanley Delahay of Heart's Ease, Church Lane, 'a faithful worshipper and benefactor'. Every few weeks he would march down, on his own, to eight o'clock communion. Nothing passed his lips beforehand, so breakfast on those days would be his favourite – kippers, followed by hot oatcakes with bitter marmalade. In the years since his death, she'd grown to be quite glad of her small involvement in the church, though she'd have been the first to admit that it had more to do with habit and social connections than with faith. Even now, she thought she detected something reproachful in the gaze of the winsome Jesus.

Just the same, successive vicars had made it clear that, no matter what one's shortcomings were, God would forgive. Also that he would answer the prayers of even the most unworthy supplicants 'as would be most expedient for them'. She closed her eyes and prayed, urgently and straightforwardly. She didn't ask for guidance, which was too complicated, but for deliverance.

But, even as she beseeched, like a child, 'please God make it stop', there was a part of her – her heart? her memory? – that hummed, like a long note stroked on a violin . . . its soft vibrato stirred her hair and stippled the smooth skin of her forearms. Her desires and petitions were not straightforward.

After leaving the church, she pushed her bike back down the path and through the lychgate. She set off home via a longer route, taking in the hamlet and the stretch of main road, as far as the turn off at Keeper's Cottage. By the time she reached the house she was hot, her legs were tired and her bottom sore. The physical discomforts provided a distraction. She would leave her bike in the porch and go straight to the larder for a glass of homemade lemonade, a recipe that always reminded her of her mother. Maureen had finished for the morning and would be back for two hours in the late afternoon to help with supper and any other odd jobs. Barbara decided not to seek out Ron, who would be having his sandwiches in the shed. She found herself praying for the second time in one day, this time that everything would have been sorted out in her absence. That the problem would have gone away.

The house was cool, a little dark on this sunny day and smelt of polish. The copper jug, full of rhododendrons on the oak blanket chest in the hall, seemed to give off a soft, pink light. Everything was quiet. She could hear the glutinous tick of the grandfather clock in the dining room and the gentle insistent 'Croo-croo' of the wood pigeons. Was the upturned bucket still beneath the window? She had to brace herself to go into the larder and moved so quickly with the jug, that she slopped some of the lemonade on the stone floor.

She returned with her glass to the hall, and hovered cautiously for a moment before stepping out into the loggia. This was her favourite place in the summer; the sense of being neither indoors nor out, but both at the same time, was agreeable to her. You were sheltered from rain, wind and sun, and also largely from view, while commanding a wide prospect of the garden, where the rough, sloping lawn was surrounded by towering rhododendrons in full red, pink and purple bloom. To the right of it was the Fort, with its ragged coronet of scots firs. On the far side of the low wall, which separated loggia from lawn, was an unpruned fuchsia, now a haze of scarlet and blue, around which a hummingbird hawk moth shimmered and darted in the sunshine.

She set her glass on the bleached wooden table and unfolded a canvas chair, disturbing a long-legged spider that scuttled away into the wigwam of old racquets and golf clubs. Stanley had been an orderly man, but the orderliness did not extend to sports equipment, which he clung to as a parent might have clung to pictures by, or of, their children. Perhaps the kit reminded him of a different younger self, one Barbara had never known; there were even two ancient ski poles among the clutter. She could have got rid of it all, but had never been able to bring herself to. Everything else – his clothes, hairbrushes, uniforms, even his cufflinks (with the exception of a pair she had made into a brooch) – she had disposed of. Yet to throw out these things would have been callous, a violence; so here they stood, as a ramshackle memorial and home for spiders and woodlice.

She did not at first take in what she saw on the Fort. The image touched her retina without registering. When realisation came it was swift and scalding. There was a figure in one of the trees. The firs with their long, bare trunks weren't easy to scale without a ladder, but one of them stood next to a broken stump. This made the lowest branch accessible and it was on this branch that Johnny stood, with one arm round the trunk, leaning out and gazing upward, like a jack tar in the age of sail, inspecting the rigging. He did not look in her direction and she remained very still, sure he hadn't seen her. After a few seconds, Ron Dexter appeared from behind the Fort, took two long, rising strides to the foot of the tree and stood there, also looking up, giving the bark a slap as he did so. The two men were in discussion.

Barbara sat motionless, but the inside of her head swarmed like a bell jar full of flies. Her chest rose and fell rapidly, her palms were dank and the tendons in her neck taut. Johnny raised an arm, caught the branch above his head and hoisted himself up, his feet scrabbling for purchase on the trunk, his free arm flailing. What did he think he was doing? He was going to fall and he wasn't supposed to be here anyway, how could Ron have been so stupid as to let him? But then that's what happened to people under his influence, they were not themselves. Who knew that better than her? She was ashamed of her relief when he was safely perched on the higher branch. Now, he lowered his head to say something and pointed in her direction. Dexter nodded and began making his way towards the loggia. So, Johnny had known she was there all along.

It was too late now to scuttle, like the spider, for cover. But neither could she stand, her legs wouldn't support her. Johnny sat there, a shadowy figure, legs dangling, watching. He raised a hand slightly, though whether it was to shift his position or to acknowledge her, she couldn't tell.

Dexter stood just beyond the fuchsia's soft burst of colour.

'Sorry madam, I didn't realise you were back. I didn't spot you there.'

'Who is that on the Fort?'

He glanced over his shoulder. 'That's Mr Eldridge madam.'

'I thought, *I said*, I don't want him here.' Her voice shook. 'We don't need him.'

'He wanted to have a word with you in person, because of knowing the Brigadier, I think. I was just showing him a few things that needed doing.'

'I see.' It appeared the other way round to her, as though Johnny were showing off, pointing things out, leading the way. 'That doesn't look very safe.'

He chuckled affably. 'I told him that, but he would do it – swarmed up it like a monkey.' He looked over his shoulder again and this time when Johnny raised his hand there was no doubt that it was a wave. Her own hand twitched in her lap, she clasped it tight in the other and the skin stretched white.

'He asked me to say he'd be over in a minute.'

'If he must. Ron, I'm not terribly pleased about this. My husband didn't care for him.'

Again the chuckle. 'Oh, he told me and I can well believe it. Chalk and cheese, eh?'

Of course, Johnny would have made a joke of that, putting himself in the role of the likable ne'er do well and Stanley the slightly stuffy, retired officer. He didn't even need to lie to get people on his side.

'He looked up to the Brigadier though, Madam. Respected him I think.'

'Perhaps.'

She watched Dexter walk back to the Fort and say something. Johnny replied, then stood unsteadily on the branch, clasping the trunk and craning to look at what was over his head. He was too high, it made her head spin, but then he knew she was watching. He looked down and spoke to Dexter again and, once again, Dexter laughed. Johnny lowered himself on to the next branch and jumped the rest of the way, landing with bent knees and arms stretched out. Part of her had wanted him to miss his footing and make a fool of himself, but another, greater part was relieved at his clean landing. He walked towards her, head lowered as he dusted the seat and knees of his trousers and the palms of his hands. She felt almost faint, as if time were folding round her, squeezing the breath from her body.

'Hello Barbara.'

He stood at the entrance to the loggia, below the shallow step, one hand resting on the wooden upright. Still, she couldn't summon the strength to rise. The powerful strangeness of the moment threatened to overwhelm her. The garden was quiet and sunny, Dexter had discreetly disappeared, but she sat there, buffeted by a storm no one could see.

The years had scribbled lines on Johnny's face, grizzled his hair and he was thin – too thin. But the essence of him was the same, and there.

He said her name softly again, 'Barbara, I'm sorry if I frightened you the other night.'

'You shouldn't have done that.' Her own voice sounded childish and sharp.

'I know and I apologise.'

She was gripping the arms of the chair. 'I don't know what you're doing here now.'

'I came back to make my peace and fell into conversation with Ron.'

'We don't need any work doing.'

He tilted his head, 'We?'

'Mr Dexter and I.'

'Ah. Actually, he seemed to think there were some jobs I could do.' He glanced over his shoulder, then back. 'There's quite a bit of dead stuff up there and on those silver birches over by the path at the back and the sweet chestnut by the gate.'

'Goodness, you have been looking around.'

'Ron showed me. He's a nice chap.'

She didn't answer, but now she managed to stand. She felt more in control, firmer.

'Why are you here?'

'Oh Barbara . . .' He took his hand from the wooden upright and rubbed his palm roughly over his face. 'Can't you guess?'

'No.' What she couldn't say was *I don't want you here.*

He looked at her. 'Honestly? I think you do. Do you mind if I sit down?'

She glanced round at the other folding chair, but he was already sitting on the step fishing cigarettes and matches from his pocket.

'This – do you mind this?' She shook her head. 'I remember you didn't often smoke.'

'Never, these days.'

He lit a cigarette and put the dead match back in the box and turned sideways to lean his back against the wall, one knee bent up. She was left stiffly standing.

'I don't want paying,' he said, 'if that's what's worrying you. I just need something to do. Healthy outdoor work isn't going to wreck me more than I'm already wrecked.' This last sentence was said without self-pity.

Her feelings were hurt by his reference to payment. Once again she might have said *I don't want you here, paid or unpaid.*

She sank back on to the chair. '*Are* you wrecked?'

He pulled a crooked smile without looking at her. 'No of course not, I'm being dramatic to attract your sympathy.'

'You don't look very well.'

'Ah, but that's easily corrected. I've always been a scruffy so-and-so. As I say, I need something to do and, Barbara, if that something brings me close to you that would be my whole happiness, complete.'

My whole happiness, complete. The words' direct simplicity unmanned her. She felt the sweet sting of tears. To cry would have been a relief, to touch him . . .

He continued mildly, as if thinking aloud. 'All these years I've thought about you, wondered how you were and how I could have been such a bloody fool as to lose you. You've been the one shining thing in my squalid mess of a life.'

Hearing him say this was like watching him deliberately cut himself, she couldn't bear it.

'Don't say that!'

'I'm not after your sympathy this time. I have to remind myself why you'd be entitled to send me packing. I was chancing my arm coming here, but I had to try. I had to. You're my redemption, Barbara.'

'That can't—' Her voice snagged. 'That can't possibly be true.'

'But it is, beyond question, I know it. I've always known it. How could I have let my chance go like that . . .? Not just let it go, but sabotage it in that mean, stupid, shameful way . . .' He pressed his cigarette into the ground next to the step. 'I suppose I was afraid.'

'Afraid? Of what?'

'Of you.' He tilted his head her way, without looking at her. 'Of change, of the opportunity to be better. Take it from me, that's frightening. If I'd won you, I'd have had to deserve you and that was going to be beyond me. So I blew it all up, didn't I? Lit the blue touch paper and ran for cover.'

'You stole!' she cried and felt the scar tissue in her heart crack. 'From my parents! *My parents* who'd been so good to you.'

He dragged the heel of his hand over his eyes. 'There's scarcely any point in my saying how sorry I am.'

'No, Johnny, no!' This was the first time she'd used his name. 'You hurt us all! What you did was mean, and wicked, and destructive—'

'You're right. I was destructive, self-destructive mainly. I hurt other people but the worst injury was to myself.'

'Really? Is that what you think?'

'Molly pointed that out.'

Molly. She had all but forgotten her. Molly, who she'd cut adrift when Johnny had gone, who she could not have faced. Reflexively she asked the polite, routine question.

'How is Molly?'

He shook out another cigarette. 'She died.'

Barbara gasped. She wanted to say, *but Molly wouldn't die, she wouldn't do that!*

'Hard to believe, isn't it?'

'Yes.' Her voice didn't work, she tried again. 'Yes. How? What did she die of?'

'She had a fall, broke a lot of bones. She was laid up for months, then she got pneumonia, the old man's friend and apparently hers too. She was always a skinny creature, like me, but the difference was she put up a helluva better show.'

Now Barbara had a reason to weep, she did so freely, dragging her hankie from the pocket of her skirt and pressing it to her nose and mouth. She was glad Johnny didn't come over to comfort her.

'Poor Molly . . .' she said when she was able to.

'Yes. Poor Molly. She took up with a rich bastard who admired her and then was jealous of her. She was loyal of course, always loyal, but take it from me that fall was no accident.'

'But that's terrible.'

'Isn't it? Brave, beautiful Molly who could spit in the eye of the devil himself, but she let that pig push her around without a word of complaint. A lot of what she gave me must have been his.'

'I can't even imagine—'

'You don't want to. She wouldn't have wanted you to, she'd have said she made her bed and must lie on it. All through that she was my friend. I've only had two and neither of them are here any longer.' He drew on his cigarette. 'I don't count you.'

'I wasn't your friend?'

He shook his head. 'Something more and – different. You have to understand, Mol and I were practically the same person.'

It was strange hearing him say this. She knew so much more than he realised. This thought, the small advantage she had over him, stiffened her spine.

'Was there a funeral?'

He nodded. 'She wouldn't have cared for the vicar, but she'd have been delighted with the attendance. She had a lot of friends.'

'I wish I'd known. I'd have come.'

'She's not holding it against you.' He smiled briefly, sweetly. 'Take it from me.' There followed a pause. Barbara mopped her eyes and face and thrust her hankie back in her pocket. Johnny ran his hands over his head – those thin, long-fingered hands with pronounced joints and almond-shaped nails, like those of the doe-eyed Jesus in the church window.

'One thing people didn't realise about her, about Mol, was how kind she was.'

'She was always nice to me, I don't know why.'

'That's different,' he said almost brusquely. 'She knew how I felt about you. But she was kind to people for no reason, people who didn't deserve it.' He turned to look at her directly. 'Me especially, I'm only here now because of her.'

'How is that?'

'She had the sense not to marry and no dependents. She had a good job and her own flat when she died, plus a little that her mother had left her. She wasn't badly off and she left it all to me.'

'She thought the world of you,' Barbara said quietly.

'It was mutual. I'd have gone down the drain but for her, I know that. For the first time in my life, I've got money in the bank.'

'But not enough to live on, surely?'

'For a while. I'm not expecting to make old bones and I've been doing odd jobs. The less I can touch what she gave me, the more there is for a rainy day. And now—' he leaned forward, put out his hand and brushed his fingertips against her skirt, so lightly that the fabric didn't touch her leg '—as the song goes, that rainy day is here.'

Her heart was in her mouth.

'So.' He stood up, pushed his cigarettes into his pocket. 'Is it all right if I do some work here?' For the first time she detected a hint of anxiety, of need. 'Ron seems agreeable. I promise I shan't be any trouble.'

'Johnny, what do you want? What's going to happen?'

He shrugged. 'Nothing that you don't want to happen.'

'All right,' she whispered.

'Thank you.' He turned towards the Fort, where now she could see Dexter, raking pine needles. 'Better get my jacket. I didn't come dressed for work.' He began walking away. 'But tomorrow, I shall.'

Eighteen

That evening Barbara was so agitated she couldn't eat. To say she regretted her decision would not have been accurate, because she had made no decision, not really. Something had happened, some mysterious, ineluctable process which meant Johnny would be here in the garden of Heart's Ease, tomorrow. At eight o'clock, unable to settle to anything, she rang Edith but there was no reply. She wasn't entirely surprised. Edith often went to bed early with a good book and the Home Service. As she some-times did herself, she reflected, though she was not much more than half Edith's age.

There was no chance of that tonight. Her nerves wouldn't allow it. The long summer evening with its beautiful, buttery light was something she usually loved. The shadow of the Fort and its trees crept over the lawn like a gentle protective hand. The giant blooms of the rhododendrons appeared defined and sculptural as flowers in a Japanese painting. From her bedroom, she could see the bright and bold ochre headland, still in full sunshine, on the far side of the bay. The sea was a silvery blue and flat as a lake. The long curve of the promenade and the beachside path was inviting as a smile, she could make out walkers and dogs down there, and the row of painted beach

huts twinkled like sweets. The white, cream and buttermilk
Georgian houses, in their prime positions overlooking the bay,
masked the modest terrace on Coastguard Road, but it pleased
her to think of Edith over there, her wisdom and sense not so
very far away.

Tonight the light was a mixed blessing. Darkness would have
meant she could close the curtains, shut out the threats and
possibilities that lay around her. But in the broad daylight of
midsummer, with Maureen at home, albeit in the furthest corner
of the house, it would have seemed strange, even slightly mad.

Molly would certainly have called such behaviour mad.

It's ridiculous! Barbara thought. *The wonderful, wounded, sharp-
tongued Molly was gone, unbelievably, for ever.* Of all the people she
had known, Molly was the last one she could have imagined
suffering such a fate, enduring so much without complaint.
What would she have thought of Heart's Ease? The very name
would have made her throw her head back and laugh her rasping
bark of a laugh.

Barbara could almost hear her saying, 'Whose idea was *that?*'

She wished she had even a single photograph of Molly. Perhaps
somewhere, you never knew . . . She moved the copper jug of
flowers from the chest in the hall and opened it, laying the lid
back against the sill of the loggia window. In the chest were
sheaves of photos: albums; envelopes; handsomely card-mounted
studio portraits; sheets of polyphotos; paper wallets of snaps
received back from the developers and scarcely looked at again.
As well as Stanley's meticulously filed family archive going back
to Victorian times, many of them were photographs she had
brought with her on her marriage. Another instalment had found
a home here following her parents' deaths, which had been
within eighteen months of each other. Only six years ago, her
father had suffered a fatal heart attack on holiday in the South
of France and her mother had quite simply not been able to
live without him. Like a flower deprived of sun, she hung her
head, wilted and died. That was when Barbara had known she
was truly alone. Orphaned, widowed, childless, not friendless
– she was surrounded by kind, acquaintances – but with no
intimates apart from Edith.

The death of Molly, whom she hadn't seen for years – in

another age and time, another world it seemed now – was a cruel shock. There had been a certain short-lived, but intense, intimacy between them. She was sure she was the only person to have heard the story Molly had told her that spring afternoon in the park, a story which later reminded her of something her father had said.

In war, good people sometimes fail and bad people can do great things. There's no justice.

She'd asked him, 'Does that make the bad people good?' And he'd answered plainly and seriously that, until he'd been in France, he'd reckoned he was a sound judge of character. His experience there had made him more cautious, slower to jump to conclusions. *You may know a good man, but you don't know how good he'll be under pressure.*

She did find one photo of Molly. Someone had taken it at the Gorringes' house party and Marjory had made some extra prints. It showed them all out on the drive by the front door, awaiting the off for the fox and hounds. Molly was easy to spot because she stood a little apart, hands in pockets, her head turned away from the rest of the group. The brim of her hat prevented Barbara seeing her expression, but she could imagine it – bored and amused in equal measure, already planning her short cut. Barbara couldn't find herself in the picture at all – though she must have been there – unlike Molly, she was one of the herd lost in the group. Johnny, of course, had already left, to lay his long and circuitous trail to the greenhouse.

She put the photo to one side and continued looking for a while, but she was sure there would be no more – even this one photo was a surprise. She loaded the others back into the chest, replaced the jug of flowers and carried the photo to the drawing room. She plumped down on the sofa with it in her hand.

All those other people . . . the laughing girls, the boisterous young men, the ones who had wanted to dance with her over and over again. She had lost touch with them all. Most of them would be married now and nearly all would, unlike her, be parents. She had received invitations to a couple of weddings and there were always a dozen or so Christmas cards. They'd be living in substantial houses in Dorking, Tunbridge Wells,

Winchester, Marlborough, Kensington; they'd discuss their offspring at dinner parties. Perhaps her name came up some-times . . . if so, how was she characterised? Barbara had no vanity, false or otherwise, but she could picture the sort of thing they would say.

Do you remember Barbara Delahay? She was a lovely girl. Bit sweet on her myself as a matter of fact (It was Gerry Gorringe's voice she was imagining) *went off and worked on some funny, little maga-zine for a while and then got married . . . Who? What, that forbidding military chap old enough to be her father . . .? Extraordinary. I never got an invitation, did you? Did anyone? He had a place down in Devon and the two of them sort of disappeared, almost as if she was running away, frightened of something. She was — I'm sure you won't mind me saying this, darling — just about the prettiest deb of that year. Very pretty mother, that's always a good sign. And a jolly nifty dancer, too, remember that, ha ha ha . . .! We get a Christmas card, there don't seem to have been any children and then his name dropped off too. Wonder what she's doing with herself down there? Sent her an invitation to Camilla's wedding but she declined. You sort of give up after a while, don't you . . .?*

It was probably something along those lines. She could hear them because she could have written them herself. What she had at Heart's Ease, both before Stanley's death and since, was pleasant, tranquil and safe. It was her sanctuary, of a sort, in her self-imposed exile. She hadn't wanted to be found and no one, whatever their memories and opinions, had tried to find her.

No one except Johnny.

She and Stanley had had a small, unshowy wedding at St Catherine's. Her parents had willingly waived any rights to something grander in London because, both bride and groom so clearly wanted simplicity and privacy, and Stanley was a regular worshipper here (a status the Delahays couldn't claim anywhere). A brother officer of Stanley's — a man she'd never met before — was the best man and she invited Lucia, less as a bridesmaid than a confidante on the day. In the event, Lucia was plainly embarrassed by the proceedings so confidences had not been exchanged. She behaved with a nervously smiling propriety, as if recognising her friend had gone mad and not wishing to catch anything. Flirtation between her and the best man, a Major Forbes, was out of the question. The wedding was at one, followed by lunch at the Deer Leap, and then Lucia insisted on being put on the four fifteen back to London.

What might she have said afterwards to other people?

It was all so peculiar, so sort of hole-in-the-corner. Rather sad to see dear Bar having this funny little wedding . . . I felt that I hardly knew her. Her parents are sweet but I thought they were awfully subdued . . . well who wouldn't be, with your only daughter marrying such an old man in such a dreary way? I know it's rude to leave before the newly-weds, but I couldn't wait to get away . . .

Stanley had booked a week's honeymoon at a hotel on Lake Maggiore. The hotel was opulent but staid; her presence alone lowered the average age by some twenty years. They had a grand room overlooking the esplanade and the lake shore, but she could not imagine that anyone supposed them to be a honeymoon couple.

That side of things at least turned out to be perfectly fine. Nerves, inexperience and having nothing to compare it with didn't matter in the end. Stanley was concerned only with her comfort. No one could have been more gentle and considerate. At the brief moment when he lost himself, she was astonished to see tears on his cheeks. Not for the last time, did he declare himself 'the luckiest man in the world'. She did not lose herself, but believed that to be perfectly natural in the early stages and was not to know that she would never do so.

They took boat trips on the lake, a drive into the mountains. They sat companionably on their balcony, reading books or simply drinking in the view. In the evening before dinner, they joined the stately *passeggiata* on the promenade. Afterwards, they joined other guests on the terrace, to listen to the hotel's string quartet playing their repertoire of light classical music and tunes from the operettas. This post-dinner hour was when they some-times fell into conversation with other English guests, but Stanley was careful not to show any favouritism. They didn't want to 'get stuck' with anyone, but he didn't need to worry. The other people were like them – well-bred, pleasant and discreet, equally disinclined to get too involved. Though, once or twice, following

introductions over coffee, she detected a petal-drop of surprise
on one or other of the faces, reminding her that she and Stanley
together were something of an oddity.

*Obviously devoted, but I must say we did wonder what on
earth . . .?*

On one occasion, at a different time and in another location,
this reaction became overt. It was on the fourth day, during
their evening walk. They had been out for half an hour and
were now strolling back towards the hotel, Barbara's hand tucked
into Stanley's arm. The lake was to their left, the sun just beginning to dip below the mountains beyond and the last pleasure
boat of the day trailed its soft chevron of wake across the water.
As usual, there were a great many people taking part in the
passeggiata: courting couples; families with children; elegant
women with pampered dogs; old people in shady hats; handsome Lotharios in perfect tailoring and a few exuberant
youngsters. A group of young men were perched on the rail
between the path and the water, smoking and admiring the
girls. Barbara felt the gaze of the nearest one as they approached.
As they drew level, he tossed his cigarette into the lake, jumped
down from the rail and began walking backwards
in front of them. He was talking quickly, gesturing towards her,
his expression exaggeratedly amorous and teasing. Under her hand,
Stanley's arm stiffened.

'Take no notice.'

That was impossible. The young man was directly in front
of them and, though she knew very little Italian, the gist of
what he was saying was all too clear. Other people smiled at
the little entertainment, their smiles said boys will be boys . . .
If Stanley had himself been Italian, perhaps he could have taken
some pride in being with a young woman who was attracting
so much attention, or at least pretend to be amused. Yet she
could sense his rising irritation and discomfort. He quickened
his stride, but she was still holding his arm and she stumbled.
She was never going to fall – Stanley saw to that – but the boy
darted forward and caught her outstretched hand briefly, raising
and returning it to her, as if it were something precious that
she had dropped.

'Go away – now! Go! Va'via!' Stanley barked, making shooing

gestures, his face dark with anger. Unperturbed, the boy stepped away, hands raised in apology. He didn't look at Stanley but kept his eyes on Barbara and spoke *sotto voce.*

She caught 'Perché . . .?' *Why?* But couldn't make out the rest, something about a fire or hell, *inferno . . .?* She clung to Stanley as they passed the boy – he made a satirical little bow – and she could hear the ripple of laughter as he rejoined his friends.

'I'm sorry,' said Stanley. 'That is not the sort of thing I'd want you to be exposed to.'

'He didn't mean any harm.'

'Maybe not, but he was rude. He spoiled our walk. I'd be sad to think Streza was becoming that sort of place.'

'Honestly, it doesn't matter at all.' She squeezed his arm and he patted her hand briefly. He was far more upset than her, she could tell.

When they'd changed for dinner, Stanley went down ahead of her to the bar. He said he wanted to talk to the concierge about a trip they were making to the *castello,* but she knew that it was so he could have a whisky before she arrived.

'I'll see you in the dining room in – twenty minutes?'

'Perfect.'

He kissed her on the forehead and said again, 'I'm sorry, my darling.'

She knew his contrition now was for his own behaviour, not the boy's.

'Don't be. It doesn't matter.'

Before going downstairs, she tore a page from the back of her pocket diary and wrote a few words on it, in capital letters.

In the foyer she saw a waiter, one who often served them, picking up glasses from a table and putting them on a tray.

'Excuse me . . .'

'*Senora!*' He put down the tray. '*Bona sera.*'

'*Bona sera.*'

They both knew that would be the end of the exchange in Italian; all the waiters spoke good English. She proffered the piece of paper.

'I'm sorry to bother you, but would you . . . do you know what this means?'

He took the paper and gazed at it with brows drawn together and one hand on his chin, in a charming parody of puzzlement.

'*Rosa in inferno* . . . Are you sure *senora*?'

'No, it's just what I thought I heard.'

'Where did you hear these words?'

'Oh, just now, when my husband and I were out on our walk. I overheard someone talking and this phrase stuck in my mind, because it's so odd.'

'Do you know what I think, *senora*?' He narrowed his eyes, nodding sagely.

'Please tell me.'

'I think this person says *rosa in inverno*.'

'That's what I thought.'

'No, no,' he shook his head with a smile. 'Not *inferno*. Not hell. *Inverno* – it means winter.' He handed back the piece of paper. '"Rose in winter."'

'Ah . . .' She looked down at the words.

'Is all right? It make sense?'

'Thank you, yes. *Grazie*.'

'*Senora* . . .'

As she walked across the foyer and into the dining room, she folded the paper until it was very small and tucked it into her evening bag. Outside, the lake was turning silver grey and the mountains violet. The restaurant was busy and dinner was in full swing. Stanley was at their table by the bay French window, he stood up the moment he saw her. A different waiter glided between the tables at speed to draw back her chair and unfurl her napkin.

When the white wine had been poured, Stanley leaned slightly forward, his mortification soothed and composure restored by a large whisky.

'I am the luckiest man in this room. Now, what shall we have . . .?'

So, in its quiet way, the honeymoon was a success. Those few days and nights proved to her, if proof were needed, that she had nothing to worry about and nothing to fear, ever again. She would always be cherished and protected.

Nineteen

With the notable exception of Coronation Day, the weather through June and July was good. Whitsun – before the deluge – had seen a heatwave that had left everyone gasping. Since then, the sky had been mostly blue and such clouds as appeared were mostly white. The Devon coast was treated to a cavalcade of soft summer days with calm seas, hazy dawns and long, gentle dusks.

Johnny was at Heart's Ease nearly every day. Gradually, Barbara became used to seeing him go about his business in the garden. He arrived early and left late and worked hard, doing all the dull jobs that Dexter wished to be relieved of. He seemed content simply to be there and rarely came near the house. Very, very slowly she came to accept his presence as he apparently intended it – as a kind of gift, freely and unconditionally given. When he left in the evening, he made a point of seeking her out – the only time he did so – to say goodnight and would then leave by the back gate, latching it carefully behind him and disappearing down the track that led through the wood. She didn't know where he was living or what he did at weekends. She didn't ask. His whereabouts was a mystery that she didn't wish to change. Even when, knowing him as she did, she suspected that the effect was intentional, she was still susceptible to this elusiveness of his.

Over the course of those sunlit weeks, she stopped being afraid. Johnny had cast himself in the role of her squire, whose part it was to serve her, not to do her harm. Still, she had the sense that they were moving through a period of a time that was finite. Like a story complete in itself, it would inevitably come to an end and she couldn't predict what the ending might be. The peace of Heart's Ease was only undisturbed for now.

One Friday in early July she received a phone call from Audrey Bryant.

'Barbara, my dear, have you heard?'

'Heard what?'

'Oh, my dear, I do so hate to be the bringer of bad news.'

'Audrey, please tell me.'

'There's no nice way I can soften what I know will be an awful blow.' Barbara knew at once what was coming.

'Edith.'

'I'm afraid so, just this morning. Quietly at home, as they say.'

'Who found her?'

'Paul. She's on his beat for the parish news and he often drops in for a quick chat. When she didn't answer the door, he took a little prowl around and then let himself in. She'd told us about the key under the loose tile.'

Barbara remembered the two unanswered calls. 'Had she been ill?'

'Oh, you know, under the weather. Old age, is all she told us. She was upstairs, lying fully dressed on the bed. Everything was tidy in the house – well, as tidy as it ever was. Almost as if she knew, like an animal. We had a dog like that, who went away and lay down to die . . .' Barbara closed her eyes, as if by doing so she could shut off Audrey's well-meaning babble.

'. . . the sad thing is, not a single relative that we know of.'

Barbara asked to be told the date of the funeral and hung up. *Not a single relative that we know of.* The same would be said of her.

A little later, she went out into the garden to collect the week's box of produce for the cottage hospital. She found Dexter picking runner beans.

'Do take some for yourself,' she said. 'We seem to have a bumper crop.'

'These and the gooseberries,' he agreed. 'All right if I take a few of those too, Madam? My wife makes a lovely goosegog pie.'

'I wish you would, Dexter.'

'Lovely little new potatoes there too.'

'I can see I'll have to have a lunch party,' she said. Then remembered Edith, without whom any lunch party would be unthinkable. 'Did you hear about Mrs Malmay?'

'Very, very sad,' Dexter shook his head. 'She was a very nice lady. I did her pots for her last year.' He took a reflective moment, before adding, 'I'll put the box on the back step in about half an hour, Madam, unless you'd like me to put it straight in the boot for you?'

'The back step is fine. Thanks, Dexter.'

Moving away she asked, as if it had just occurred to her, 'Do you know where Mr Eldridge might be?'

'He said he was going to thin out those big rhodies, the purple ones on the south side. Lot of dead wood in there.'

'I'll go and see.'

She returned to the back of the house, climbing the short flight of steps to the terrace, walking as far as the loggia and scanning the back lawn and the shrubs that surrounded it. On the far side, facing the house, were the purple rhododendrons referred to by Dexter and a dense, flowering rampart between her and the fairway that led to the Salting beacon. Everything was still. A squirrel scampered over the Fort and up the tree at the back, the one where Johnny had perched.

She walked across the grass.

'Hello . . .?'

Silence. Was he watching her? She paused, self-conscious.

'Johnny?'

He appeared from between the bushes, with a pair of secateurs stuck out of his pocket.

'Here. Come and see.' He stepped aside, holding branches back as if opening a door. 'Isn't this something?'

She was in a twilit cave of green, twisting wooden branches snaked towards the surface. From here, the purple blooms on the outside were only just visible, like lamps in a mist. The ground was a soft carpet of moss and dry leaves. Considering how fragile the wall was between them and the garden, the sense was of complete seclusion. They seemed part of a collective held breath.

Johnny turned on the spot, looking up towards the sun-freckled 'roof'.

'I could live here.'

'Not in winter.'

'Don't let's be practical.' He looked at her, serious. 'Please Barbara, don't let's.'

She saw how much healthier he was looking than when he'd

first arrived. He had filled out a little and his skin, which had always had a bluish pallor, was lightly tanned. The long grooves on either side of his mouth were less pronounced and the twin apostrophes between his brows had all but gone. His hair, though greying at the temples, appeared thicker and less lank. Barbara experienced the tender satisfaction that she, and Heart's Ease, had brought about this transformation.

She recalled herself to find him studying her as she studied him, with that air he had of being able to read her thoughts.

'Was there something you wanted to say?'

'No, not really . . . I just had some bad news.'

'I'm sorry to hear that.'

'An old friend of mine has died. Old in both senses, so not before her time.'

'But you were fond of her.'

'Very. And she was fond of me.'

'Of course.'

'I don't—' she hesitated, not wanting to sound self-pitying. 'I don't have many close friends, not these days. I accept that's my fault.'

'Why should it be anyone's fault?'

'No reason, but I have rather cut myself off down here. Everyone I know in Salting was a friend or acquaintance of Stanley's, so they're a bit older. The funny thing is, she was the oldest of them but somehow we always saw eye to eye.'

'Kindred spirits,' he suggested. 'You're an old soul in lots of ways.'

He'd touched a nerve. 'Don't say that!'

'Why? It's a good thing to be. You'll miss her, this friend.'

'Very much.'

'Well, for what it's worth . . .' He took out the secateurs and began snipping at the spurs of spare growth that sprouted from one of the branches. 'I bet she wouldn't want you to. She – what's her name?'

'Edith.'

'Edith has gone on her way. She's set you free.'

She was thinking about this when she heard the faint sound of the doorbell over in the house. She would have ignored it but Johnny nodded in that direction.

'You have a visitor.'

'I can't be bothered.'

'You must. What are you going to do, hide?'

There was the sound of the loggia door.

'Mrs Govan! Madam?' Maureen's voice was calling.

'Go on,' said Johnny, continuing to snip. 'Go.'

As she crossed the lawn, the figure of Phoebe − organiser of the St Catherine's flower rota − appeared next to Maureen in the loggia, waving energetically.

'Barbara! I just called in to see if you were all right in the light of today's sad news . . .!'

That night in bed, she reflected on what Johnny had said.

Edith's gone. She's set you free.

Is that what had happened, then? Did people that you left or who left you by dying grant you some sort of liberty? And if it did so, why did she feel not free, but still trapped and alone. Bereft.

As well as offering sympathy, Phoebe had wanted to discuss church flowers.

'It's thee and me again in a couple of weeks and there's a wedding coming up. I was thinking perhaps we should have a bower of roses − wouldn't that be lovely?' Barbara agreed but it didn't much matter because, on this subject, Phoebe was a force of nature. 'Will you have enough in your garden by then . . .?'

'More than enough.'

There were always plenty of roses at Heart's Ease. The rhododendrons took pride of place, but there were roses everywhere − clambering over fences and up the side of the shed, rambling around the edges of the fruit cage and vegetable plot. Humble dog roses colonised any sunny corner. Old-fashioned, sweet-smelling tea roses stood in great clouds on the sheltered western boundary, bobbing their heads to the afternoon sun. Barbara picked a posy every few days, to have on the side table in the drawing room, where their scent kept her company for as long as the luscious petals lasted.

Twenty

On the day of Edith's funeral, when Barbara had just got changed into her dark dress and hat, there was a knock at the back door. When she opened it Johnny was there, carrying an enormous bouquet of roses – white, cream and coral pink – the stems were wrapped in newspaper.

'Goodness . . .!'

'I hope you don't mind,' he said. 'I did ask Dexter.'

'But what—'

'They're not for you,' he said. 'Obviously, because they're yours anyway and not mine to give, but I thought you might like them for your friend.'

He saw at once that she didn't quite understand him.

'Edith. Her funeral.'

'I did send some.'

'Of course, but these are from Heart's Ease. From you.'

The idea was perfect. That he had thought of it on her behalf was more perfect still; a present in itself. She held out her hands.

'Thank you.'

'I've snipped the thorns and put some damp sacking round the stalks. You can add something nicer over the top if you want to.'

'Thank you,' she said again, taking them. Their hands didn't touch, but there was something sacramental in receiving the flowers from him. She was enveloped in a soft halo of scent.

'You look beautiful,' he said.

She looked down at her black dress, blushed and smoothed the skirt with her free hand.

'It's my funeral outfit.'

'Plain clothes suit you. No need to gild the lily. Or the rose.'

When she'd closed the door, she was trembling.

There were perhaps fifty people in Salting Parish church and at least thirty of them could scarcely have known Edith. To Barbara's knowledge she had been at best an agnostic, but a service had been organised, by Audrey, along sturdy Anglican lines:

Praise my soul the king of Heaven, Who would true valour see (Edith would have approved of the old words, hobgoblins and all). But Barbara wasn't so sure about: *Lead us heavenly Father lead us.* Would Edith ever have wanted to be 'provided, pardoned, guided . . .?'

But the final blessing was one for which Edith had once expressed a liking:

Go forth into the world in peace; be of good courage; hold fast that which is good; render to no man evil for evil; defend the fainthearted . . . Yes, that was Edith.

Barbara wasn't sure what to do with her roses, among all the formal sprays and wreaths, (though having seen those, including her own, she was glad she'd brought them). In the end, she waited until they moved outside for the burial and laid them on the ground near the neat, baize-lined hole, waiting to receive Edith's earthly remains. At no stage did she cry, though she had expected to. The proceedings were dignified and respectful, but seemed by and large to have little to do with her wise, eccentric friend.

She stayed at the wake – tea or sherry, with cucumber sandwiches, fruit cake and platitudes, in the same parish hall where they'd watched the Coronation – for about half an hour. She knew the remarks about Edith were sincere, but their tone of rueful pity rubbed her up the wrong way. These were good people who had recognised the good in Edith, but there was something important that they were missing. She had been so much more than the 'funny old thing', brusque, brainy but good-hearted, who had lived on her own for too long. To Barbara, she had sometimes seemed the youngest of them all. The third time someone used the phrase 'a good innings' Barbara decided she could bear it no longer and made a move to go.

'Barbara! Hang on a minute!'

She was already out of the door, when an excitable Audrey caught up with her.

'Barbara . . . I've been trying to elbow my way to your side for the last twenty minutes.'

'It was a good turn-out,' agreed Barbara, this being one of the approved sayings of the day.

'It was, it was, she would have been so pleased. But look, what I wanted to say is, there's something for you.'

'Oh?'

'We popped into the house to do a little, basic clearing up, the fridge and so on, and Paul found a box with your name on it on the bureau. Perhaps she meant to give it to you next time . . . in any event I knew I'd see you this afternoon and, if you hold on for two ticks, I'll fish it out of the boot.'

Barbara followed Audrey to the Bryants' blue Ford Consul and waited while she unlocked the boot.

'There you are. Signed, sealed and delivered.'

'Thank you Audrey.'

'Lovely roses by the way . . .'

Audrey pulled in her chin, beaming indulgently as Barbara took the white shoebox, the lid secured with a whiskery cat's cradle of string. *Mrs Barbara Govan* was scrawled on the lid in Edith's large, leaping hand. She hadn't the least idea what it might contain, but was conscious of something inquisitive in Audrey's manner, as if she expected her to open it there and then, in front of her.

'Any ideas?'

'None at all. But thank you – a surprise in store.'

On the short drive home, the box sat on the passenger seat next to her and did indeed feel like a companion, as if it contained Edith's breath, voice and presence. Even the string reminded her of Edith's disorganised, long hair that was never quite contained by combs, pins or net.

She encountered neither Johnny nor Dexter and it was that time of day – late afternoon – when Maureen, if she was in, would be in her room listening to the Light Programme and reading her latest instalment of True Love Tales. Wanting privacy, Barbara went upstairs to her bedroom and closed the door. She put the box on the bed and took a pair of nail scissors out of a drawer. Then she sat down on the bed and snipped the string.

Inside, was a mass of tangled, nylon stockings, all in a service-able forty denier and all laddered. A couple had even been mended, something Barbara hadn't seen since her school days, when it had been obligatory and considered, like darning, to be character-forming. She found it hard to imagine Edith wielding a needle, but the effortful stitched ridges were there to prove it. The stockings had been stuffed into the box as protective wadding for something smaller and, sure enough, about halfway down she found the real contents.

They took up very little space. Edith must have packed them this way to disguise them. Perhaps a box, which might contain trinkets, was less freighted with importance than an envelope with its air of personal significance.

There was a letter, still in its opened envelope, the paper fragile and old, the handwriting not Edith's, and a photograph, sandwiched between two squares of cardboard. The cardboard appeared to have been added recently, the cut edges and the sellotape looked fresh. Barbara removed both of these and set them aside, before shaking out the rest of the stockings to check there was nothing else. She half-expected to find a note from Edith herself, but there was none.

She rolled the stockings and for no good reason replaced them tidily, with the string, in the box. Then, well aware that she was deferring the moment of disclosure, she walked to the dressing table and put the box down next to her hairbrush and comb. The central panel of the mirror was tilted slightly upward, so that she caught sight of her reflection; she was surprised to see that her face was a little flushed. When she raised her eyes, she saw Johnny standing between the rhododendrons on the far side of the lawn, his hand on one of the branches. He was looking straight at her. Barbara took a step back.

She moved away from the dressing table and returned to the bed. She picked up the letter and the photograph and held them in both hands, on her lap. Her heart was racing and she closed her eyes for a moment, gathering herself before opening the envelope.

My sweet darling,

I've read of hearts aching and breaking, and thought it was just words. I didn't know that loving someone and missing them could make flesh and blood hurt. But now I do know. There are plenty of things that hurt over here, but none of them cause pain like that of being apart from you. The softness of your skin, of your gentle knowing hands, the expression in your eyes, and your mouth . . . oh! Your mouth . . .

Barbara lowered the letter, for a moment, to catch her breath.

> . . . *When I'm able to sleep I tumble into dreams of you, I drown in you my darling, my love . . . I don't fear danger or wounds or anything, certainly not the poor, wretched enemy who are, after all, just like us. I fear only death, because it would separate me from you for ever. A great black nothingness of not-you. How could I stand it? Please send a lock of hair, a handkerchief with your scent, a spoon that's touched your lips, so I can sniff and suck and lose myself in you —*

So passionate . . . so unbearably personal, and private . . . Unable to read on, Barbara put the letter down. A full minute passed before she was able to pick it up and read the signature.

> *Your only, lonely, desperately longing for you*
> *K*

Kit, who had died — she looked at the date — only a few months after writing those words. The thing he feared and dreaded most had happened. The great black nothingness had swallowed him up.

Yet it was not that — the dread, the nothingness — which struck her most. It was the humming heartbeat of life, the vivid force of memory in every word:

. . . *your gentle, knowing hands . . . your mouth, oh — your mouth . . .!*

There was nothing elegiac here, nothing stoical or accepting. All was impatient ardour and desire. Hot blood pumped by a young and yearning heart.

She didn't want to replace the letter in its envelope, not right away. Instead, she left it on the bedspread. The decades-long fold in the single sheet meant that it reverted to a half-open state, like a child's paper boat or a flower with unfurling petals.

She turned her attention to the photograph, slipping the point of her nail scissors under the sellotape and prising off the cardboard.

She was looking at a postcard-sized print of three people on a beach. The centre focus was of a couple, a man and a woman, leaning back on a breakwater. The day was sunny and they both held hats. Perhaps they had been told to remove them for the picture. Their faces were bright, eyes narrowed against the light and there were short shadows at their feet. They appeared to be in early middle-age and not fashionable, but from the woman's long coat and bobbed hair, Barbara guessed the period to be the twenties.

She turned the photo to the window to examine it more closely. The woman was Edith, even without the particular circumstances, she'd have recognised the tall figure. She seemed energetic, even in repose, and the fine-boned, long face, with its humorous, enquiring expression rebelled slightly against the requirements of the photographer. She held her hat in front of her, both hands clasping the brim. The man was beaming, no, laughing, open-mouthed, a picture of happiness. He stood with one hand resting on the top of the breakwater behind him – behind Edith – as if just about to put his arm around her. Because of the accompanying letter and his air of exuberant pleasure she might have taken him to be Kit, except that the picture was clearly too late for that.

She turned the photo over and her heart tripped.

Me and S G, Salting July 1922

Looking again at the picture, there was no doubt. It was Stanley, of course, but not as she had ever seen him. An almost unrecognisable Stanley translated by – she sought the word – joy. Yes, joy; occasioned, unmistakably, by love.

Barbara laid the photo face down next to the letter and sat very still, her hands braced either side of her on the edge of the bed. Beyond the windows, the tops of the pines stirred against a pale sky. The weather was changing.

After a few minutes, she put photo and letter on the bedside table, heeled off her smart shoes and lay down. When Maureen tapped discreetly, to ask if she was all right and what would she like for supper, she told her that she had a headache and asked her please to lock up.

It was the beginning of August and by mid-evening day was turning dusk. There was no need to draw the curtains as she undressed and returned to bed. She didn't put on her nightdress but lay between the smooth sheets bare as a newborn, in her strange new world.

Edith has gone on her way. She's set you free.

Twenty-One

Maureen had the weekend off, but Barbara was glad to be solitary. The weather had turned restless with a moist breeze from the south west brushing grey clouds before it. The spell had been broken. In spite of the cooler temperature, the air inside Heart's Ease felt stuffy as it had not done during the weeks of sunshine, when windows and doors had stood open. In contrast, the garden became unsettled, the full-blown flower heads swinging and trembling, ready to fall, and the tops of the trees switching like irritable cats' tails. The rhododendrons, with their green internal caves, seemed to take great breaths, heaving and subsiding. No rain fell, but it was coming, you could feel it, borne on the back of the breeze.

On Saturday, she laid an oil cloth in the boot of the car and loaded it with roses, the least-open ones she could find. With the cooler weather and in the enclosed shade of the church, she considered that they would last. She left early, arriving at St Catherine's not long after eight o'clock, when the verger unlocked the door. Normally, she would have timed her session to coincide with Phoebe, but now she wished expressly to avoid her. Exceeding her usual brief she created two large arrangements – exuberantly flowing and informal – for the altar and another, smaller one, for the font near the south door. There were still some stems left, so she found a bucket in the cupboard at the back of the nave, filled it with water and placed all the remaining blooms in it except one. Then, leaving the bucket in the south aisle where Phoebe would see it, she went out, closing the door with its massive iron latch behind her. She passed through the porch and turned right, following the path that led between the ancient, lichen-covered graves. Then went up the gentle slope to the top of the churchyard, where the more recent burials were, the resting places of those who had died this century.

Stanley's, at his own request, was a simple soldier's grave, an arched white stone with his name, regiment and dates. Barbara hadn't wished her name to appear on it, nor on the plaque in the church.

The churchyard was well cared for, the grass mowed and the graves weeded. A few bore metal containers like upturned colanders and three contained flowers in varying states of decay.

She felt a warm rush of affection for Stanley, the strongest and most genuine she had ever experienced. Stanley, who had said to her when he was ill, but before she had accepted the inevitable,

'Organise me something simple and serviceable Bar, no quotations and whatnot. You know me well enough. And don't feel you have to deck me with flowers, what would I do with them?'

So she hadn't. She had done as he asked and left him alone, as he had left her: heeded, taken care of, remembered, but alone. Tears ran down her cheeks as she laid the golden rose at the foot of the plain white stone. They had had more in common than they knew, but understanding had come too late.

For Stanley anyway. Barbara got to her feet and dusted her knees. Now she wanted only to get away before Phoebe arrived. Before reaching the lychgate, she looked once more over her shoulder and saw that her offering was already on the grass, brushed aside by the wind.

All day long on Sunday, she moved around the house and garden: remembering, looking . . . Seeing. Her slow tour had much in common with the very first time she had come to Heart's Ease with Stanley. The day he had proposed and when she had refused him. Nothing had changed; everything was cared for, then and since. But Barbara realised that, in her whole time here, she had made no impression on this place. It remained her husband's. For nearly twenty years, both with him and on her own, she had inhabited it like one of those tiny crabs that makes its home in a discarded shell.

In the afternoon, she placed the photo of Molly and that of Stanley with Edith, on the drawing room mantelpiece, with

Kit's letter tucked behind them. She moved Stanley's polo and golf trophies aside to do so. She folded the *découpage* screen and propped it in the corner.

Out in the loggia, she dragged out the old golf clubs and tennis racquets and stacked them on the terrace against the wall. Squeamishly, she opened the deckchairs and those that were rotting with mildew she also threw out. The piles of flowerpots she set a few at a time on the table. The tiles revealed by this exercise were a different colour, a warm terracotta unbleached by the sun, though littered with insects (dead and alive), dry leaves and a fine powder of desiccated potting soil.

By the time she'd swept the floor, she was sweating, her arms ached and she went to pour herself a cold drink in the kitchen. Everything now cried out for her ministrations: the pantry, with its glass-fronted cupboard full of grand, seldom-used glasses; the old-fashioned kitchen with shelves of enormous meat plat-ters; the heavy saucepans and chipped, enamel pie dishes standing on the stove. What did she want with such things? What had Stanley wanted with them? The weight of it all squeezed the breath from her and she had to sit down on the only uphol-stered chair, the one she thought of as Maureen's. The wireless stood on the dresser and she reached out and turned the knob until she found music that she half-recognised, sombre but tuneful. She laid her head back. In the hall, she heard the phone ring, quite persistently . . . stopping, ringing again. She ignored it.

She fell asleep and when she woke it was to a faded, grey light, the wireless crackling with interference. The wind had dropped, but rain freckled the windows. Disorientated, she looked at her watch, half past six. She finished the squash in her tumbler and walked, a little stiffly, to the dining room, where she poured herself a glass of sherry. For almost the first time, she took pleasure in the stealthy enlivening heat of the first sips hitting her stomach and spreading through her veins.

She had still not turned on the light. This evening, in spite of the rain, the house and garden seemed of a piece and at peace. When she opened the door and stepped out into the loggia still carrying her glass, she was not surprised to see Johnny standing there, below the step. He wore a jacket, but no hat, the rain was soft and beads of it lay on his shoulders and on his hair.

'Barbara.'

'Hello Johnny.'

'I wanted to see you.'

She took a slow sip and set her glass down on the table. 'Here I am.'

He glanced slowly around. 'You've been busy.'

'Better late than never.'

She was never sure which came first – her step forward, or his outstretched hand. But just before her fingers touched his, she heard him say,

'Will you come with me?'

What she would always remember – when she needed to, when everything that came later seemed to disappear in dry smoke – was the greenness. She'd remember: the tender half-light, which was like being under water; the sweet, poignant smell of the damp earth and leaves; the tip-tapping of the half-hearted rain. This was Johnny's place – she saw he had been sleeping there – the eldritch cave, where he had watched and waited for her. She remembered that, except for their mouths, they were cold. Their smooth damp skin moved on smooth damp skin, like two mer-creatures. She remembered his long and beautiful Jesus-hands, with their calloused palms, that seemed to draw patterns on her, swirls, feathers and rosettes . . . A slender fern of black hair grew up his belly and spread at the start of his ribs. The wet hair on his head was ruffled into points. His eyes were bright slits, barely seeing her. She remembered her passive, spellbound ecstasy, and his glorious devouring of her, as the leaves over his head melted into one another and lost their greenness to the dark.

With the dark, their mood changed. They were shivering with cold and with crazy laughter at themselves.

'Come on!' he said and they ran over the grass, clutching their bundles of clothes.

'Maureen . . .!'

'To hell with Maureen!'

Across the hall and up the stairs they scampered and into her room. This was the other thing she remembered. How, when they had closed the door behind them they had fallen, still laughing, into her bed, their cold limbs warming up as they wrapped them around one another.

Alongside stood Stanley's empty bed, quiet as a catafalque.

Twenty-Two

They found the letter long after Barbara Govan had gone, with no forwarding address. The new people in Heart's Ease had painted the house pink and glassed in the loggia to make a conservatory. They had also put up a tall, wrought-iron gate, so passers-by couldn't simply stop and admire as they used to do.

The letter was slotted into an album of hand-coloured post-cards of the area. Edith had left them to the village museum, but they weren't interested in all that – times and tastes were changing – and it was a year before they looked through the album and found the envelope. This time it was simply addressed to 'Barbara', so they gave it back to Mrs Bryant who had brought in the album and who might know.

The Bryants realised at once who it was for and found them-selves in a quandary as to what to do. So much time had passed and so much water had gone under the bridge. Barbara Govan, whom they had all been prepared to like, not least for her husband's sake, had left Salting without so much as a goodbye and under the most peculiar (and, it had to be said, unsavoury) circumstances. Maureen Parr and Ron Dexter, who had worked up at Heart's Ease, were not to be drawn on the subject and loyally unprepared to condemn. At least, everyone murmured grimly, she wasn't a bolter; she hadn't run off in this extraordi-nary way while Stanley was still alive. But her behaviour cast a disturbing backward shadow. After all, what else might have happened, clandestinely, during Stanley's lifetime? And what might have happened since his death, when they had all rallied round and kept an eye on her, the funny little thing?

The Bryants considered opening the letter, but not for long.

It was not intended for them and Barbara had severed all her connections with Salting, with all of them. They dropped it into the ideal boiler and replaced the lid as if shutting a snake in a basket. The paper curled, crackled and was gone.

Not that it would have meant anything to them.

> *My dear Barbara,*
>
> *It occurs to me that I should have explained the contents of the box; although I know that you'll surely cotton on. The letter from Kit tells you why I was quite unable to respond to or care for anyone else. The expression on Stanley's face says everything about what he hoped for. He was a dear man and very lucky that, in due course, he met you.*
>
> *I have no idea whether you were happy with him and it certainly isn't my business. But your life is yours again now Barbara, and has been for years, so — forgive me — don't be afraid of the freedom. On with the dance! Kick up your heels and wave your arms about, if you want to.*
>
> *I am feeling very groggy at the moment, so shan't be joining in.*
> *Fondest love,*
> *Edith.*

It would have meant a great deal to Barbara, who thought often about Edith. Not many days went by when she didn't keenly feel the loss of her old, true friend. Their conversations hung like lanterns in her memory of those dim, constrained years after Stanley's death. The last one especially, with its urgent, loving advice, had been like guiding light, without which she would never have found the courage (she thought of it as Edith's spirit) to do what she had done. Even now, the realisation of her own daring had the power to snatch her breath away. This evening, Barbara wondered if Edith was watching her as she got ready to go out and, if so, what her expression would be.

The bedroom of the Bayswater flat was big but, like the large drawing room, had an empty, under-furnished appearance. Thanks to Stanley's provision for her, and the proceeds from Heart's Ease, they had been able to buy the flat, but neither of them had the inclination or aptitude to select and purchase things to go in it. Johnny's line was that, as long as he had her and somewhere to hang his hat, he couldn't care less. And she had no experience of homemaking, having moved into a ready-made one when she married Stanley. She went to Whiteley's and self-consciously ordered basic furniture and kitchen equipment, sure the staff were laughing behind their hands at her incompetence. The result was that they had only what was necessary and none of it suited the Victorian flat. She had no confidence in her taste either, so wasn't able to dress things up with the little touches and grace notes that other women were good at. So everything felt rather impermanent.

That feeling extended to the two of them. They were going to marry, but had not yet got round to it. Johnny said that he wanted to look after her – once he got up, he was busy, in and out all day, and often had meetings with useful contacts in the evening.

Barbara wouldn't have minded a job herself, but *The Country-woman* had closed down some time ago. She still had her shorthand and typing, and some useful experience, so she was sure she'd be able to find something, but Johnny wouldn't have it.

'I may not be the Brigadier,' he'd say, pulling her against him, growling into her ear, 'but I have my standards.'

She no longer had friends in London and didn't know how or where to start making any. Her loneliness was exacerbated by not having enough to do. She employed an amiable, rather slatternly woman to help with the cleaning, but there had been no option but to learn to cook and she was terrible at it. Johnny often breezed in late in the evening with a bottle of scotch to find her in tears amid some ruined experiment, but his line was that he didn't care. They would open the scotch and have fish and chips. But *she* cared and it was becoming increasingly hard not to show it. She had fled headlong to happiness. Now it seemed happiness was fleeing her and she could not catch it.

This evening, they'd been invited by a pal of Johnny's (he had many 'pals', most of whom she had never met) to join him for dinner with a well-known actress (he mentioned a name she didn't recognise) and some others. Johnny was keen on the idea of working in the expanding field of PR – he had

had one or two freelance jobs – and the pal had assured him that the actress and her coterie would be fertile ground. He was febrile with excitement and impatient with her hesitation: *come on, they must go! It would be fun!*

It was now seven thirty. Barbara wasn't sure of the evening's timing. She wanted to be ready when Johnny got back so that, if necessary, they could leave right away. She stood before the wardrobe mirror. The black taffeta dress was his favourite, one that he had persuaded her to buy; she herself would not have bought it without his persuasion. Her hair needed cutting, but he liked it long and she had rolled into a loose chignon that was a less tidy copy of the one her mother used to create when Barbara was doing the season. Johnny also liked lipstick, 'a bit of glamour', so she had put on a little, hoping it didn't make her look like a clown.

The door of the flat opened with a rattle and closed with a bang.

'Anyone at home? You ready?'

Barbara heard him in the kitchen – the clink of a glass, a tap running, a snappish 'Blast . . .!'

'Hello darling – yes, almost!'

Was she ready for Johnny? She tweaked the neckline of her dress, patted her hair – there was something missing, something he would notice. Just in time, she remembered and went quickly, breathlessly to the dressing-table drawer.

'Barbara!'

'I'm here,' she cried. 'Coming!'

The will o' the wisp of happiness flew before her, as she touched her hair once more and turned out the light.

For the Salting crowd, there was a final postscript to the Govan affair, a public one. Dick and Evelyn Keyes took the Express and happened to spot it in the William Hickey column. The photograph was of a glamorous, British film actress surrounded by admiring hangers-on, sitting at a nightclub table crowded with bottles and glasses. She was the star, the subject of the accompanying small story and the focus of attention. Closest to the camera and the only one looking straight into the lens was, unmistakably, Barbara Govan. Her neckline was rather too low for a woman of her age and her eyes were dull and exhausted. The man next to her, who may or may not have been her companion, was turned away, paying court to the actress.

The *décolletage* was altogether too much. And then – oh dear, such a mistake! – there was that ridiculous *rose*.

The End